CAPTAIN
OF
NEMAIN'S
REVENGE

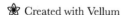 Created with Vellum

"Your words surround you like fog and make you hard to see."

— EDWARD 'BLACKBEARD' TEACH

For those with wanderlust

CHAPTER I
NEMAIN'S REVENGE

Nemain, the Goddess of Death, would not make an appearance until later in the evening.

The night was young, but it was the longest night of the year. Even though temperature rarely changed with the seasons in the Carriwitchet Isles, there was a sharp coolness to the night. A foreboding of sorts, but the omen was not for him, rather from him. For what he was about to bring upon the Temple of St. Angeles.

He was the oncoming storm, the villain in the shadows, the pirate the people of Samsara had come to fear.

The Temple sat atop a cliff face, looking out over the sea, similar to the much larger Fortress sitting only a few miles to the West. It had a sharper shape to it than the other buildings in Samsara. A dark gothic gloom emanated from its cone shaped steeples and sloping rooftops.

Below the Temple, waves crashed against the cliff and rocks, shaping them. They would only grow more harsh and rapid as the night continued. Once Nemain's crimson moon appeared in the sky, the world below grew more wild and raged.

That, and there was a storm brewing. It wasn't anything he could describe as much as an acuteness for being at sea for so long. But it was coming.

Steps creaked the floorboards of the deck behind him.

"Captain Phantom."

Phantom smiled faintly as he stared at the Temple. The moniker he used as Captain was the legend itself. It served him well.

He turned to the old man, wrinkled by age and a life under the sun. He couldn't be more than fifty years, but his hair became white early. The long strands were tied to his nape and a large hat rested on his head. Even though the man was a former Kalonite slave, he spoke like a nobleman, clear and defined.

"It's a fair night, would you agree?" The old man pressed. Kalonites had an odd coloring. Their skin was warm and bronzed, but their eyes were light, usually blue or grey. Mr. Ramirez's eyes were grey although Phantom suspected they used to be bluer.

"For now." Phantom's voice was more raspy than he intended. In the act, he was always confident, but before plans went into motion, dread and nerves settled into his stomach. He couldn't afford something to go wrong. "Are you certain?"

Ramirez knew what he was referencing. He had been Phantom's scout, watching and asking while the Temple was open for visitors whether their prize would in fact be there tonight.

"Without a doubt, Captain." The man pulled out a cigar, lighting it on a match then tossing the match into the sea. Smoke wafted around the man in a cloud. Ramirez was so often right that it sustained some of his nerves. He returned to his task of shoving a handful of slippery glow kelp into his satchel, careful to stifle the soft green light it gave off.

A small trilling noise floated from the dark red sails above. A small smile parted Phantom's lips as an adolescent dragon flew down from the mast to land on his shoulder. The creature had white scales that rippled blue and reacted to her surroundings. When she was excited, they would ripple faster, when sleeping they would disappear altogether.

Serena had two set of wings and a near snake-like narrow body with four stubby legs and whiskers trailing her face. She was a remarkably beautiful creature and very likely the last of her kind. They understood each other in that way.

He scratched under her chin, right in the spot she liked, her scales rippling blue in reaction to the blissful feeling it gave her. "Lock this one up before I get back. Can't have her causing trouble."

The old man nodded. "Must you go alone? Black? Earhart? Any one of your crew would aid you." The smoke still curled around Ramirez in puffs.

Yes— yes he must. The crew did so many things for Phantom. He collected them because they were the best and every time he promised them freedom. Freedom to roam. Freedom to wander. Freedom that could not be achieved while anchored to these Davina-forsaken isles and their backwards politics.

He had an entire ship, including himself, to keep his end of the bargain to.

Serena chirped before taking off to patrol the ship.

Phantom put a hand on his mate's shoulder. "Not to worry about me." He smiled broadly, although not entirely genuine. "I'm just a story meant to scare children. Just a myth. A fable." He turned abruptly, jumping to the railing of his ship and taking the rope tied to the cliff's edge, then he pulled his hood over his head. "A phantom in the wind." He pulled on the rope, making sure it was secure. "And you can't kill a phantom."

Ramirez offered a bemused twist of his lips. "Right," he said in a weary tone.

Phantom laughed at the sight, then began the climb.

The room was dark, as expected. Ramirez never left out any details in his report. The black and grey marble reflected no moonlight or starlight. The walls and dome of the temple room held no entrance for light to seep through, except at the very center.

It was a blessing to be sure that Phantom remembered to bring the glow kelp. It cast a light green sheen over the black room, even if it left his hand feeling slimy. His mouth twinged upward as he took in the dark room. It wouldn't take the officers long to notice the broken back door. Or one of their comrades out cold in the alley.

Phantom had little time to gain in bearings. He had visited the Temple as a child. He knew the object never left the pedestal in the center of the floor below the dome. Good thing, since over a decade later, it would be his prize.

As he approached the middle of the dome, the Stone glowed in answer to his presense. The colors within swelled.

Glittering beads of silver and streams of lilac intertwined as if the Stone itself was glass and the spirits of two Goddesses were trapped beneath the surface.

That's if, Phantom believed in such powers. His Goddess glowed red.

A small flicker of red emerged from the Stone, like a drop of blood. Right, the crimson moon was to appear soon. It was the entire reason he waited months for this heist. The crimson moon scared superstitious officers from chasing after him. He could sail the seas during the crimson moon, but they could not. Or more likely, were too afraid to.

But he had a Goddess on his side. One who ruled over the seas and lives of men.

The Stone glowed in the shape of an oval. It stood on a pedestal with warnings to not touch it. Silly warnings for a thief. If they ever caught him, they would hang him anyway.

If they caught him.

Another smile tugged at his mouth, causing the otherwise still hairs of his face to flicker in response. He threw a black velvet cloth over the Stone, stifling it's light. It seemed to purr in response to his hand.

Cold, sharp metal bit at his neck, right at the base of his chin.

"I don't believe that belongs to you." The melodic voice chimed with feminine grace. It was hard to see her in the darkness though. Since he stifled the light of the Stone, only Davina's muted silver glow from above and the faint sheen of green from the kelp in his hand shed any light. But she had a large hood draped over her head, same as Phantom.

He smiled, hoping she could see it regardless of the darkness. "I wouldn't be here to steal it if it was, would I?" He let his voice drop dangerously low, in that way he knew made most women's toes curl. Yet the shadowed figure seemed unaffected.

She pressed the sword further in, but it didn't cut through his skin. The sword was dull then, likely something she pulled off from the walls of the Temple. The Priestess displayed swords of ancient warriors, but most of those pieces of metal weren't much use as weapons anymore.

The cutlass at his hip however—

"Don't." It was as if she could read his thoughts, but he supposed it was the easy conclusion to draw. He raised his arms, covered Stone in one hand, glow kelp in the other. He wanted to see how this would play out.

"What's your plan? Gut me and take the Stone for yourself? I noticed you've yet to call for the officers."

She inhaled as if gathering patience. "Put the Stone back and I'll let you go."

He resisted the laugh that bubbled up. "Sorry to disappoint, but no."

She swung the sword, but it was heavy and she was too slow with it. He knocked it away before she could make any use out of it. It clanked easily to the ground. He stashed the kelp, sending the room into near darkness, with only Davina's light above them.

Before she could fully register her new situation, he pocketed the Stone and pulled the cutlass from its sheath, placing it at her chin which he could barely see under the darkness of her hood.

She sucked in a breath. "I give orders, I don't take them, love."

"I'm not your love," she spat, her breath growing quicker as her nerves grew taut.

"So incredibly brave. Tell me, who is the girl who fights off thieves in the middle of night?"

She said nothing. Not even deigning to give him a fake name.

He replaced the tip of his cutlass with his finger as he sheathed the weapon, then with his free hand, he pulled the hood back revealing a head of blonde silky locks and gold eyes the shade of treasure. Like the coins he coveted so often. He almost wanted to steal her away like the treasure she was, but he resisted. He had a plan to enact.

The angry furrow of her delicate brows was so adorable he nearly laughed. His finger was still under her chin, tipping her head up to look at him, their bodies so close he could feel the warmth of her.

Footsteps stomped from the direction of the door. About four sets if he wasn't mistaken and the muffled voice of command.

Right on time.

"I'll see you again soon, love." Phantom smiled down at the beauty one more time, then took off. The air seemed colder than it did before.

He ducked into the hallway and heard footsteps come after him. The door he picked contained the staircase to the roof. He lowered his boots against the steps in an attempt to be quiet. The groaning stairs would not allow it; as if sounding their own creaking alarm.

The door to the staircase flew open. The officers beat their boots against the steps, not even trying for silence. They mumbled chatter to each other as if it would make them any faster or any more likely to catch him.

Phantom barreled through the roof door and was greeted by a less-than-flat roof. A set back. Nothing he couldn't handle. He dropped the glow kelp at his feet. It served only one last purpose.

He set out to the middle beam of the roof toward the sea that always called to him. The beam was thin, as if the architects of the temple designed it to discourage escape. But, he persisted and put one foot before another. He was a decent twenty paces from the door when it swung out and a familiar face emerged.

The officer had honey colored hair and fair skin with freckles that decorated his cheeks. Phantom used to tell him how he would have been such a pretty girl. But now, the man before him was only soft in that way. His body had taken to manhood. His broad shoulders and strong legs nearly rattled the roof.

His voice boomed into the night sky, "Stop, thief. The Stone is disgraced by your hands."

Phantom remembered that his old friend could not see his face beneath the hood. Yet, the temptation was too great to resist. How is a heist worth it anyway, if he did not receive the credit for it?

"Commodore," Phantom purred loud enough to be heard over the whistling winds. The Commodore's eyes widened before Phantom let his hood drop behind him. The Stone hummed in his pocket as the sky drowned in crimson light.

Perfect timing from his favorite Goddess.

The red moon appeared above them in full.

It never rose. It never set.

It only appeared long enough to bathe the ground in blood.

Phantom could not contain the smirk as it landed on his face. "Come now, is that anyway to speak to an old friend, Commodore."

The Commodore huffed as a bull before a matador. An interesting challenge to be sure, but one Phantom had no time for. He let the smile twinge only slightly further before snapping himself into a sprint. A chase it shall be then.

Delightful.

The Commodore was flanked by two officers. One slipped on the glow kelp Phantom left for them. That officer slipped into another with a yelp, leaving the Commodore alone on Phantom's trail.

Just like old times.

When Phantom looked over his shoulder, the Commodore huffed so violently, his face turned a new shade of red. He appeared like a ripe tomato in the crimson moon light. Phantom audibly chuckled at the sight, nearly losing his footing as a result.

He halted at the end of the building. Below him was a cliff and then the sea. A drop that was only mildly dangerous normally, but with a crimson moon in full bloom above them, it was exponentially more so. Below him, waves crashed into the cliff as if in attack.

The Commodore's bellowing laugh echoed across the building at his apparent victory. As Phantom turned, a crimson shimmer caught his eye. The Commodore's blade was drawn and aimed for Phantom's navel. He lifted his hands in response, the Stone dangling from his lifted hand in black velvet. Such a true black that even the crimson light did not reflect from it.

"Give it up and I'll take you in. Resist and I will spread your entrails over the roof of this holy place. A mess and dishonor I wish to avoid." His voice held a hint of the playful tone Phantom remembered from childhood, but it was altered and fashioned to sound menacing. Yet to Phantom, it might as well have been the whisper of kittens.

"Take me in to be hanged you mean?" The smile still refused to be contained.

"You are a criminal and I have a duty." The Commodore inched forward.

"You always did take our games too seriously."

The Commodore flinched forward, but Phantom made no move of fear from the blood glinted blade. "And you always didn't take them seriously enough."

Phantom frowned mockingly then tossed the velvet bag to the Commodore. Someone he once called brother. He often wondered what would have happened if he had stayed in Samsara all those years ago. Even though Phantom doubted there would ever be a version of him that didn't crave the sea.

The Commodore caught the bag with ease, taking his eyes off Phantom.

Phantom inched to the edge of the building as the Commodore tied the bag to his belt.

"Now, old friend, come with me. Die with honor."

Another smile flickered on his mouth. "Oh, have you forgotten me so thoroughly, brother?" Phantom knew the rage it caused the Commodore to be called brother. The rage flamed in the Commodore's eyes and Phantom drank it in.

Realization flashed on the Commodore's face. He grabbed the velvet bag again, palming the stone inside it. The stone inside was no more than a rock. When the Commodore's eyes flicked up, Phantom held the Stone in his hand, his callouses drifting over the smooth surface. The beads of silver and streams of lilac were now joined by freckles of red, like specks of blood.

"Another time brother," Phantom said, a hand to his forehead in salute as he let his weight take him backward.

CHAPTER 2
THE STORM

"**N**o," the Commodore shouted, lunging for Phantom with his blade. Wind swept by him as he spiraled into the darkness. He turned to dive into the water and crashed beneath the rolling waves. Breaching the surface of the waves, he took in the sweet air, wiping his dark hair out of his eyes.

The Commodore and the other officers looked over the edge of the building. They were in no hurry. Phantom's odds were to die in the rocks or be arrested on the beach. It was a miracle he was still alive after the fall.

Or so they thought.

From behind of the bend of the cliff sailed the love of Phantom's life.

Nemain's Revenge sailed into the cove where Phantom treaded.

The Commodore shouted at his officers. A muffled sound above the crash of waves. Phantom put the Stone between his teeth as he swam to his ship.

When he reached the hull, the crew threw out a rope for

him to take hold of. He hugged his feet over the knot at the end of the rope as it was lifted to the deck. He dripped sea water over the deck as the rope swung. The Stone proudly fisted in his right hand.

"Aye men, here's our prize," Phantom shouted with no small amount of pride. The crew shouted and cheered. It hummed in response. As if it joined them in celebration.

Phantom planted his feet to the deck. The crew swarmed in to take in the Stone. A legend in its own right. It was said that one touch of the sacred stone could kill a man. Yet, here he stood, his calloused fingertips with dirt imbedded underneath his fingernails, holding the Stone with no issues.

The Priestess would call it a miracle, a sign he was blessed by a Goddess. And he knew exactly which one.

The Stone's glow tempted the crew members to reach for it. Phantom snatched it away. "We'll admire the Stone once we get very far from here boys and not a moment sooner." Disappointment flashed across their dirty faces.

"Captain," a young voice shouted from above. A boy dangled from a sail with absolute ease. He was no more than twelve years old with freckles and hair like sand. He always reminded Phantom of when the Commodore was that young. When they both were.

"Yes Robin, what do you see?" Phantom shouted back at him.

"We have company." Robin pointed beyond them to a ship already sailing. A ship known as *Davina's Will* came rushing from around the cove. The Commodore jumped from a dip in the cliff onto the ship. The only ship known to man that was a match to *Nemain's Revenge*. The only ship faster was the legend known as *Macha's Demise*, which was at the bottom of the ocean.

That is, outside Brettanian war ships.

"To your posts boys," Phantom shouted and the men scrambled across the deck, realizing the immediate danger. "We are about to play with the big boys."

Phantom ran to the main cabin stairs in the middle of the deck, trotting downward. A couple of drunkards were playing dice in the sleeping quarters beyond the stairs. *Pirates.*

"Straighten yourselves you bilge rats," Phantom snapped and the men reacted immediately. One man flinched so hard he lost most of his dice to the filth of the lower deck. The other snapped to attention. "Get above deck, we're on the run boys. Time to earn your keep."

"Right away sir," Hyne said with crumbs in his beard. Tick nodded, his coloring matching Rameriez with soft blue eyes and warm skin. "He says *we'll be on it Captain*," Hyne said in a voice a pitch higher than his own.

They took to the stairs right away. Hyne and Tick. They were an inseparable duo. Tick didn't speak, so Hyne spoke for him. Usually accompanied by voices or accents. As inconsistent as they were, Tick never argued.

Once they were out of sight, Phantom continued to the treasure room. It was mostly barren. The crew cleaned it of its worth a fortnight ago. Bottles of rum and moonshine decorated the walls instead. Since Phantom set this plan in motion, they didn't have time to pillage the citizens of Samsara as usual, betting on a steeper prize.

A chest stood at the far end of the room. It was where Phantom and his crew kept their most prized and valuable assets. Phantom fished a key from the thin rope string around his neck. He clicked open the chest and placed the Stone inside. There was no use bringing the Stone into battle, especially with a storm drawing near.

Before he slammed the door, he felt a heaviness at his back, a sixth sense one gets when they are being watched. The decks of *Nemain's Revenge* carried many spirits, heralding its namesake. But this was no spirit—

A sly smile etched the corner of his mouth, but he resisted its further spread.

A quick shift, then he slammed the lid down and stuffed the key back into his shirt against his hairy chest. A mirror stood above the chest and caught Phantom's reflection. His eyes were a blue so dark they matched the ocean during a storm. His nearly black hair was ruffled, but that wasn't new. He wore black usually, but a red vest was his newest addition. Black ink traveled up his golden sun-kissed neck. The tentacles of a kraken wrapping around his neck.

The ship rocked with impact. Phantom steadied himself before running back to the upper deck. The men continued to scramble and shout. The ship they were escaping from was gaining on them. They had front facing cannons and aimed to take the entire ship down. An oddity Phantom didn't factor in since he thought the men too superstitious to be seafaring during a red moon.

The sea was still coated red and he had to remind himself that he was fully here, his monster nowhere near the surface.

He recalled the look of horror on the Commodore's face when he saw the Stone in Phantom's hands. The legend states that no man can touch it since it carries the presence of all three Goddesses. He challenged their views in taking it. The blasphemy was a greater risk than losing the Stone. He should have seen it sooner.

No matter. The stakes had thickened, nothing more.

"Captain," Earhart summoned from the wheel of the ship, snapping Phantom from his daze. "We need you on the helm."

"Aye," Phantom purred. "That you do, Mr. Earhart." Phantom climbed the steps to the quarterdeck of the ship. The crimson light still spilled over the crashing waves, the wood of the deck, the dark of the sky, and the men. It appeared like a massacre that had yet to occur.

Earhart backed away from the wheel to join the others on the main deck, while Phantom's dirt caked hands took firm grasp of it and spun so violently the crew nearly stumbled with the movement.

Phantom searched the waters before him then turned his eyes to the sky and grinned wildly.

"Captain," an older man with spectacles rushed to the wheel. "A storm is coming Captain." Indeed, the waters below rushed and the skies ahead were full of dark unforgiving clouds. "I suggest we head North and dodge the oncoming storm."

"Smith. Have you learned nothing? Nemain is on our side. We sail West and the storm will serve *us*." Phantom was nearly giddy with the good fortune that presented itself. Laying West, was not only a storm, but an arrangement of sharp rocks, islands, and sand bars. This part of the sea, Phantom knew like he knew every freckle and sun spot on the back of his hand. He knew the Commodore was too much of a landlubber to have that sort of knowledge.

Still his crew was shaken. They doubted him.

"Who are you?" Phantom shouted. Still the crew wavered. "I said, who are you?"

Dr. Smith replied, "We are the Eleven Devils, Captain."

"Eleven Devils, you say? Are you sure it's not the eleven cowards? Or the eleven seagulls of Cerriwitchet?" Phantom continued to shout. "No, because when *Nemain's Revenge* docks, the land trembles. Because Phantom and the Eleven Devils is a name that strikes fear into the minds of our enemies. Because we will not be defeated!"

The crew cheered in response.

Phantom tossed his head toward the pursuing ship. "Those are the bastards that try to cage you." They booed in response. "Those are the men who see fit to hang us!" They booed louder. "And now, they want to sink *Nemain's Revenge* so She has provided a way out for us. If any of them," he pointed back again, "survive the storm, they will tell of the fearlessness of the Eleven Devils and the Phantom they call Captain. They will call us impossible. We will strike fear into any sailor who spots our colors." They cheered louder than ever. He looked up at those colors flapping violently in the wind. A crimson red flag with a black skull painted upon it. The sight fearsome against a red sky.

"So I ask you again men," Phantom belted. "Who are you?"

"Eleven Devils!" The crew shouted at once.

"Then show them who you are!" Phantom shouted louder than he thought he could. But this moment, he had been born for it. The crew scrambled again with renewed purpose and their hearts hungry for the legends they would become.

When Phantom stared back, *Davina's Will* had fallen

back. He laughed at the sight. The officers feared the storm and waited to see if they would back from it, but they did not. Apparently, the blasphemy Phantom committed was offensive enough to warrant a chase, one that sent them into the belly of the beast.

The rain hit like a sheet of ice slamming into them. Phantom kept two hands on the wheel to control the ship against the raging currents of the storm that wished to overtake them.

"Captain," Dr. Smith screamed. "We must take down the sails before they tear."

Phantom's eyes snapped to the sails that flapped uncontrollably in the inconsistent shifting winds. Then he looked back at the ship in their wake. They were about to enter the storm. "Not yet, Dr. Smith. But be ready." A flicker of doubt shown in his eye before he spit the orders back at the crew. The smoldering embers in Phantom's eyes enough to burn his doubts.

The men got into position to reel in the sails as *Davina's Will* entered into the waves and rain. They flinched, but Phantom remained. "Steady."

The winds picked up with raging intensity, as if scolding Phantom for his recklessness. The following ship veered back and forth against the currents. Then they steadied and Phantom knew his old friend had taken the wheel. After all, he learned from Phantom.

Perfect. It was a stalemate then.

The sound of ripping cloth echoed over the winds. "Captain," Robin begged, straining to hold down a rustling sail.

"Steady," Phantom shouted with a head tossed over his shoulder. Then he whispered to himself, "Come on, brother." Two long minutes held out before sails of *Davina's Will* folded like the wings of an eagle.

"Now," Phantom shouted over the winds and the crew reacted. The sails folded violently against the threatening winds.

But he should have paid more attention to the sea before him. A reef laid too close to the surface in this spot. It rocked the ship.

Robin lost his grip on the mast and fell to the deck. Smith was at his side before anyone else, but the sail unfurled on one side. The other men had their hands full.

"Mr. Earhart."

"Yes, Captain."

Phantom took his hand and placed it on the wheel. "Keep her due West and try to keep her out of the currents."

"But, Captain," he argued.

"I'll be back soon, Earhart. Try not to steal my glory in the meantime." He winked before jumping off the quarterdeck to a low hanging rope. He swung onto the main mast, then climbed up the mast to secure the sail himself. Ripping cloth sounded like coins falling from his pockets. He'd have to replace the sails, but red was not an easy color to come by.

Making it to the top of the sail, he rolled up the sail with the other crew members until everything was completely secure.

The ship rocked again against a rock Phantom would have remembered. It was a small rock by any means, by it still rocked the ship enough for Phantom to lose his footing. He held onto a rope as rain dripped down his face and waves violently crashed against the hull.

He stared at the Commodore's ship again. The ship swayed against the wind, but mostly held firm. It learned from their ship what direction was safe and what wasn't. They were lasting longer than Phantom anticipated.

He jumped from the rope and landed on the deck, absorbing the shock with bent knees. He marched across the deck back to the quarterdeck. Earhart was more than willing to give up the violent pull of the wheel to Phantom.

"Alright men," Phantom ordered. "Time to show them who we are." They cheered again as they went to their posts. Then, the storm seemed kinder and it wasn't pulling on them as violently. Phantom suspected their pursuers had the same such luck.

Phantom spotted the sign. A rock shaped like a human head that was half decayed. It was due North so Phantom turned the ship toward it. The ship behind them knew what the decaying head meant. Death awaited beyond.

"Hyne and Tick," Phantom shouted, somewhat worried he was relying on drunken bastards until he remembered they performed their best work in such a way. "Secure the mast to the hooks. And be ready." The duo went to work right away, tying a rope around the main mast that ended in iron grapples. The two moved flawlessly besides being drunk off their asses. If this experience hadn't sobered them, nothing would. But Phantom had to be at the wheel, so he relied on them, he had to.

The ship sailed right to the opened mouth of the decaying beast. A hole toward the back of its head revealed clearer skies toward the northern horizon. Phantom sailed it smoothy into the mouth, careful to stay in the middle, even against the waves that continued to crash. It was a good

21

thing for the sea to be at low tide. Otherwise, more damage would have been caused to the masts and the hull.

As suspected, the Commodore's ship rounded the corner. It was close enough now to see the crew running about the deck and the Commodore with eyes trained to Phantom in a way that promised death. He wouldn't get his chance today.

They breached into the sunlight of the opposite side of the cave.

"Now," Phantom shouted. Hyne and Tick both threw their grapples to the jagged grip of the rock's edge on the port side. The grapples caught onto their mark yanking the ship to the left with such force it knocked most crew members to their hands and knees. Phantom let go of the tension he held onto and let the wheel fly.

It turned the ship sharp enough to turn their trajectory back West. It still rained on this side of the rock, but the waves didn't crash as violently. Phantom grabbed the wheel again before it could pull them into the rock itself. The force strong enough, he almost couldn't hold it.

"Cut her free!" Phantom shouted as Hyne and Tick sliced the ropes that held the grapples, leaving them and the Commodore behind. *Davina's Will* sailed straight North, into presumably smooth waters.

Their ship turned West slightly before knocking into the first sharp rock. It significantly slowed their pursuit. Then the second rock pierced the hull. The damage was visible from where Phantom stood.

The men screamed as they realized the doom that awaited them. It was a land mind of sharp rocks. By the third impact, the ship was sinking. There was enough nearby land that most of them would survive, but they would never catch Phantom and the Eleven Devils.

Phantom turned their ship South, right back into the storm. The last thing the crew of *Davina's Will* would see would be *Nemain's Revenge*, the last remaining Goddess ship, disappearing into the storm, fearless and undefeated.

CHAPTER 3
TREASURE

B y the time *Nemian's Revenge* cleared the storm the crew was singing.

OH WHOA THE BOTTLES EMPTY
OH WHOA THE CREWS ALL TIPSEY
OH WHOA THE SHIPS NOT SINKING
IN THE STORMY BLUE
HEY!

It was an intoxicating upbeat tune that sent even the most reserved of privateers to their feet singing or dancing. Even with the sour meaning behind the song. Legend had it, doomed sailors would drink whatever they had left and sing until the ship went down.

The song's popularity grew during the Necromite War thirty years ago. Ships were lost to the sea often around that time. With no port left to dock in and the land infested with necromites, they simply let the sea take them.

The sky was still dark and even though Nemain's

appearance was brief, the silver moon of Davina and the lilac moon of Macha still decorated the sky in varying degrees.

Phantom stood at the quarterdeck, looking over the main deck and his cheering crew. Mr. Earhart took the wheel to guide their path, but Phantom would not join the singing even as the fiddle was pulled out by Tick to play.

A Captain had to be sure his treasure was secure.

He descended down the stairs to the cabins below. The song muffled behind him as he unlocked the door to the treasure room, the old hinges groaning in protest.

Phantom's eyes searched the room, landing on an empty plain. The chest was gone.

He fumbled for his key, but it was still around his neck. Did he forget to lock it in all the rush? No, he never forgot to lock the bloody chest. He knew his crew wouldn't have dared to touch it, so there must have been a thief.

Phantom sniffed the air as if the stale sea air would provide him with clues. Then that heaviness at his back returned. Whoever they were, they never made it from the treasure room. His smile kicked up to one side as he drew the cutlass from his hip. A familiar weapon that felt molded to his hand.

"I know you're here," he sang. "I can smell you." He couldn't actually smell the rat, but he knew it was there all the same. "Come out and I might not split your throat open for stealing my prize." He turned about the room. There were plenty of places to hide, depending on the smallness of the intruder. Behind rum barrels— In cabinets recently emptied—

"I won't dock this ship," he started, peeking around a barrel. "Until I've discovered you. So you may as well end your little game before I grow tired of it." He checked inside a cabinet to find only empty shadows and a spare gold coin.

A faint scratch. Not the intruder, but a bilge rat skittering along the wall. It came from behind the cabinet. By dust patterns on the floor, the cabinet had been moved, but whatever squeezed behind it couldn't be large at all. A foolish child. A thin, quiet burglar. Whatever it was, it was not something to fear.

Phantom set his sword down on the nearby table and reached a hand into the empty ally behind the cabinet. His hand snagged a fistful of a finely threaded coat and yanked at it.

"Alright, lad." He threw the intruder to the floor before him, but before he could threaten the thief, a flash of blonde hair and gold eyes passed by. It wasn't the sweaty musk of a poor burglar or the unwashed stench of a homeless child that filled his lungs, but the sweet scent of roses and the undercurrent of smoke.

Phantom narrowed his eyes at the woman holding herself up by her arms. She wore a long white night dress with small silk slippers. Her form was petite and delicate, much like the flower she smelled of. It was as if a life size doll had been deposited in his treasure room. Yet she breathed frantically.

It was the same brave woman he came across in the Temple. Except her hood was gone, replaced by a coat. The steely determined glint in her gold eyes had vanished, replaced by a wide eyed gaze.

"A pleasure to see you again so soon, love," he purred.

Her face was soft and exquisite. Not a single flaw or speck of dirt interrupted her perfectly beautiful face, but the navy blue coat she wore was decorated with golden ribbons and badges of honor. It was Commodore Ashby's coat.

And *there*. In her hand, was the chest.

Phantom held his hand out and the beautiful creature flinched. He felt sorry even through the anger of her trying to steal his prize. "I won't harm you. Now, give me back the chest."

The fear in those eyes didn't fade as she breathed, "No."

"No?" He pulled his hand back. "What was your plan then? Swim to shore with the chest? Break it open. You don't think through your plans very well, thief." His hand roamed into his shirt and pulled out the key on a rope around his neck. Her eyes snagged onto the key. "That's right, love. No way to open the chest without this." He waved the key around a bit as she stood.

"What's your name, love?" Of course, he knew. He recognized her the moment he pulled that hood down, but she didn't know that.

She blinked at him, but said nothing. "I'm inclined to only call you 'love' if you don't divulge." He chewed each word like caramel candy.

Then, there it was, the fire he spotted earlier in the night. Her eyes narrowed, the fear disappeared. In one hand was the chest, but the other held Phantom's discarded cutlass. She held it up to Phantom's chest.

"Clever girl," he purred. "Not as innocent as you appear?" Her face was as cold as stone when she lifted the blade to the base of his neck. "Sadly, you can take the key off my corpse, but this ship doesn't port without my say so. Some civility just might save your life, love."

She began to lower the blade.

"Good girl," he purred. With a flick of her wrist, the key

was released from it's rope. She snatched it before it hit the floor, but he was ready. Phantom jumped at her, but she dodged. Again, the blade was at his throat. He let out an exasperated sigh. "I tire of these games. Put down the sword."

"No," was all she said before she turned to run. She might have even made it to the deck had Earhart and Black not been there to block her path.

Phantom sauntered to block her escape back into the cabin. Not that there was any kind of escape for her.

"What trouble is this, Captain?" Earhart said, brows raising up and wrinkling his forehead.

"Trouble." Phantom mused. "That's a perfect name. Thank you for your assistance, Earhart."

"Anytime, Captain." Earhart and Black drew their blades, metal singing. If there was anyone to avoiding dueling with, it was those two. It was a good reason Phantom had chosen Earhart as his first mate. That, and the fact that they stole a ship together, but it was Black who should be feared above all else. Phantom still remembered the first time he saw what Black could do with a blade in hand.

"Don't worry." Phantom winked as those golden eyes found him. "I'll still call you love." Something like a snarl lifted her upper lip as she swiped at Phantom's throat.

"Captain," Black barked. Both devils came to his rescue as the girl pushed him back into the cabin. Her bravery made Phantom giddy. He put a hand up and Earhart tossed a cutlass into Phantom's awaiting palm.

A flicker of fear returned to her golden gaze, but she held her blade up against his.

Phantom grinned uncontrollably. This woman's bravery

and determination was near admirable. "Are you sure you want to be doing this?" Phantom's eyes simmered in the lamp light. "Crossing blades with the infamous Phantom aboard *Nemain's Revenge* in the middle of the sea." He ran his blade against hers in a caress, metal ringing out. "It would be foolish even for a skilled swordsman." He let his gaze drop, appreciating what he could see of her curves. "Or woman."

Rather than responding, she firmed her grip on the cutlass and tightened her stance, too stiff to be well experienced with a blade, but too poised to be unfamiliar with one. She really was a beautiful little creature.

She struck, but he was off-guard, distracted. He managed to parry her strike before the sword went through his arm. He smiled again. This was the kind of game he liked.

He struck at her cutlass instead of at her body. The body she possessed was delicate, and worth more to him unharmed. It was likely hard for her to even hold the sword, let alone absorb the shock from his as well. Again and again he struck her sword and she backed up, unable to hold her ground.

He held the cutlass on hers, slowly applying more pressure. It pushed her into the wall next to the cabin stairs. Their faces were only inches apart with only the sharp barrier of their swords between them.

"Why are you here anyway, love?" He knew damn well why, but he could sense her foresight to lie to him and he wanted to hear what lies she would come up with.

She huffed at the effort of holding him away.

"Surely, it wasn't for a chat." His eyes dipped to her lips.

They blossomed like a rose, full and tempting. "Perhaps, it was for a bit of company."

"No," she yelled, snapping her head to his and knocking him backwards. Pain flooded his forehead. It gave her enough distance to escape up the steps. Earhart and Black flinched as Phantom put a nursing hand to his head.

"Stand down. That glorious creature is *mine*." He smiled as a trickle of blood ran from his mouth. He bolted up the steps, boots pounding against wood.

The chorus of crewmen had stopped their singing and surrounded her, the chest still clutched in her hand as she rotated with her sword raised.

Phantom reached for the chest since her back was turned and ducked in the same instance, narrowly missing her swing. Stepping out of her reach, he threw the chest to Ramirez. "Safe keeping and all that." He turned his eyes to the crew. "No one touches her. She's mine alone."

Before he could set his eyes on her again, she attacked. Not Phantom, but Ramirez, who was less inclined to swordsmanship, but surrounded by crew members who were.

Black deflected her blow and tossed her back to center deck.

"Naughty, naughty," Phantom purred. "If I'm going to tell my crew not to touch you, the least you can do is return the favor." He spread his arms. "Me, however. You may hurt me as much as you like." She glared at him.

Hyne shouted, "Are you sure she speaks Brettanian, Captain?"

Phantom didn't let his eyes meet Hyne's. Instead, he kept them straight on the girl's, like a heading. "Quite certain. Aren't I, love?" Her eyes simmered with the new morning sun that blinked over the horizon. "Now," he said, holding out his hand, palm up. "Hand over the key."

She attacked again, but he was focused now. He parried her swing and used his wrist to knock the sword from her hand completely. The key along with it. Black dived for it before the little thief could even think about retrieving it.

The woman stood in the middle of ship, surrounded by devils, with nothing left.

"A spot of rope, Robin," Phantom ordered and the powder monkey dropped a length of rope from his perch on the mast. He sheathed the sword to his belt.

That fear from before flickered behind her eyes. He was almost sorry for its return.

He waltzed up to her like it was the beginning of a tango. "Put your hands out before you," he commanded her, but she raised her chin in defiance. The smile returned to his face as he reached for her hands. She did not resist. What else could she do?

He wrapped her wrists in the rope, tight enough to discourage escape, but loose enough to prevent burn. "There's no sense in gagging ya," Phantom whispered. "Besides, I'd like to hear your story, love."

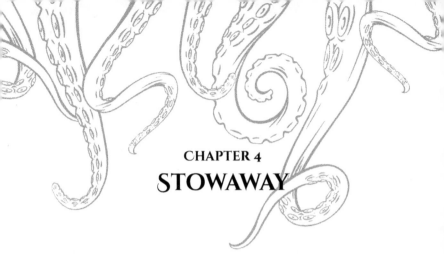

CHAPTER 4
STOWAWAY

P hantom passed the rope tied girl over to Tick and Hyne who each took an arm. She struggled against them, her gaze steeling to stone. Whatever thoughts rolled around in that pretty head of hers, Phantom wanted to know. What did she know about him? The Samaran people didn't exactly like him, often exaggerating the stories, but what exactly sparked such hatred in that molten gaze?

A hairy arm patted Phantom's as he was about to follow Tick and Hyne into the Captain's quarters. He nearly glared back at Earhart who was flushed with worry. Although his demeanor was small, Earhart had tree trunk arms and broad shoulders. Not quite like Jon, the muscle of the crew, but it was an odd shape. As if he was too top heavy. His dark beard covered how enormous his neck was, but they served time together in the Navy, so Phantom knew everything there was to know about his first mate.

Such as that crinkled forehead of worry, which grew

more and more frequent the more he added devils to the ranks. After all, who else was there to look after them?

"Be careful with her, Captain." Earhart's gaze trailed the stowaway.

A laugh spouted from his lips before he could stop it. This girl was no more dangerous than a kitten. A couple strikes of claws, but nothing more.

"You're joking, Earhart." Phantom pointed back to him as he dropped his hand. "A new look for you. A little lacking in delivery, but I do believe I'm finally rubbing off on you."

The man's fuzzy eyebrows knocked together in confusion or maybe offense. They never did have the same sense of humor. "No, Captain. I'm serious. This girl is worth more to the Minister than any trinket you could ever steal from him."

Phantom's lips turnt up into a cruel smile. "I know," he whispered. The gleam in his eye was not mistaken by his first mate. "That's the entire point, mate."

He leaned back as if his Captain had struck him. "It was trap," he breathed, blinking away confusion as if it were sea fog.

Phantom's smile grew wider then he drew a single finger to his lips. "Keep this between us, Earhart."

Earhart's eyes narrowed into slits. "You kept this from everyone?"

"If the trap doesn't know it's a trap, neither will the mouse." Earhart blinked. Phantom straightened under his stare. "I made a promise to the crew I intend to carry out. We weren't going to get there with a glittery Stone and a victory shanty."

Earhart nodded. "Of course, Captain."

With a curt nod, Phantom passed over his first mate to

visit his newfound treasure, his boots stomping against the damp floorboards of the deck, his belts, chains, and buckles all jingling along. An announcement all its own. The devils snuck peeks at their Captain passing by. A new firmer energy radiated from him as he turned the knob to his own quarters.

Inside was the blonde girl, no more than twenty years old. An age that seemed like a child to him. Even though he was only twenty-seven. Life hadn't been kind to Phantom and often times he felt centuries older than he was, but those gold eyes didn't look so young to him.

She breathed heavily, almost stinking of fear. An emotion that didn't even roll off her when she stood surrounded by devils on the deck only moments ago.

It took Phantom too long to realize that Hyne and Tick had relieved her of the Commodore's jacket before they tied her to the chair she sat upon with her arms firmly fixed behind her back. And her dress—

It was scandalously thin white cotton against her sun-kissed, freckled skin.

Hyne and Tick stood on either side of her, waiting instruction like good deck pups. They must have taken the jacket out of spite. There was no small amount of hatred on this ship for the Minister's Navy, but with the look of fear in her eyes, she clearly believed they were preparing her for their Captain. For him to—

He'd ram their heads together later for their idiocy. All the devils knew that if they were to ever defile a woman in such a way, they'd lose their hands, if not their heads, by their Captain's hand himself.

"You're dismissed," Phantom said dryly with an enormous amount of patience. Hyne and Tick glanced at one another as if they expected to stay for the interrogation, but with how uncomfortable they made her, they would be doing more harm than good by remaining.

When they made no move Phantom shouted, "Out!" All three of them flinched and he instantly regretted it, because she was trembling.

Hyne and Tick scrambled out of the room wordlessly.

As the door shut behind him, the girl's body grew impossibly tenser. As if every muscle in her small body was poised and ready to attack. A gag was positioned over her mouth, but he could see the word "no" try to form on her lips. Phantom moved a single finger to the side of her face and she flinched, but he continued to drag the gag down her face until it dropped to her throat. Her fast breaths didn't relent.

"I do apologize Miss," Phantom let the sincerity of his words roll with his tongue. "My crew have been at sea too long to remember how to treat a woman." She spat in his face, her saliva traveling down his cheek as he straightened. "I'm going to allow that, love."

He marched over to his wardrobe at the side of the room as he lifted his sleeve to wipe away the wet spot on his cheek. It clicked open, moaning at the hinges. "I do hope you can forgive me." He pulled out a brown longcoat that would dangle behind his knees when he wore it. It would serve someone else today.

Stuffing the coat in his arms, he unsheathed the dagger at his hip. Any of her muscles that had relaxed became taut once again, but he moved behind her as she began to struggle.

Phantom let his blade slice open the bounds that held her arms to the back of the chair. In disbelief, she moved her arms before her. He cursed to himself that they let her fear grow as much as it did.

She gaped at her empty hands as he placed the longcoat over her shoulders. The Commodore's jacket was like armor to her, but Phantom couldn't stand to look at it. So his longcoat would have to do.

Unsure hands grabbed each side of the longcoat as she pulled it across her chest. It was big enough to cover her completely rather than envelop her like the Commodore's jacket had.

He cleared his throat, not about to take that personally.

While she was still in shock that he not only freed her arms, but gave a stowaway his coat, he tucked the knife neatly and quietly into his desk behind her. The desk was at the very back middle of the room where a window revealed a dawning sky. Not a single, pathetic ship followed them.

Inhaling, he circled her chair dragging one along with him that he placed before her, backwards. Squatting in the chair, he placed his black leather clad arms over the back of the seat. A barrier he knew she'd appreciate.

He watched the fear trickle out of her eyes, but it was replaced by equal parts shock and determination.

"Where is the Stone?" She boldly asked, the fear no longer decimating her beautiful features.

"And here I thought I was the one interrogating a stowaway." He let his lips curve in amusement. His normal Captain demeanor was gone, no straight back or stern eyes. His relaxed form encouraged hers to relax as well. Or was he doing that on purpose? He couldn't always tell.

"You stole it from St. Angeles. I saw you," she accused. Her voice was soft, but since she tried to sound firm, the melody was cut off too quickly.

"Ah," he purred. "So you were the woman in the Temple?" He pursed his lips into an uncommitted frown. "I might have guessed." She only seethed under his gaze like a cat about to show him her claws. "But, more interestingly, what was a girl like you doing in the Temple that late at night? No one is allowed in there after dark. Unless you were trying to steal my prize first."

Her face twisted at the thought of being a thief. He'd have to keep her away from the crew's gambling tables.

"Yes, that's what I thought," he mused. "A proper burgular would know not to wear night dresses and would have weapons strapped on every inch of their person." He flitted a hand before himself as if the thought wasn't worth entertaining. "But you," he breathed, pointing a finger in her direction. "You see an infamous pirate steal a religious artifact and you scamper off to steal it back by stowing away on the most dangerous ship sailing the Sumerian Sea. All for this?" His right hand was in the air so much that her eyes didn't even trail his left hand, where a glittering silver and lilac smooth Stone rested. Her breath hitched at the sight of it.

Good. He'd use it against her later.

"You really must be a fanatic. To risk your life over a slab of rock."

Her eyes narrowed. "Do you not believe in the Goddesses?" Her voice was less firm now, revealing the sweet music her voice produced. Alas, only a small hint of it.

"I believe—" He said curtly, readjusting the Stone to his pocket. "I believe they exist, but I do not worship Davina like the lot of you on Samsara do." He paused, contemplative. "I don't even worship Macha like they do on Kheli." She blinked in astonishment. It was clear, she was unaware there was any other way to worship the Goddesses. "I worship Nemain." His voice cherished the word like a lover's name. "For it is Nemain who rules the sea and that is where I belong." There were more reasons than that, but it was the one it all came down to.

He looked out to the sea beyond. It was a rare magic where the Sumerian Sea and the Keraunos Sea entwined. In the peak of summer, the seas could visibly be seen colliding in swirls of blue and green.

He found her gold coin eyes again. This time they were curious. "To the people of Samsara," she whispered, "saying you worship Nemain is damning yourself to Hell."

These were the moments he lived for. His smile twisted.

"But the Priestess conveniently forgets that Nemain is from Heaven and she does not dwell in Hell. She dwells in the sea, in the push and pull of it. In the waves that crash against the rocks and mold to Her will. She dwelled in its depths when serpents of the ancients ruled these waters with blood. And She will dwell in its shallows when the earth has gone completely barren and there are no more people for fate to torment." Phantom didn't realize he had gotten so carried away in his Goddess until the woman's eyes sparkled. The glint of her curiosity could have easily been missed, but it did not escape the captain.

She quickly steeled her features as he grew quiet. Part of his smile kicked up again. He understood.

Curiosity.

She wanted to know more about the Crone Goddess. He almost obliged her.

"What's your name, love?" He asked instead.

Her eyes shifted then glued to the floor. Silent as the grave.

"I will continue to call you *love* if you don't provide me with an alternative," he spoke lightly. As if the air itself lifted his words. "Love," he added with a puff of air. Her glare was back, pinning him to his seat. He smiled at the challenge.

"Rose," she breathed. "You may call me Rose."

"Ah, now we are getting somewhere Rose of Samsara." He lifted himself from his seat, dragging it against the wood planks beneath. "Although I must say," he chimed, nearly brimming with excitement. "I am surprised you didn't provide me with an alias." He slammed the chair against the rug that encircled his desk.

The sounds matching the realization that spread across her face. Her eyes danced in front of her before she blinked long and hard.

"It was a trap," she whispered.

Phantom popped open the cork on his personal bottle of rum. It wasn't always filled with rum. Really it was for whatever libation he could sink his claws into. Before bringing it to his own lips, he handed it to her, but she stared at it in awe and a hint of disgust.

He breathed deep. "If I wanted to kill you, there are much more interesting ways than poison." He took a swig to prove his point. "Not to mention, the amount of trouble you went through for us to capture you."

She glared at him through her lashes and he was nearly weak at the sight. She was going to be difficult to give back.

After he pushed the bottle into her hand, she finally tipped it back into her mouth. Her twisted face of disgust was adorable.

At last, he noticed the pendant around her neck. The circular shape seemed thick enough to be a locket. The outside of it was an exquisite silver design, but he was too far away to make it out, yet he could see the middle of it depicted a rose. The necklace must have been pretty special to her if she was unwilling to part with it for her self-inflicted mission. Although, sneaking onto a pirate ship was the last place it should have been if she was attempting to prevent it from being stolen.

At Phantom's attention to her neck, she hugged his longcoat tighter around her chest, covering the interesting pendant. Clearly, she was unwilling to acknowledge it.

He put out his hand expectantly and she handed him back the bottle. He accepted it and wiped the smile from his lips.

"Let me make things as crystalline as possible, love." He set the bottle down on his desk again. One drink was more than enough and he'd need to retain his wits. "I am motivated by two things," he said, raising a hand with two fingers pointed in the air. He hardly paid attention to her expression, but he could feel it, how increasingly irritated she was becoming. "Coin and freedom. Both of which you can provide for me." He took that moment to look to her. "Well, your doting father can provide for me as Prime Minister."

She blinked slow. He expected a reaction that she did not deliver. So much so it spiked Phantom's suspicions. The woman had no facial filter before. Why was it suddenly working now? Unless it was practiced.

When it was clear she was finished speaking for the moment, he launched himself off his desk. His boots pounded against the floorboards as he crossed to the door. His crew would only wait so long for an explanation.

"Why?" She breathed so quietly, he nearly missed it.

He turned slowly to her. "Why what?"

"Why does a pirate seek freedom?" The curiosity in her eyes had returned. It softened her brow whereas her glare would have hardened it. Her lips parted ever so slightly with that curiosity. A piece of her blonde hair fell into her face delicately. She was like a goddess-damned angel.

"It is not my own freedom I seek." That was a lie and not at the same time. He and his crew could sail the world and never return to the Isles of Carriwitchet, but there were ties here they couldn't yet break. Ones that kept them nearby. Ones preventing them from following the stars to somewhere grander.

Her eyes narrowed in suspicion. She must have been surprised that an infamous pirate such as himself would be motivated by something selfless. Phantom tried not to let the offense twist his features. A difficult feat, since he had to bite his lip to do so.

"Perhaps, when we ship you back to Samsara—" He didn't care enough to sweeten the bitterness of his tone. "You can ask your Commodore friend."

She blinked. Her only sign of surprise.

But he didn't care. Turning on his heel, he freed the door from its frame. The dawn light trickled in, but it halted when he slammed the door again. He turned the key in the door knob to seal in his real prize.

The dawn air felt like liberty as it kissed his skin. He was so close to victory.

As he turned to the ship deck, his devils waited for him, standing at attention with curious eyes and a stupor to match.

Phantom breathed deep as he reached into the barrel next to him, freeing a juicy apple from its pile. He hadn't eaten since yester-morning and their expectant faces made him famished. He wiped a speck of dirt from the apple onto his coat as he said, "Can I assume you lot were listening in on the entire conversation or will I need to catch you up?" He bit into the apple and the juices dripped down his days old scruff.

Robin dropped down to the deck. "Where's the Stone?" He said tentatively. Jon smacked the back of his head lightly, but Robin complained anyway.

"You mean this?" He had pulled out the Stone before anyone realized he reached for it. The apple doing its job. He snickered to himself. Honestly, how many times was he going to be able to pull that off?

The crew stared at the glittering, swirling purples and silvers ebbing and flowing within its glasslike surface. They were instantly mesmerized. Especially, as Phantom threw it to them. Black caught it in his leather clad hands, marveling at the treasure.

"The Stone's only purpose was bait." The crew snapped their heads back to him as he threw his head back to the door behind him. "The real prize is currently rummaging through my desk."

They blinked in astonishment.

Hyne interceded. "You said they'd pay a fortune for the Stone."

"And that it would be the last job we ever do." Russet, a man with a beer belly and a long red beard, retorted.

Robin dared another look. "You said we could buy Kheli."

Earhart stood in stoic silence with his arms crossed. He already knew the answer.

Phantom spread his arms before him. "Gentlemen," he

mused, tossing the remaining apple core overboard. "Have I ever failed to deliver a deal for you?"

"No, but you enjoy leaving out the details," Jon mumbled. A picture of tall muscle and unamusement. The brute was dark skinned with even darker hair and eyes, a permanent scowl defining his features.

Phantom placed a hand over his heart. "That hurts, Jon. And I thought we knew each other." Before the brute could react, Phantom danced by him to climb the steps to the quarterdeck. "Devils, we captured ourselves the songbird of Samsara."

Their faces dropped in awe. Rose was known for more than her father's wealth and power. The island of Samsara spent every Sunday listening to her sing hymns in worship to Davina. They called her gifted. "Blessed by Davina" to sing so beautifully. Little tricks like that kept Samsara tame. Kept it oppressed. Kept it docile.

Everything Phantom tried to prevent happening in Kheli.

"They won't only pay us to get her back. No, she's more valuable than that. They'll give us Kheli to get her back. Then, you devils can do whatever you want with it." His smile was broad, almost showy.

"What if she isn't worth it to them?" Smith chimed.

"Oh, my dear doctor, she's the daughter of the Prime Minister. There isn't a price he wouldn't pay to get her back."

"Then let's get back to Samsara. Get our ransom," Hyne shouted, Tick nodding his head in agreement.

Phantom put out his hands, waving them downward. "Not so fast. Let the Minister chew on her absence for awhile longer. Let him decide what she's really worth to him. In the meantime," he said, bending over behind the ledge. "Let's celebrate our incoming reward." He pulled out a large bottle Black had managed to smuggle onto the ship when they were docked on Samsara. The island had the strongest mead he'd ever tasted.

The devils instantly perked up at the sight of the familiar bottle. Phantom tossed it to Hyne, who would have tossed himself overboard to catch it. But there was more where that came from. Black had managed to smuggle five bottles onto the ship.

Phantom passed the bottles out. "Drink up boys, but be ready for tomorrow."

CHAPTER 5
THREE DAYS

A	s night fell, the men were so filled with the anticipation of the upcoming victory that they filled their bellies with mead and rum. Although, some crew members kept their decorum such as Ramirez and Earhart. Even Black drank, but he avoided a full drunken splender.

Earhart would normally join, but opted to manage the ship. He never did like it when the devils celebrated prematurely. Something about bad luck.

Russet, Hyne, Tick were the main culprits of the drunken singing. Their pitch was so deafeningly high that it was to the point of irritation.

Phantom laughed as Hyne dropped to the deck, losing the support Tick had provided him. Russet bellowed so loudly it was a whole new type of comical.

Even Jon had cracked a laugh or two as the liquid had melted away his usual stoic nature. Jon was the tallest and biggest member of the Eleven Devils. He came from Draiocht before it fell to the necromites. His face was shaved, but his dark hair came to his shoulders in a curly mess. Robin would often land on his shoulders like an overgrown monkey. Not that Jon ever complained.

The stars above blinked as if they laughed with the drunken sailors.

"What say you, Mr. Earhart?" Phantom prompted. Earhart whipped his head to his Captain. "What do we do with a drunken devil?" Phantom swaggered toward the lopsided devil, who toppled over with every swell of the sea.

Earhart huffed before answering. "Lock them in the brig, Captain."

The laughter continued and Russet set a hollowed out horn to his lips, drinking the rum like it was air to breathe. It ran down the front of his shirt and soaked his beard.

Phantom grinned only slightly before turning. "What say you, Black?" Black stiffened at the attention. "What do we do with them?"

"Tie them to the mast!" Robin blurted as he dropped to the deck. "Upside-down." Robin used his arms to showcase his idea.

Phantom grabbed Robin's head playfully. "Now, that's an idea, but I was asking Black." He forcibly turned Robin with an arm around his shoulders to look directly at Black. "What should we do with these drunken fools?"

He smiled under his hat. No beard ever grew on that sharp chin. He claimed he couldn't grow one. His hair was cut short around his head, but buried under a feather hat. A small smile protruded from his face.

"Dress them up as ladies, Captain."

"Oh," Phantom sung. "I like that." He raised his arm from Robin's shoulders. "Earhart!"

"Yes, Captain."

"Do we have women's clothing aboard?"

"We do not," Earhart said with a disappointed expression.

"Oh, but we do." Phantom nearly beamed with excitement. He shoved off Robin toward his quarters. "Gentlemen, I shall return. Please be certain Russet has relieved himself of everything but his undershorts."

Before the crew could respond, Phantom unlocked the room and shoved himself inside. The room was dark save for the lone candle Rose must have lit, but the girl herself was nowhere in sight. She'd turn up soon.

He clamored against the wardrobe at the side of the room. Through the doors, he pulled out a white puffed shirt and a pair of brown trousers. A cold piece of metal pressed against his neck and he smiled.

"I was hoping you'd find that," Phantom purred. He quickly turned around before the pressure of the knife was too much to slip from. Not smart, but he had to see what her face looked like when she held a blade to his throat. He missed out on it the first time around.

There she was. Her blonde hair swept back. The Commodore's coat around her shoulders once more. And her face. There was a beautiful determination set to her delicate features. Her brows were low, somehow looking down on him from a foot below. Her gold coin eyes looked through her brows and her mouth was a stern line.

Phantom considered the consequence of kissing that beautiful brow. Instead, he smiled and she pressed the knife further into his throat.

"What exactly do you expect to accomplish with this?" His eyes traveled to her hand then back to her eyes.

"Let me go," she breathed.

He licked his teeth then laughed. "Let you go where?"

She blinked.

"You could walk the plank if you'd like, but we are in the middle of the ocean, love. Not an island in sight. Even if you do manage to swim to one, all the ones near here are deserted. You'd starve before your Commodore in threaded blue could save you."

Her face faltered only slightly, her scrunching brows giving her away, but she reasserted herself, pressing the knife tighter to his throat. "Then take me back to Samsara."

Phantom dramatically sucked in a breath. "Can't do that, love." She pressed in further and a small trickle of blood rolled down his chest. "Are you going to kill me? Because that won't do you any good either." He watched as she swallowed. "My crew will still ransom you to the Minister regardless of what happens to me." He paused for a moment. "That is, of course, if they don't kill you for murdering their Captain."

She breathed and it seemed physically painful for her to release his neck, but she did. Her eyes drew to the floor as she lifted the blade handle to him.

"Keep it." He fiddled with the clothes still in his hands as she gaped at him. "If it makes you feel better, I won't deny you the weapon." Then he bit his smile as he purred. "As long as you promise to always greet me that way."

A disgusted look flashed across her face, but she flipped the knife in her hand then in a second she threw and impaled it into the adjacent wall. The blade landed perfectly in the face of a painting of Phantom. It was a younger version of him, painted in Kheli. There were fresh tears littering it. She had been practicing.

"Bloody Hell!" He cursed. "That is a very expensive

painting." And there it was. A small smile broke her face. "Stealing my knife, practicing with it on my very *irreplaceable* painting." Then he smiled. "You've been a naughty girl." As fast as it came, her smile disappeared. Her glare returned. It seemed she had no intention to make this easy.

"Put these on." He threw his clothes at her and she managed to catch them.

"No," she said dropping the clothes to the floor.

"I thought," he started, "You'd want to wear something other than that flimsy dress."

She didn't move to pick up the clothes.

"Or you can keep the dress on," he offered, letting his smile grow and his eyes drop. "I do enjoy watching your nipples peak from underneath—."

Her eyes widened. That broke her stubbornness. She immediately reached for the clothes, covering her chest with them. He almost regretted causing her to be uncomfortable. Instead of apologizing, he threw his head to the foldable screen at the corner of the room. It was covered in red cherry blossom paintings. A beautiful piece stolen from an empress in Koi No Yokan before the mother country fell.

Defeated, Rose walked to the screen.

"Despite what you may think, I don't enjoy making you uncomfortable." Phantom started, running his hands over the holes in his painting. Her accuracy was both worrisome and exciting. The Prime Minister's daughter was made of more than he could have predicted.

"Don't you?" She asked from behind the screen.

"Well in theory, I do." He used a handkerchief to wipe the blood track down his chest. The cut wasn't deep at all. He'd made deeper cuts shaving. "I keep expecting you to retort to my attempts at making you uncomfortable."

Only silence came from behind the screen. "You are very quiet, Rose."

A few beats of silence followed. "Perhaps, I was meant to be silent." Her voice was so soft it could have been mistaken as a whisper.

There was a sudden unfamiliar urge to slice open whatever monster convinced her that was true. He nearly entertained it too. "I don't believe that for a second."

More silence followed. Somehow her words were worth more now, but she didn't indulge him. Instead she threw her discarded dress over the screen.

He poked his fingers into the warm fabric and pulled it from the screen. "My apologies, love." She poked her head out from behind the screen. The glimpse of her bare shoulder nearly had him on his knees before her, but he managed to resist. She was here for a purpose, fraternizing with the cargo wouldn't help.

He lifted the fabric in his hand. "I won't be able to return this intact. Consider the shirt and trousers yours in replacement."

He forced himself to turn to the door, managing to nab the Commodore's coat as well.

"Phantom—" Rose scolded. His name sounded sweet on her lips, especially since he could hear the anger in her tone.

"Don't worry, love. It's going to a good cause." He spread his arms in invitation, even though her head went back behind the screen. "You can join us on deck if you'd like to see."

She only huffed as he escaped the room, slamming the door behind him. For a moment, he considered locking it, but decided against her imprisonment. After all, she was only trying to steal back what he took. She was as good as a guest on his ship.

The deck was filled with the sounds of a new shanty. It was light in tone at the expense of the drunken devil.

Jon had taken the lowest notes, Black carried the melody and Robin took the higher harmony. Other sailors filled out the rest of the notes, most sloppily, but they weren't singing for the Priestess.

OH YO WHO STOLE THE CAPTAINS RUM
OH YO WHO STOLE THE CAPTAINS FLASK
OH YO WHO STOLE THE CAPTAINS RUM
IT'S THE SCALYWAG SWINGING ON THE MAST

Phantom climbed the steps and threw the Commodore's coat to Ramirez. "Safe keeping," he said, winking. Ramirez caught the coat with swift ease and tucked it under his armpit.

OH YO CAPTAIN SAYS
THROW HIM OVERBOARD
SWIMMING HIGH, SWIMMING LOW
OH YO CAPTAIN SAYS
HANG HIM BY THE ANKLES
SWINGING HIGH, SWINGING LOW

Phantom laughed at Russet who tumbled against the rail of the ship. A bit of fear in his eyes and nothing to cover his white belly. Yet, he smiled at his Captain. The crew went silent as Phantom approached the drunken sailor.

Black sang directly to his Captain.

OH CAPTAIN SAYS

Phantom shouted, "Put him in a dress." He tossed the dress to Jon, who rejoined the singing.

PUT HIM IN A DRESS
TWIRLING HIGH, TWIRLING LOW

No one on the crew could keep the song going once Jon shoved the dress over Russet's red head. They rolled to the floor in belly laughs, wheezing, snorting, and coughs. Russet's red hairy chest stuck out the top of the bust, the seams on the side bursting with his beer belly. His shoulders seemed uncomfortably scrunched in the puffy sleeves.

Leave it to Russet to let himself in on the joke. He clasped his hands together, placing them next to his head as he batted his red lashes. Jon was the object of his drunken flirtation. It wasn't the first time Phantom had seen the brute uncomfortable.

The crew erupted again in even louder laughs. Hyne rolled on the floor as Russet lifted the dress, prancing around the deck.

Phantom's arms crossed before him as a flicker of metal flashed in his peripheral, like the glint of a drawn blade. He ducked backwards before the blade crashed down on his neck. As he whipped around, drawing his own blade, he saw the men sneaking aboard his ship. Men in blue Navy uniforms.

Phantom's devils drew their swords and pistols immediately. All drawing attention to the rail where the officers climbed aboard. Earhart and Jon would be searching the rest of the ship for a counter attack.

"Come now, gentlemen," Phantom cooed as he straightened, letting his arms fan out before him. It wasn't a defensive position, which was mocking enough. He made it clear, the Captain of the Eleven Devils did not fear them. "This is increasingly rude. If you had told us of your arrival, I would have had a bed prepared for you. Russet could have personally seen to it." A glance behind him revealed the perfect sight of a burly red bearded fellow in a white dress holding out a cutlass before him. He winked at the gentlemen who let their feet drop to the deck.

The officers showed no reaction. They were finer soldiers than Phantom remembered.

The two who had dropped to the deck stood at attention as they waited for their commanding officer. Sure enough, clean honey hair and freckles appeared over the railing. He really would have made such a pretty girl.

Commodore Ashby was still without his coat. Such a shame. He let his immaculate boots land on the dirty ship planks before Phantom.

"James," Ashby addressed. It was the one thing. The one name that stoked Phantom's fire and upset his calculated demeanor. Yet Ashby let the side of his mouth curve upward when Phantom flinched at the name.

"If you want something from me, Sebastian, you will need to address me properly."

The Commodore's eyes narrowed. "As a Captain?" Phantom inched his way to look over the railing of his ship. "With a stolen ship and an outlawed crew? Hardly applicable."

Phantom bit back his smirk as he stared off the side of his ship where a small sailboat floated off to the side. "And that, Commodore?" He threw his head over toward the sailboat. "Is that your magnificent ship?"

He enjoyed the way the Commodore's nose flared when he was angry. Phantom noted that two men was all his old friend managed to supply. A small sailboat couldn't possibly house an entire Navy, but two men was pathetic. No wonder they preferred the element of surprise. An element they quickly lost.

Black stood at attention before the Commodore, watching his every move. As much as he would enjoy the sight of Black knocking Ashby on his ass, this was his fight.

Phantom drew his cutlass to the Commodore who raised his in return. The Captain smiled. "Good boy."

Ashby's eyes narrowed into slits. "I don't want any trouble, just give her back."

So he did know. It made the game easier. "Oh," Phantom feigned ignorance. "You mean, the stowaway I caught trying to steal my treasure." Right on cue, Black tossed the Stone to Phantom who caught the glittering Stone with his left hand. "How much is she worth to you?"

Then, it was the Commodore who faked his expressions. "Nobody. A servant girl to the Priestess. Just let us return her and we can negotiate for the Stone."

Phantom hummed as he circled the Commodore. "You should know better than to lie to me, Bash," Phantom whispered loud enough for Ashby to hear and the hope dissolved from his eyes. "Miss Rose Davenport will be staying with us for awhile," he bellowed. "Isn't that right boys?"

The devils cheered and shouted in agreement with their Captain.

As if just noticing, the Commodore's eyes landed on

Russet and on the dress he nearly ripped to shreds. His voice turned into a growl. "If you harmed her in any way, I will gut you."

"Relax, Commodore, she remains unharmed," Phantom chimed, watching the Commodore's shoulders drop. "As long as we can come to an arrangement."

Ashby stiffened. "What sort of arrangement?"

"I'd prefer to discuss that with the Prime Minister himself. I'll accept nothing less." Phantom whistled to Ramirez and the old man tossed the jacket he held to his Captain. "You look a bit chilly, Commodore." He threw the coat to Ashby's face and he caught it in his free hand. "She won't be needing this anymore."

There, his nostrils flared again.

The songbird found the perfect moment to test out her sea legs. She strode onto the deck in the shirt and trousers Phantom had loaned her. And to his utter delight, she wore the longcoat he had provided her with that morning. He snuck a glance at the Commodore. A vein protruded from his forehead and his jaw tightened. Phantom smirked at the sight.

It was Rose who didn't realize that the Commodore had come to rescue her. She clearly was coming out to join the crew. Phantom sagged a bit at the realization. He would have liked to see how she would have handled the devils.

"Rose," Ashby called out. She snapped her attention to him and he nearly barreled over the crew to get to her. Black's cutlass was positioned to cut his throat open if he did. The other two naval officers in similar positions.

"Sebastian," Rose cried. Phantom was almost jealous of the melodic way she said his name. Like it was a prayer. She lunged for him, but she didn't meet resistance.

The crew wouldn't touch her, following their Captain's orders.

Phantom slid his cutlass back in its sheath and spread out his arms to stop her.

"Let me pass," she demanded. The devils cooed at of her bravery in low "ooo"s.

"I don't think so, love." Phantom caught her around the waist in an attempt to stop her pathway to the Commodore. She struggled against his arm with albeit weak muscles.

One look back at the Commodore was confirmation. He had guessed before that their relationship was more than what duty required, but with his stiff position, flaring nostrils, and tense jaw, and that damn vein in his forehead, there was no denying it. But a gut feeling warned Phantom that it was not what it appeared to be.

Phantom leaned in to whisper to her delicate ear. "Put on a good show, love."

Rose shoved off him, not bothering to get to the Commodore anymore, but needing distance from her captor. Perfect, she wouldn't try to pass him again.

Phantom turned to the seething Commodore. "In three days time, I will expect to meet the Prime Minister on the island of Bashtir. He is allowed only three guards."

"You will not harm her," Ashby demanded.

Phantom rolled his eyes. "Yes, she will remain unharmed." He tipped his head upward. "Now, off my ship before I need to make an example of *you*, Commodore."

The naval officers waited for their Commodore to break his stand off with the Captain of *Nemain's Revenge* before they began their decent. Ashby followed closely behind them.

The devils spat at them, shouting insults.

"Brute beasts!" Black shouted.

"Blue coat mackerel!" Hyne yelled.

As the three men got back to their sailboat, Phantom turned and Rose tensed. But instead of giving her attention or shoving her back into the Captains's Quarters, he passed right by her.

She followed right after him. "Captain Phantom," she addressed, a bit too formally.

"Yes, love," he cooed in retort, not bothering to turn or even stop.

"Aren't you going to lock me back up?"

Phantom turned so quickly she jumped back. "Are you a danger to my crew?" The nearby crew members quietly tended to the ship, pretending not to listen in.

"I—" she started, glancing around at the devils. "I could be."

Phantom smiled faintly. "I doubt it." He turned again, walking away. He wasn't heading anywhere in particular, but he enjoyed the way she chased after him.

"Well if I am to stay here for three days, where am I going to sleep?" She changed the subject quickly.

"In the main cabin, with the rest of the crew." He had no intention of leaving his prize with them, but he was curious at her reaction.

Hyne took the opportunity to sweep in, careful not to touch her. "You can bunk with me, sweetheart. Tick isn't much of a cuddler." Tick set his smile to a straight line.

Her face twisted adorably in disgust, shoving Hyne away. He nearly whimpered at her rejection. Then she continued after the Captain.

"You have to have other arrangements," she demanded.

He twisted. Then he was walking into her, shoving her into the ship's railing. Though, he was careful to keep physical contact to a minimum. He latched his arms to the railing on either side of her until they were only a breath apart and she was caged in.

"Would you rather share my quarters, love?" He purred.

Before he could tease her further, her knee came up between his legs. Hard. Exploding pain greeted him there. He hurled over in pain and she took the opportunity to escape his hold.

"Don't call me love," she shouted back as she cantered to the Captain's quarters. She shoved the door closed before any of the crew bothered to stop her. They were too occupied staring at their Captain in astonishment, then amusement. Soon they were doubled over, laughing at his expense.

"Very funny, boys," Phantom said gruffly, barely swallowing a wince, still hunched over in pain.

Earhart came up beside his Captain cackling softly. "I'm afraid you've met your match, Captain." He crossed his arms and faced the door she disappeared into. "It's about to be an interesting three days."

Through the pain, Phantom shot a look promising death to his first mate.

CHAPTER 6
DAY ONE

Rose Davenport had confiscated the Captain's quarters.

When Phantom had attempted to reenter his room, she managed to lock it from the inside. She swiped the key from his pocket when he had caged her against the railing. The little songbird was almost as good as him.

When he banged on the door, she simply did not answer. It was as if the siren wanted him to think she had escaped. Clever ploy, but escaping would only earn her a ticket on Nemain's carriage. The trip to Kheli had no islands and lots of open sea since it laid East of Samsara.

She was in there, but Phantom was too exhausted to fight that battle and too cheap to damage a perfectly sound door.

So he slept under the stars, bunking with the devils was hardly an option. Jon and Russet snored like piles of chains. Not to mention the only bunk available was occupied by piles of rusted junk. If he was honest with himself, he hadn't thought through her sleeping arrangement because he didn't think she'd be staying longer than one night.

Bargaining for three days was probably the most selfish thing he'd ever done, yet the thought of her leaving so soon prickled something hot in his blood. Each moment he spent with the songbird made the feeling stronger, but it wasn't something he recognized.

Perhaps it was pure spite after seeing that look on the Commodore's face. He clearly cared for her and taking away something that belonged to him felt satisfying. But that wasn't it—

He twisted in his spot on the deck. With only Robin as a lookout on the mast, these were the quietest moments on *Nemain's Revenge*.

He had three days to figure out why he needed more time with Rose Davenport and why the Commodore looked at her like that. It wasn't enough, but he wasn't enough of a bastard to delay their victory any longer. More than anything, he knew once she was in the Commodore's clutches, he'd never see her again.

Between the hard deck floors and his racing thoughts, Phantom evaded sleep, even as the sun rose over the horizon. They'd be in Kheli by the next morning.

Phantom heard the flap of membranous wings before the little beast could trill. A flash of white and blue scales, then Serena's heavy talons landed directly on his gut.

A pained groan escaped him. *What is it with the females on this ship causing me pain?*

Serena's curious head shot to Phantom then turnt sideways, seemingly assessing his foul mood. The little dragon wasn't exactly little. From nose tip to tail, she nearly spanned Phantom's height, quite smaller than the legends and histories proclaimed. She pounded once more causing a frustrated grunt to rumble from his throat.

"Smith!" Phantom called into the night that was quickly melting into daylight.

Footsteps pounded against the planks and the doctor rounded to where Phantom had huddled for the night. "Terribly sorry, Captain." He whistled and the little beast's ears shot backwards, followed by its head. The doctor propped an arm up to one side, allowing Serena to land easily on his arm.

Smith smoothed a knuckle under the dragon's chin, right in the spot she liked, causing her scales to ripple with blue. "Let's see what Wilson has made up for you this morning, how does that sound?" The beastie chirped happily in response to the prospect of food. Like any other animal, even a dragon could be motivated by something tasty.

The doctor wasn't quite as old as Ramirez, but close. His grey hair was kept short and his beard trimmed. Even among pirates, the man regarded his appearance highly. He had a straight nose and a narrow face to match his relatively lean body.

Smith was one of the many devils who didn't hail from Samsara. He came from the peaks of Meraki. A holy land to any devout Davinian. Although, Phantom never had the honor of witnessing the peaks himself, Smith spoke highly of their beauty. To the Merakesh people, doctors were holy men, just as they believed science and faith to be related rather than separated like many in Samsara.

Phantom watched Serena bob with every step from the limping doctor as they descended to the main cabin.

The tragedy of doctor Rylan Smith was the absence of

his leg. He amputated it himself after the unfortunate incident of a necromite bite. If one severed the limb seconds after the bite, there was a chance to stop the spread of infection and save the patient's life. Or mind, since it was arguable that the corpse that still walked afterward was still alive.

At least, that was how Smith would put it. Bloody Hell, his thoughts were starting to sound like the doctor's. Phantom couldn't imagine having to do the act himself. Although, he would, given the alternative.

He stood as the foggy morning air began to clear, leaning over the railing before the helm. There were very few men on deck yet. Some would need to be woken by force soon.

The door below him rattled and a blonde head peeked out. Instead of announcing his presence, Phantom decided to see what she would do.

With soft steps she walked out to the deck, still wearing the clothes he had given her. The trousers fitting tightly around her hips. Clearly the seams were made for a male figure and as petite as she was, her hips contained feminine wealth.

Not that he was looking.

When she discovered that the deck was empty, she didn't roam. Instead, she cantered to the main cabin. Those noiseless slippers still covered her feet. It didn't take him long to realize she was searching for food. Strange, since she refused anything he brought to her thus far.

Was she a prisoner or was she a stowaway? Hostage? Treasure?

The definition grew foggier with each passing hour.

Phantom considered following her into the main cabin,

but he didn't want to interrupt if it meant she wouldn't eat. Instead, he decided to sneak into his own room, to surprise her when she came back. He toed around the deck, careful not to alert the cabin below of his whereabouts.

Softly, he strode into the Captain's quarters to find them dark. The sun rose in the East, which was their heading. The glass windows faced West on this journey, shrouding the cabin in a foggy splendor. The expensive painting of himself was shredded to ribbons on the floor. The wardrobe door was open, revealing his clothing being rifled through. And of course, so was his desk.

Nothing he didn't expect.

Yet, a glint of something caught his eye toward the nightstand. As a pirate, Phantom had a eye for anything that shined. He strode to the bed where the blankets laid crumpled and disrupted. On the nightstand laid that necklace he had spotted on her before.

For something that seemed to hold value to her, she didn't exactly keep it close.

He lifted the pendant, considering taking it to remind her of the criminals she was dealing with, but as his eyes studied the strange engravings, he grew fascinated. What was it about this necklace?

There was a seam along the edge, indicating the contraption's opening. A locket perhaps? Phantom might have considered throwing it overboard if the Commodore's portrait lay inside.

He studied the necklace further, running a callused finger over the delicate lines that portrayed a rose and its petals. At the very end of the rose's stem, the metal seemed to dip out a bit. He pushed the piece in and the pendant snapped open.

Sweet soft chimes swirled from the pendant. A beautiful melody that reminded him of a lullaby. The notes continued lazily, hitting each like a small wind bell would in the breeze. There was an odd calming effect the music brought as if forcing peace on him, making him feel as if he were lounging on a beach in the sunlight or floating in the waves of the ocean, letting Nemain control the direction of his body.

Another feeling followed. One that sparked a part of him that only came out when it was time to battle. A rising anger came with the feeling, as if his body rebelled against the idea of being calmed forcibly by music.

He snapped the locket shut, dropping it to the nightstand before it could cause further damage, the feeling receding like a wave.

Phantom no longer had a desire to surprise Rose, so he left. The crew would be up and about soon enough with the way the light began to wash over the room. He snuck out before she could realize he was there.

A few crew members mulled about the deck, searching for their duties. Robin leapt off the mast and landed before his Captain. His mannerisms were so monkey like there would never be any mistaking him. He landed on all fours, but slowly rose with a small grin on his face.

"Sleep well, Captain?"

Of course he saw everything. He saw his Captain get locked out of his own quarters. Saw him struggle for sleep on the top deck. His locket induced spout of anger was too recent to keep himself in check.

Phantom steeled his expression. "You keep this attitude up and you'll be on lookout duty every night. Is that understood?"

Robin's smile wiped from his face and he stood straighter. "Yes, sir." The boy turned to the main cabin to enjoy some sleep now that his shift was over.

Phantom was too sleep deprived and had too little patience to deal with his teasing. He rubbed his head in attempt to banish the building headache, but of course that did little to ease the pain.

"Captain?"

Phantom flinched, a small irritated sound coming from him.

"Are you alright, sir?" Earhart asked.

Phantom waved him off. "Yes, what is it?"

Earhart pursed his lips. A sure sign of displeasure from his first mate. Phantom, of course, knew this would come. As his first mate, Earhart was inclined to point out actions he disagreed with.

The first mate looked more closely at Phantom, at his eyes which were likely darker than they should have been. But apparently not enough to worry Earhart, so he spoke, "The men are worried we will lose our victory, Captain."

Phantom cocked an eyebrow. The mere suggestion of gossip was enough to sour his mood further. "Does the crew often talk in whispers of their disagreement toward their Captain's decisions?" He paused, letting the offense land on his old friend. "Or is it just you?"

Perhaps, it was the lack of sleep that pricked at his patience or the narrowing of Earhart's eyes. The first mate was never afraid of his Captain. He had always been quick to discourage others from becoming too forthcoming, but something about this particular scheme might be the invisible line Earhart couldn't cross.

The thought alone had Phantom grinding his teeth.

"Why three days Captain?"

He could lie. He was exceptionally good at it. Even to his first mate. The man wore a tanned billowy shirt. His arms were so disproportionate to his torso, that the shirt clung to his arms then hung loose around his chest. He was shorter than Phantom, possibly the shortest devil, save for Robin. His dark hair was cropped closely to his scalp and his dark eyes radiated a sort of brilliance. After a moment of evaluating his first mate, practically his brother, a blonde head caught his attention.

Earhart sensed the shift in Phantom's attention, his eyes scanned for the source behind him. When he saw the songbird come out from the main cabin, smiling bashfully as Hyne no doubt flirted mercilessly, Earhart's face flushed red. Not in embarrassment, but frustration.

His voice was low and deadly when he whispered, "Is this because of Sebastian?"

Sebastian. Earhart would be the only one to say the Commodore's first name. It was how the first mate knew him. Phantom often forgot that Earhart was his friend as well and when the time came to choose sides, he chose Phantom.

Phantom snapped his eyes to his first mate, tipping his head up.

"Do you want to take something else from the bastard?"

"Mr. Earhart," Phantom addressed and Earhart stiffened. The first mate was an obedient solider through and through. He would always need leadership. Someone to make the hard decisions. So his Captain approached him with arms crossed around his chest. "Why do you think the Commodore slipped onto our ship with only two men?"

Earhart lowered his eyes, for only a moment.

"Desperation. It isn't just his own need to have her where he deems *safe*. I know Sebastian. He would have come alone, and probably would have been successful in retrieving her. But he came, expecting to have to find her. He came, expecting I would have her under lock and key, not roaming about the ship."

Earhart's eyes narrowed, as if he too, wanted to ask that very question.

"When he looked upon her, it was not love or some affection." He watched his first mate retrace the encounter, searching for details. "There is a big difference between love and greed, mate. And that was greed lacing the Commodore's face. He expected me to lock her away, because he sees her as something to possess." Finally, Earhart's eyes widened, realization hitting him.

Phantom's eyes shifted to the songbird on his ship and what secrets she held onto.

"He looked at her the same way I look at treasure." Her gaze fluttered about the ship until it landed on Phantom. A cool determination set her jaw as she lifted her chin and marched in his direction. Without breaking eye contact with the stowaway, Phantom whispered, "And I have three days to find out why."

Rose's steps came determined as Earhart gaped at his Captain. She ignored him, clearly having her own reasons for approaching. "Captain Phantom," she addressed.

"Yes, love," Phantom purred with no small amount of satisfaction as Rose let out an irritated breath. It broke her determined face for a fraction of a second before she recovered. He didn't understand why he enjoyed irritating her, but any reaction from her felt like an enjoyable one. So long as he caused it.

"You will be negotiating with my father for my life soon, is that correct?" Her tone was unyieldingly perfect, as though speaking every word carefully would help her cause.

"Yes," Phantom purred again. He didn't miss that his low register and growled undertones made her tense. He relished in it.

"Then, I will negotiate for the Stone." Her hands were firmly at her sides and her back was as straight as a plank, but those gold coin eyes held no amount of fear.

Phantom nodded to his first mate. A simple dismissal, but he didn't need her words influenced by another presence. He took two strides toward her, but she didn't yield. Even as they were a breath's width apart. Even as he could feel her body's warmth, just as he knew she could feel his. Not even a gasp escaped her lips.

Even as a small woman aboard a ship of a dozen devils, she exuded the confidence of a woman with nothing to fear. "Will you now?"

If she could feel his purr rattle her, she didn't let it show. Phantom pulled the Stone from his pocket. She nearly reached for it, but lowered her hand before she could. He let the glow of the simmering silver and lilac wash over her steeled features as he drew it close to her cheek.

"The Davinians on Samsara may pay a pretty price for it. But I have feeling that trading it to the markets of Atlas would bring me much more profit."

Her eyes glowed with fury. Just the idea of the Stone being in foreign lands. Especially, with the Atlatics who insisted upon twisting the Triple Goddess religion to suit their own needs. Oh— Phantom knew that would make her blood boil. No traditional Davinian had anything nice to say about Atlas.

"What could you possibly give me in exchange?" Phantom let the glittering purples and silvers land on his face instead, showing her who held the power of fate over the Stone.

But Rose was not so easily deterred.

"Play me for it."

Phantom tipped his head back in surprise. Of all the things he thought she would say, that was not one of them.

"A game of Kazeboon. If I win, I get the Stone."

Kazeboon was a Draiocht game that Jon brought aboard. It translated to "liars" in his language. It was a game that solely depended on a person's ability to lie. He could easily win against her. Lying was a sport to him and from what he had gathered of the songbird thus far, it was not her strong suit.

But even more curious than her choice of game was the fact that she was not bargaining for her life or safe return home. She only cared about the Stone. She had already given away something vastly crucial. Something he wouldn't hesitate to take advantage of.

His lips curved into a smile as he leaned down to her. "And if I win?"

There. A flicker of fear in her practiced diplomatic determination. "What do you want?" Her breath was shaky. This would be an easy win.

He leaned back, pretending to consider for a moment. Then he leaned in again, whispering into her ear. Her flinch did not escape him as his breath drifted across her ear and down her neck.

"I want," he started, relishing in the shiver that floated across her spine. "Information."

She jerked back. "Information about what?"

"Relax, love." She did anything but. "I won't ask you about Samsara, or your father, or even your precious Commodore." Her eyes narrowed, but her shoulders were still tense. "All I want to know, is why you want this so badly?" He held up the Stone. "Truth only, and if I win a game of Kazeboon against you, I'll know if you lie to me."

Her brows crashed together. "That's all that you want?"

Phantom's smile kicked up. "Now that you mention it, I would like to be able to sleep in my own bed again."

She looked him up and down. Perhaps determining if she could fight him off if need be. Not that she would have to. Phantom really did want to be able to sleep in his own bed again, but he could understand her concern since he had no intention of letting her sleep anywhere else either. "And when I say sleep, I do mean sleep."

"Are you actually suggesting that we share a bed?"

"Yes, I thought that was clear," he intoned. Not even a hint of his earlier purring made an appearance. It was critical for her to understand that he was simply keeping his treasure close. Not fraternizing with it. No matter how tempting. When she seemed unconvinced, he held up a hand as though in court. "I swear I will not touch you." But with no small amount of pride, his purring returned. "Unless you beg me too."

She let out a noise of disgust right before she declared, "Deal!"

He let his smile creep up. "Excellent."

CHAPTER 7
KAZEBOON

The game of Kazeboon was played with specific tiles containing Draiochet runes. Most of them geometric in shape. Triangles, lines, squares, circles and mixtures of each laid out on one side of each tile. Each rune represented a god or goddess from the mythology of the people of Draiochet.

Each of the gods and goddesses of ancient Draiochet were split into three categories. Although, the meaning of these three categories can never be fully agreed upon.

Aaru were the highest ranking tiles. In this, the King of Gods, his wife and any other deities loyal to the heavens or associated with the sky would belong. Most scholars believed these gods to not only be tied to the heavens, but to represent the past and the journey to glory. Loyalty and worship were treasured highly and blasphemy was treasonous.

Geb were the tiles closely related to humanity. They represented grounding in the earth and were supported by gods and goddesses that associated with the earth, youth, beauty, and the wilderness as well as the present. Fertility and free will were prized most of all and death was feared.

Duat was death. They were the deities that would exist long after the rest have gone. They were the future. Any gods or goddesses associated with rot, death, wisdom, time, or the afterlife were connected with Duat. These gods treasured nothing and they feared nothing.

There were forty tiles altogether. Twenty-five of those tiles belonged to Geb and were the weakest, although, they varied in power. A few of them were more powerful than some Duat or Aaru tiles. Ten tiles belonged to Aaru and only five to Duat.

The tile belonging to the King of Gods, Ran, could ultimately crush any other tile, even though the Duat tiles were the strongest.

The devils had accumulated on the main deck by the time Jon returned with the pouch containing the tiles of Kazeboon. Phantom crossed his legs in front of himself as he sat, waving an arm where he expected Rose to sit. "My lady," he purred.

She hesitated, her breaths shallow. But it was too late to reconsider. Even so, Phantom thought perhaps a proper taunt would encourage her.

He pulled his arm back. "Unless, of course, you've lost your courage, love."

Taking the bait, she straightened, then sat across from him on the deck, crossing her legs. The devils began dealing out their bets, most in favor of their Captain, but Jon always did like an underdog.

"No cheating," Phantom warned as Jon placed his bet.

Jon spread his arms low. "I wouldn't dream of it."

Phantom raised one eyebrow at his ship's brute right

before he retreated to lean against the mast. Robin dropped next to him, clearly not tired enough to miss the action.

After shaking the pouch, Phantom angled the opening toward his opponent. She blinked in response. "Love," Phantom said at her elongated pause. "You have played Kazeboon before? Haven't you?"

She blinked, clearly sensing her mistake. "I've studied the game, but I haven't had the chance to play myself."

Victory rippled off the devils behind him, but Jon's face didn't falter for a moment. The idiots assumed she was telling the truth. Kazeboon was a liar's game and the lying started long before tiles were drawn.

Phantom played along though. "Draw five tiles from the pouch and keep them to yourself. Every time you use one, you will draw another tile from the pouch until the tiles are gone." He plucked five tiles from the pouch himself to demonstrate and she followed the action. "Since you challenged me, my turn will begin the game." He was careful to explain, even if he knew those attentive eyes already knew. Phantom wondered if she would cut her act if he lied about a rule. Thief and pirate he was. A cheater he was not.

He scanned the tiles before making his selection, holding the tile in his fist for a moment. "Whoever possesses the turn, must say out loud which rank that tile belongs to. This, of course, does not have to be the truth." He set his tile down before her, scanning her eyes before saying, "Aaru." His voice was a near whisper as if he wished her to chew on the word long before making her decision. There was so much strategy in saying that one word. Such as claiming to have a Duat, then possessing a low-ranking Geb to con the opposition into throwing away a good tile. Or claiming Geb to then crush one of their higher tiles with a Aaru tile. All of this, of course, depended on the liar across the tiles.

At first, Phantom's strategy was to use simple tricks to dissuade her, but after her show of pretending not to understand the game, he evaluated his opponent much differently.

"Once you set a tile down and we both reveal our play, the winner will take both tiles into their winning pile. The tiles cannot be used again, but the pile will help us determine a winner in the end." She scanned her tiles vigilantly, but she still made a show of knocking her brows together. As if not understanding what the runes meant. But Phantom knew, she wouldn't have suggested the game without knowing exactly what each rune symbolized.

The first few rounds with a new opponent were crucial to understanding what kind of player one found oneself dealing with. The Captain watched the songbird intently to see if she would pick it up, he feigned a nervous tick, rubbing at his nose. A soft tell, but one she'd pay attention to if she was any good. Of course, he had no tells, but she wasn't going to know that.

She slammed her tile on the floorboards without hesitation, face down. There, a small gleam in her eye told him her meekness was an act and she knew exactly what she was doing. It was there and gone in an instant.

Phantom's smile kicked up. *This game is going to be so much fun.*

They both flipped over their tiles. Phantom's tile was a circle with a line diagonally piercing it, if not slightly off center. Rose's tile had two triangles mirroring each other. Phantom's smile kicked up wider. Both tiles were from Aaru. A strong round to start the match.

The circle and line represented the god of truth, Amet. An ironic tile for a game of Kazeboon. It was a high ranking god, but just under the goddess of balance, Maram. Rose had won, but Phantom got his confirmation. She did know what she was doing. That was the best move she could have made.

Beginner's luck.

With a false bashful grin, she swiped the tiles to her side which Robin leapt to protect. His monkey was to guard her winnings.

The minutes ticked by. Kazeboon was not a long game, but it felt like chess with the amount of contemplation and strategy it required. The devils behind Phantom were close enough to feel the warmth of their breath. An uncomfortable arrangement, but he was careful to not let it show.

Their two piles were evenly spread. He lost as much as he won. Although he never let the grin fall from his face, she was better than he could have anticipated. He attempted to make the even game seem like he was toying with the songbird, if only for his own pride. Her face never faltered away from its concentration, as if she could cast better runes to appear on the tiles, but he knew better than to believe the innocence of her face.

Delicate light eyebrows pinched together as if she couldn't quite place what the rune was. But all the runes were in play now and the King of Gods had yet to make an appearance. He didn't have it, so she must possess it. That single win would not win her the game, as it were. There were six runes left, which meant, if he could win the other two rounds, he could take the game.

He peered at his tiles. The God of the Harvest, Flit, a Geb. And two Duat goddesses. Phantom had to be absolutely certain the Geb was conquered by the King of Gods, because Flit will concede to nearly every rune that existed in the game. It would be a complete waste for her to use her best tile on that. But if he lost one of the two goddesses to Ran, she would win. His only chance was if the other two runes she tentatively thumbed through were low enough to be beaten by the Duat goddesses. It was likely, but it had to be executed perfectly.

She set down a tile and whispered, "Geb." Phantom's head rang with alarm bells. Did that mean she lied? Not enough evidence. He studied her. Those gold coin eyes sparkled, clearly she was up to something, but she didn't let her body move an inch. It was a lie, certainly, but the intention was clear. She wanted him to believe that the lie meant she set down Ran. The little minx wanted him to waste his Geb on another rune.

It was surely not Geb, but it wouldn't be Aaru either. The songbird was good, but no one can lie to Captain Phantom easily. It was why he was self-deemed the reigning champion of the game.

He set a tile facedown and they both flipped their tiles over. On his tile was a crescent moon with a small dot in the middle of it. Hect, the Goddess of Magic and Consequences. A Duat Goddess. A powerful rune. Rose's tile contained another Duat God. The rune with two circles slightly overlapping one another, was Delmec, the God of the Gates of Hell. The one who guarded the world below, a prison guard more than a protector and the largest in size of all the Gods. A God who happened to be Hect's lover and husband. Ironic again, because Hect was just powerful enough to be above her husband.

An almost cruel smile tugged at Phantom's lips. He guessed right. She lied, but not the obvious lie that he waited patiently for.

She sighed slowly and closed her eyes. She was losing faith in her ability to win this game. He could see it in the way her shoulders dropped and her hair cascaded into her face.

"Last chance, love," he breathed, unsure why he felt the need to give her an out. Her chances of winning this were just as great as his was. Perhaps, it was to save himself the embarrassment of losing in front of his crew or the dying light in her eyes. "Forfeit now, and I won't hold you to any part of the deal."

The devils booed behind him. Clearly, he was ruining their fun. Jon still remained impassive at the mast. Robin was downright giddy, swaying back and forth on his crossed legs.

Rose's eyes narrowed, her mistrust amplified by the game. Phantom's foolish heart faltered at that. A feeling he immediately tamped out, unwilling to examine that brief emotion too closely. Not in the middle of a liar's battle. She glanced down at her tiles. Phantom knew she wouldn't surrender. Not with the King of Gods in her hand, feeding her courage. But the offer made him look stronger.

"I challenged you, Captain," she said with no small amount of mirth, making a mockery of the title. "Don't cow on me now."

Oh, this woman was going to be the death of him.

His lips curled into another cruel smile. The challenge

was understood. Whatever strength he displayed by offering her a way out was immediately crushed by her confident response.

After a moment of examining her, he laughed. A sound that earned a rather nasty look from her.

Perhaps she does fit in with a crew of devils.

In the midst of his laughing, he placed a tile facedown before her. "Aaru," he announced and she seemed stunned into silence, unprepared for the play to happen. He knew, damn well, that the only Aaru tile left in play was the King of Gods, therefore she knew he was lying. The word left her with no more knowledge than she had before. It could be seen as a temptation to use her strongest tile against him, or the taunt itself was meant to dissuade her.

Either way, he rubbed his nose to solidify it. When he caught her eyes tracking the movement he knew he won.

She set down her tile and they both flipped them over.

His tile displayed a line with smaller diagonal lines jutting upwards from the top of the larger line, resembling a stalk of wheat. The God of the Harvest. A Geb tile, easily thrown away.

There— on her tile was a circle with triangular lines bouncing off it, depicting the sun. There he was, the King of Gods, finally in play. Wasted.

His smile grew to wicked delight on his face and she huffed at the sight of it. She won this round, making their score even, but she lost the war, wasting the best tile on a lowly Geb.

She cursed as he clapped his hands together.

"You haven't won yet," she snarled. And oh, he loved the temper she had. From what he'd seen of it so far, she let it slip so very little.

"Oh, love, but I have," he purred, plucking the tile from her hand. It didn't matter, she had no more to choose from. Whatever the outcome, she had no way to stop it. No way to end it. No way to avoid it.

He set the tile face up before her. It was three wavy lines and it represented Ily, the God of Song and Merriment. A powerful tile, but still only a Geb.

Phantom's smile grew to an impossibly large reach. The tile he flipped over was a line with two smaller lines diagonally jutting upwards creating a fork-like symbol.

It was Nemain, the Goddess of Death, his Goddess. Although, the people of Draiochet refered to her as Nephthys, but he knew his Goddess well. The King of Gods and only the King of Gods could beat Nephthys.

The men behind Phantom stood and cheered, patting their champion Captain on the back. They made mocking noises to Robin and Jon for their poor choice and Rose's poor luck.

Jon stood on the mast, glaring bullets at his Captain. Phantom narrowed his eyes. Somehow the look granted him a hole at the pit of his stomach, warning him that he may have made a mistake. When his eyes tracked the blonde's form, he understood why.

Her eyes filled with unrivaled despair. He knew the Stone meant a lot to her, but perhaps he underestimated her drive. Those gold coin eyes shifted up to her opponent and she steeled her features, even with the glisten of tears lining her eyes. Tears she never let fall.

There was an urge to help her. To do something. Maybe hand her the bloody Stone and be done with the look on her face. But he was frozen. Unable to act, he watched as she drifted away from the cheering devils, a sinking feeling accompanying all the others.

The devils were all too occupied with exchanging their bets to notice. All except one. Jon still stood at the mast, gazing at Phantom. The man knew too much for his own good. Phantom had considered killing him on more than one occasion for that knowledge, but the man had shown too much unparalleled loyalty to even consider it.

But that look was all too damning.

CHAPTER 8
CAPTAIN'S QUARTERS

T he day billowed on into night and no shanties filled the air. The anticipation was great since they would arrive in Kheli at dawn. The only land any of them called home. Although, Phantom knew, his home would always be the sea. The land never felt quite right beneath his feet. No, he was born with salt water running through his veins.

This trip was less cheerful because every time they arrived in Kheli, news was worse. There was less food, more expensive taxes, or unwelcome visitors. Phantom and his devils built their reputation as high as they could for that reason. If they were feared enough, perhaps it would discourage raiders and thieves.

Lately, desperation seemed to be running higher than fear.

Often times, there were unfamiliar raiders, sailors, and would-be pirates attempting to take advantage of the few places left in the world that held rich land and unprotected people. In a world mostly shrouded in death, all visitors were unsavory ones.

With Samsara oppressing them and the rest of the world trying to conquer them, the people had little to place their hope in. Phantom felt a pang of shame in letting them believe in even a small hope. For that reason, they didn't know about the deal and they wouldn't until Phantom could be certain Samsara would never touch them again.

Freedom may be the reason he stole *Nemain's Revenge* in the first place, but it was never his own. Maybe one day, it would be.

The crew yawned and clamored into the main cabin, some with bottles in hand. Russet almost always had a bottle of rum in hand, as he did now, dipping his head below the low clearance of the cabin entrance. Before descending Hyne shot a wink back to his Captain. Hyne wasn't exactly young. He was in the middle of his third decade, but he always carried the air and mischief of a child. His honeyed hair hung in waves loosely around his face, a simple light brown cloth tied around his forehead to keep the sun from scorching his skin.

Tick stood behind him. Silent as always, but it was never uncomfortable. Tick's was a soothing kind of silence. His hair was an ebony, near black color that was cropped near his ears and hung over his forehead. He had a limber build, but still strong. Tick had surprised his Captain on multiple occasions of his strength. He dipped his head silently before ducking into the cabin after Hyne.

Ramirez was on night watch. Phantom wondered if it was a mistake, letting him keep watch, but the man enjoyed the night too much. He wouldn't doze off on duty.

The old man was at the helm with a weathered hand on

the wheel. His white and grey hair tied back at his nape and a hat resting atop it. Ramirez always went for a cleaner look than the other devils. It served them well when a little propriety was needed.

Phantom climbed the steps to stand with him. With one hand on the wheel, the other held a book with his thumb firmly placed between the pages to hold the spot.

"What do the stars say tonight?" Phantom mused. He knew the old man's favorite pastime. It's why he didn't have the heart to keep Ramirez from night watch. It would break the poor man's heart to not gaze at the stars, especially on a clear night.

A gleam in the old man's crystal eyes told him he asked the right question. He pointed to the left, where a cluster of stars decorated the horizon.

"Do you see that star, Captain?" Amongst the cluster shone a bright star he knew all too well.

"The Star of Nemain?" Phantom wanted to follow that star more than anything. It was said that the star hung above the Gates of Hell. Some would call it Necropolis. The city of the dead and keeper to the Gates. He had once sworn to himself that he'd find Necropolis one day. One day when the people of Kheli didn't need him anymore.

The old man's nose crinkled up. "No, boy," he spat. Phantom hated when Ramirez called him a boy. He pointed again, this time, Phantom could see a small, faint star below the Star of Nemain. "That small star that could be easily missed was not there two days ago."

Phantom whipped his head from the star to the old man. "What? How do you know?"

Ramirez shot him a glare that dared to question him,

which promptly brought Phantom's jaw to his skull. There was always a good reason to listen when it came to Ramirez.

"Do you see the star above it, to the right of Nemain's star?" The man's accent was hushed and slow, as if he could take eons to make his point.

Phantom didn't need to squint to see the star. It shone brightly, even next to Nemain. Although, in the times he spent staring at the Star of Nemain with dreams of running away, he never remembered the star shining so bright.

"The bright one is referred to as Asad or the Lion." Ramirez spoke with a hint of wonder. "That one appeared in the sky about twenty eight years ago and has slowly grown brighter as the years have gone by." Phantom forgot how old the man really was, for him to remember when a star was born. "It encircles Nemain every year, but that little dim star is now in its path."

Ramirez sucked in a breath as if in remembrance. "I suspect, that the dim star will grow brighter and by the time Asad arrives, they will glow together, brighter than the Death Goddess herself."

Phantom huffed out a laugh. "You have much faith in a dim little star."

The old man let a smile grace his lips. A small peek of yellow teeth exposed. "I've seen it before, Captain. Thirty four years ago, when the world ended and necromites roamed the earth. Asad joined with another star that grew from dim to bright in a matter of months before it disappeared completely."

Phantom blinked at the notion, but Ramirez continued.

"I've always wanted to visit Atlas and ask the scholars of Kalopsia if they knew why the stars appeared and disappeared. Then again when Asad reappeared in the night sky." He seemed to let his mind drift him there. To the library of great knowledge, kept away from the world.

"Why haven't you?"

Ramirez blinked for a moment, coming out of his momentary daydream. Then those crystal eyes pinned Phantom in place. As if they could nail his boots to the floorboards below.

"Why haven't you followed Nemain to the ends of the earth?"

Phantom's heart skipped or stopped altogether, but he knew the answer was the same as Ramirez. Because he was a devil of the *Nemain's Revenge* and his job would never be complete until Kheli's people were safe.

With a nod, Phantom dismissed himself from Ramirez's presence. As beautiful as his stars are and his attentiveness to the condition of the sky, Ramirez's gaze felt heavy. An added weight to Phantom's burdened shoulders.

Plus, there was a blonde haired beauty waiting for him in the cabin below. Reluctantly waiting if not downright fuming.

He turned the knob to the Captain's quarters easily. He frowned slightly, expecting it to be locked and likely barricaded, but she was honorable enough to keep up her end of the deal. She would have expected him to hand over the Stone if she won. It's only fair.

Phantom wandered in to one candle lighting the dark cabin. An eery sort of calm swept over him as he turned to the bed. She sat on it, her soft shoes tossed to the side and the longcoat draped over one bed post. There was a glimmer of resolve in those gold coin eyes. Of defiance.

One look at Phantom had her balling up one blanket and pillow from the bed and heading to the desk chair.

He blocked her path, one hand out before her. "Just what do you think you're doing?" His eyebrows rose high.

"Forgive me, Captain," she spat, not a single ounce of respect in her tone. "But I have no intention of sleeping in a bed that you occupy." She took the moment to scan him, her eyes narrowing. "Even if you are a man of your word."

He grit his teeth, ever so slightly, but he managed to beat back the offense enough to even his tone. "I am." She let her head drop, pointedly staring at the desk chair. "Tell me, love, are you a woman of yours?"

A fraction of the tension bunching the muscles of her back eased as she feigned ignorance. "Meaning?"

He huffed a laugh, stepping away from her to shrug off his coat. "It's only me here, no need to pretend, love."

She whirled on him. "I'm not pretending."

It was an effort to keep his grin to a minimum. As he suspected, figuring her out was like remembering the lyrics to a lullaby he hadn't heard in ages. New and familiar all at once.

Phantom stepped out of his boots almost lovingly, making her wait for the response he clearly had.

"Did you know you force yourself to relax right before you lie?"

She blinked. Clearly, she didn't.

"It's a small movement, but when I could pinpoint it," he began, inching closer to her. "I can see the very moment you decide you will lie. But you're astronomically brilliant at lying, so much so that your tell is actually the body language of someone who is telling the truth."

"Maybe because I was!" Her voice was louder this time. The sweet music of it even more intoxicating with the volume.

"Or maybe," he continued, keeping his arms tucked into his chest, but with his and her feet bare, every step closer seemed more intimate. "You've grown accustomed to lying so much, that your body is as deceptive as you are." His ocean eyes pinned her where she was. She refused to budge on pure spite. "You've trained yourself to react to lies as if they were truth."

He couldn't contain his smile this time. "I wonder," he whispered, close enough to touch her. He resisted the urge to press his fingers to the tender pumping pulse on her neck. "Does your heartbeat quicken when you speak the truth?"

Rose stepped back as if breaking the trance, her breathing fierce. "You said you wouldn't touch me." He hadn't even realized he lifted his hand, but he shoved it back to his chest. There was something new on her face.

Fear— raw and real.

He found himself wishing he could take back whatever put that look on her face. To destroy whatever villain put that fear in her in the first place. Survivor's instinct would have kicked in much faster. This fear was learned.

He'd find the villain and be their worst nightmare.

Phantom let his wrath slip away as he faced her, gathering all the seriousness he could.

"I won't— I apologize if I made you feel as though I would." Her breathing slowed only by a fraction, but her stance remained tense, as though she would run at any sudden movement. "Let me make something quite clear, love. I, nor any soul aboard this ship will touch you without your consent. Have I made myself clear?"

She blinked, but nodded. Phantom released a breath. He'd have any one of the devil's heads before he allowed them to take another's freedom of choice away. Aside from the kidnapping and ransoming, but she did stow away. Technically, the choice had still been hers.

Somehow she still managed to say, "I'm still not sleeping with you."

He let a sigh roll out of his nostrils as he held out a hand. "Let me have the pillow and blankets you seem to be clutching to." As if now realizing that her fist was balled into the linen of the pillow she quickly dropped it into Phantom's awaiting grasp. "Thank you."

Rose gazed at him as he strode to the side of the bed, then dropped the pillow and blanket to the floorboards beside it. He kneeled down to the floor before positioning himself on the hard floor, head on the pillow and arms still folded in front of himself. The floor was no better than the deck above, where he slept the night before, but at least it wasn't so cold. And that pesky little beastie couldn't disturb him.

The songbird was stunned in place, staring at him as if she were trying to solve a riddle.

He tossed one arm at the bed. "Your carriage awaits."

"You—" she cleared her throat, her voice coming out too soft the first time. "You will stay there, all night?"

He shrugged, an awkward gesture while laying down. "Have a little faith, love."

"Yes, well, I don't exactly trust you enough to have faith."

Phantom cleared his throat, then twisted where he laid, propping himself up on one elbow. "You stowed away on my ship," he started.

"Which was a trap," she countered.

"You tried to steal my treasure."

She squinted. "You stole it in the first place."

"You put a blade to my throat."

"You locked me away."

"A blade, I know you still have," he slowed. She had no response to that. "It seems to me I should be the one fearing for my life sleeping near you."

She kept her face as impassive as possible, but he saw the truth of it in her stick straight spine and hard eyes. It was no fool's gold her eyes were made of.

"How do I know you haven't hidden away some weapon in your trousers or shirt?"

His grin was unleashable. "By all means, love." He spread his arms in a welcoming gesture. "Search me. I assure you, it would be enjoyable for both of us."

She scoffed, charging for the bed. Not to him, but to the soft bed. A show of defiance against doing anything close to touching him. "Don't call me that," she muttered as she arranged the bed, clearly planning to sleep on the side of the bed furthest from him. She pinned her eyes on him over the mattress. "I'm not your love."

Phantom's smile faded, but not completely. He had no intention of dropping the nickname, but he sensed it would be best to leave it alone for the night.

"You still owe me an explanation," he mused and he heard the sheets glide against her clothes and the bed frame creak. After a beat of silence he added, "About the Stone." He could no longer see her face, but he figured it would help the truth come out if she couldn't see his. "All those things I just listed, you didn't do them because you could. You risked all that and probably more for the Stone. Why?"

"It's a sacred Stone that belongs in the Temple," she blurted, giving herself away.

Phantom let his tone sharpen. "*Los cojones.*" *Bullshit.*

A beat of silence.

His voice dropped down again, gentler. "Why is it so important?"

The silence stretched on for so long, Phantom was near ready to flip over to his side and attempt sleep. Then he heard her take a long breath.

"When I was little, my mother used to take me to the Temple. She taught me to sing there. Songs no one else knew. The acoustics made it sound like an entire choir was singing with us. She told me it was because the Stone could capture voices and it would sing with us."

A brief pause and a breath.

"I was eleven when she passed." Her voice was strained, like she held tears at bay. "I visited the Temple whenever I could because it felt like visiting my mother." Rose huffed a laugh. A pitiful sound that held no joy. "Some part of me held onto the belief that the Stone captured my mother's voice and if I sing with it— it's like she still singing with me."

Phantom didn't know what he expected, but it wasn't that. He knew the reason had to be personal for her to cross so many lines, but he wasn't prepared for the knowledge. The Stone seemed to hum against him in answer to her voice. It was buried in the pocket of his pants. She was less likely to risk stealing it if it was on his person as he slept, yet with this new knowledge, he wasn't so sure.

He'd do anything to have even a piece of his mother back. There wasn't limitations on the lines he'd cross to hear her voice again. Even for a moment. He couldn't even remember her face anymore.

In a split second, he wanted to give it all back. The Stone. Her. But he was still too much of a bastard to let her go so easily. There was an urge in his chest, begging him to give her the Stone, be the reason she smiled, instead he said, "I want to hear you sing."

She laughed again, cruel amusement seeping from her words. "No you don't."

"I am quite serious," he said, resisting the urge to add "love" to the end.

"I'm not going to sing." Her steely resolve bled through her tone.

"Tell you what," he started. "I challenge you to another game of Kazeboon tomorrow. If you win, you get the Stone. If I win, you sing for me."

She was silent for too long before stating, "I will not sing for you." Ice coated every word.

"Then win," he retorted. He grew very familiar with the color and shape of his ceiling as he waited for her response.

"No."

That was the line she drew. The point of which her determination to retrieve the Stone vanished. Sure, singing before another was a vulnerability, but no more vulnerable than she had made herself in pursuit of the Stone. A flash of that previous fear he spied in her face reminded him that she agreed to that. She knew she feared sharing a bed with a man, yet she risked it for the Stone.

The Stone that was a living memory of her mother.

Yet, to sing was too high a price.

Before he could finish mulling over her words, Rose blew out the candle on the nightstand.

CHAPTER 9
DAY TWO

R ose Davenport was up before Phantom could realize
she was gone. Surprisingly, he was able to sleep
soundly on the hard conditions of the floor of his
cabin. Likely due to exhaustion from the night before. Rose
had even made the bed before she escaped the room, her
slippery shoes and his longcoat gone with her.

He'd have to buy her new shoes when they ported in
Kheli. The only benefit those shoes had was their silencing
ability. He didn't particularly like someone being able to
creep around his sleeping body without him knowing of it.
The thought made him jolt.

The little minx.

He searched his pockets, checking his trousers in a rush,
before landing on the hard lump of the Stone, but he
invented the swap trick, so he wasn't about to go on faith.
He pulled the velvet black pouch, before sliding the Stone
out. It was there alright, its silver beads and lilac streams still
giving off an eerie glow. Its patterns and life like movement
would be impossible to replicate.

Of course, that was the entire point of why it was so valuable. If humans could replicate what the Goddesses could do, what was the point of them?

Sunlight glided through the windows in beams, illuminating the dark room as Phantom rubbed at his eyes. Shouts from the crew littered the air above his cabin. It was later than he intended to sleep.

Phantom breached his quarters after readying himself, complete with a black leather tailcoat that reached his calves along with a half buttoned shirt and silver rings. He even went so far as to put his small silver hooked earring on, looking the part of pirate captain was perhaps the excitement of porting in Kheli, not that he resisted the ensemble in Samsara, but the purpose was different. In Samsara, he wore it to keep to his image. In Kheli, he wore it because he liked to.

A mix of crisp morning mist and salty sea air kissed his cheeks. Clouds rested heavy amidst the ship, but visibility wasn't unbearable. The crew swarmed the deck in a mess of shouts, sails, and ropes. Robin knocked over a barrel of fruits before jumping onto the mast and climbing up to the sails. Russet promptly righted the barrel, taxing an apple from its contents.

Hyne and Tick climbed up nets on either side of the deck to pull the sails in. They were upon Kheli, there was no doubt. Phantom scanned the devils in search of one body in particular, stepping to the middle of the deck to expand his view. As he suspected, she was at the front of the action, taking in the landing from a front row seat. Her blonde hair was braided behind her. Likely, because she quickly learned of the windy day.

Phantom glided to her side before leaning his arms against the rail. "First time to Kheli?"

Rose's smile was so broad it blinded. An anticipated shake coursed through her, sending gooseflesh to her arms. There was even a pink glow forming over her cheekbones and nose. A result of the sea and wind. A nuisance she barely seemed to register.

"First time anywhere," she breathed, as if it were the first breath she ever took. Closing her eyes, she leaned into the scent of the air, the wind, and the sea. It was as if she could feel every drop of water on her skin, every change in the wind.

As her eyes opened, they landed on him. Her eyebrows knocked together, as if she just realized it was him who had spoken to her and she wasn't thrilled with the idea.

"What?" Her voice had lost its wonderful airiness.

Phantom frowned, then looked her up and down. "You are not what I was expecting, love."

All the muscles in her face that had relaxed went taut at the nickname. "What were you expecting, *Captain*?" The mirth in her voice somehow tasted more bitter than before. "A cowering little girl who'd rather paint in her room all day than see the world?" Her delicate brows rose in question. He noted her choice of mundane activity. What was painting to her?

Phantom had to stifle a laugh. "Come now," he started. "If I believed that was who you were, I wouldn't have bothered to set a trap for you." It was his turn to close his eyes and take in the morning air, seagulls chattering in the wind.

"Then what is it that you find so unexpected?" She

leaned her forearms against the railing, but kept her gaze sharply on him.

A smile threatened to creep up his face, but he kept it down. "You are being held at ransom and yet you seem to have no desire to go back to Samsara." Something changed in her face. He couldn't quite pin point it, but it was something that ran bone deep. "It's almost as if you are breathing real air for the first time." His voice was softer than he intended, but it was as if the very winds died down to hear what he had to say. "I know that look. The sea beckons you as She does me."

Rose broke the stare, looking to her hands instead. "You're wrong," she said too softly for it to be the truth. As if her own voice, her own body, didn't have the strength to deny it. A small strand of hair fell to her face, waved due to the salty air. Phantom resisted the urge to push it away from her eyes. He hadn't earned the right to.

A white blur entered Phantom's peripheral vision, along with a soft trill. "Nemain spare me," he grumbled under his breath, earning a furrowed brow from Rose. That is, until the little beastie slammed into Phantom, huffing pleasantly. The creature was the most active when the sun rose.

A small yelp escaped the songbird, causing Serena's ears to perk and turn to her. Phantom wrapped a hand around the beastie's belly, cradling her to his chest as a low rumble trembled from deep in her throat. She assessed Rose as a threat, but the songbird's eyes were wide with wonder, not even flinching at the clear warning growl.

"Is—" She blinked and shook her head, expelling the possibility of dreaming. "Is that a dragon?"

"Indeed," Phantom sighed heavily. "With the exception of the fire breathing bit." If the creature was more useful, her habits would be less annoying. As it were, her only purpose was to reduce the rat population and keep a certain devil aboard the ship. "Smith!"

The old man came running to his side, Serena growling at his approach. It meant the doctor would attempt to pry her away from the Captain. Phantom wasn't certain he could be rid of her if he tried.

The doctor withdrew his prying hands at the beastie's hostile reaction. "I don't think she'll let you go for some time, Captain." Smith had an amused smile on his face as Phantom's twisted into discomfort.

"Perfect," Phantom said with no small amount of ire.

Rose's mouth still gaped at the creature. "She's quite small."

Smith answered, "She's only an adolescent, Miss. Another century or two and she'll be fully grown."

"Century?"

It wasn't surprising that Rose would be ill versed with dragons. Most believed dragons to only be myth, particularly the white dragons of Merakesh. Phantom was just as ignorant and amazed when he first met the beastie. Back before he knew her temperament. The wonder was short lived.

"Serena is in her third decade already, but the aging process for dragons spans centuries." Smith grew giddy when speaking of dragons. When Phantom discovered the doctor's love of the creatures, it was the only bargaining chip he needed to recruit the doctor. He was more than willing to drop his life in Samsara to become a dragon toddler's nursemaid.

"How did she end up on a pirate ship?" Somehow Rose kept the bitterness out of her tone.

Gleefully, Smith answered, "She imprinted on the Captain here a few years ago when he visited Kalon."

She rose a brow at that and Phantom twisted his lips. Smith made it sound like he was the little beastie's mother. To make matters worse, Serena choose that moment to slither around Phantom's chest landing around his shoulder and nuzzling his neck to purr softly, as if marking her territory.

Though the action seemed to have the opposite effect as Rose's hand flew to her mouth, stifling the soft laugh there.

"She loves you very much."

Phantom settled his hands on the scaly body, blue rippling where he touched her. "So it would seem."

"I dare say, Captain, you are not what I expected either."

Phantom's eyebrow shot up, his smile following. "And what is it you expected of the infamous Captain Phantom?"

She raised her chin in defiance. "An old burly man, missing an eye, with a head too large for his body."

Smith covered a snort of a laugh, but Phantom only grinned wider. He knew that's not what she expected of him. She likely thought the worst, just like everyone else in Samsara, a cruel monster capable of heinous acts, but he didn't expect her to admit to fear.

He leaned in closer. "And what did you find instead, love?"

Her lips parted, but no words came out.

Before he could pressure her further, Robin's voice carried over the ship. "Land ho!"

Smith returned to his duties, leaving Serena in his care. He didn't mind so much with the smile it put on Rose's face, but her attention turned forward.

Finally, the mist cleared enough to see the outline of green that was Kheli. The shore and the port were still some distance away, but it was close enough to see the brown etched into the green island. A small village if anything, much smaller than Samsara, but it was far more beautiful.

Phantom snuck a look at Rose to find her wondrous gaze had returned. Her gaze fluttered all over the island as it glimmered before her. Samsara didn't have much green left, but Kheli had an abundance of lush life and giving rain.

"That," he began, "is the price you are worth, love." Her attention snapped to him, but she tightened her jaw. He let his head drop and looked at her through lowered lashes. "Your safe return to Samsara is going to buy that entire island their freedom."

No emotion trailed her features. "Or they will just earn a new leader." Her eyes were pointed directly to him. Serena shifted nervously on his back.

Phantom's jaw tensed. He raised his head, looking down at her. "I do not seek power, Rose." She stiffened at the sound of her name, but her eyes softened. "I don't want to chain myself to an island."

She looked away, as if she couldn't have been bothered. Another act, of course. This time she was covering disbelief. He wouldn't call her on it though. There was nothing he could say to change her mind. He could only show her.

So, down to business. "When we arrive in Kheli, do keep your identity to yourself."

"Why do I need to do that? You're afraid someone else will take off with your prize?" She did not glance in his direction. Instead, she stared at the incoming shore. The wonder gone again.

"Now that you mention it, yes, it would be tiresome to rescue you from a less curious host," Phantom mused.

She gaped at him. "Yes, you are such a gentleman, kidnapping, thievery and all," Rose said in a near lyrical way. It reminded Phantom how unwilling she was to sing.

"First, some unsavory characters would find your lack of imprisonment all too tempting. I have no lack of enemies." He let that fact sink into her, letting her taste the fear. "Second, the people of Kheli don't know what we plan to do. I rather not bring them hope to take it away if your father is less than negotiable and third—" He let a smile grace his lips. "I'm always a gentleman."

She leaned a hip against the railing so she could face him completely. "Scoundrel is more like it."

"Oh," he purred, letting the note of his voice sink. "I like the sound of that, especially the way you say it."

Her mouth opened in rebuttal, but sadly, Black called out, "Captain!" The warning came in time for Phantom to catch the pistol the swordsman threw to him. The act made Rose flinch and Serena whine. For a flicker of a heartbeat, he felt bad about it. But in truth, she'd have to get used to things like that aboard *Nemain's Revenge*.

"We'll be docking soon," he said while strapping the pistol to the holster at his side. "So do yourself a favor, stay close to the devils. No wandering off."

She scoffed. "You really don't kidnap very many women, do you?"

"Only the ones who stow away on my ship," he retorted before winking back to her, but walked across the deck before she could reply.

The landing deck was nearly before the port side of the ship. Already, a crowd of cheering villagers had accumulated on the dock. Mostly children came to greet them. Usually it was the offspring of some of the devils, but other children came to watch them dock too. Many wanted to see what new treats and goods they would provide. A sad smile crept up his lips. They didn't have nearly as much as they usually did since they hoped to bring news of their freedom.

A pang of guilt settled low in Phantom's gut. Because of him, their victory was delayed. Because of him, the crew was forced to lie about Rose and who she really was. Because of him, they took the risk in capturing her instead of acquiring more goods or food to bring back. Although the guilt weighed heavily, it was a familiar burden.

The people of Kheli felt the effect of his decisions. Their impeding freedom was the only thing that kept him steady. One day that freedom would be his to grasp and he could follow Nemain's Star as far as She would let him.

But for now—

He set his shoulders back and jumped to the landing below.

Immediately, children swarmed him, merrily shouting. Serena squawked at the small humans approaching. He struggled to hold himself upwards and not topple onto the small ones as tiny hands and arms encircled him. He'd barely managed to get his pistol out of the way in time, lifting it above his head.

Serena mercifully leapt from his chest as soon as the first grabbing hand grazed her, a weary chirp coming from her as she flapped back to the ship and landed on a sail.

Phantom caught Rose's gaze as she gaped at the strange site. He called up to her, "This is why I don't wear a sword here." Rose averted her gaze before she could seem too interested.

"Which is very much appreciated." A soft voice came from his other side and he turned to see a dark skinned beauty in a simple red dress. Flowers embroidered the edges of her food stained apron.

"You get more beautiful every time I see you Angelica."

The woman cast a look he'd seen her use on unruly children. Some of which were currently tugging on the tails of his coat.

Earhart nearly leapt off the ship, bypassing the ramp altogether. "Get your own woman, Captain," Earhart tossed before consuming himself in Angelica's embrace. The two made an odd couple. His reddish pale skin against her glowing sepia skin. His barrel thick arms against her thin, petite frame. The fact that she stood several inches above him. The two made no sense at all and yet, he couldn't name a pair that was more in love than the first mate and his wife.

CHAPTER 10
TAVERN

The morning had just begun when the crew finished unloading the spirits and foods. One trunk of fabrics and threads was provided as well. When the Samsaran fisher boats came, they taxed the people out of life and limb. Most of the food they presented to the people each visit came from Kheli itself. With the thin state of the boys who took the barrels from them, it was clear, their visits weren't often enough.

These people were not nobles. They were farmers, bakers, seamstresses and mostly women and children. The Prime Minister commissioned every able bodied man above the age of seventeen to join the Navy rather than stay behind to protect their families. The only men in Kheli were elderly or those considered unsuited for the Minister's Navy.

A large bearded man came from behind the side alcove of the supply room.

"Phantom!" He bellowed with every ounce of friendly charm he'd ever seen from the man. Both of his considerable arms were stretched wide. His clothes were mostly worn from hard labor.

"Roger," Phantom said, a genuine smile etching the side of his mouth. He grunted as he set a barrel down with Black.

Roger was one of the few men who lived on Kheli. His overweight size the disqualifying factor in his recruitment, but one punch from him could rival Jon. Phantom hoped he'd be there the day that match happened, just to witness the sight.

He leaned into Roger's embrace without a second thought. The man rewarded the embrace with a solid pat on his back that threatened to steal his breath.

"Handsome as ever Roger," Phantom mused. It was more of a jab than a compliment. The man looked like he had wrestled a bear and lost.

Roger lifted one burly finger in his direction and squinted his eyes. "I'll be havin' none of ya fine words Captain." His northern accent rang loudly. He came from Toska before the war and he never did shake that accent. "Ya have a prettier face than most the women 'round here." Black and Hyne both stifled a laugh behind their Captain. Jon snorted. "Don't be running off with any of my daughters now."

Phantom wasn't certain if he should be flattered or offended, but he learned not to take things personally when it came from Roger. "I wouldn't dream of it."

Then Roger's blue eyes shifted to Phantom's left. To where Jon stood near his back.

"Hello," he cooed. "Who do we have here?"

Phantom's head snapped to his left. He didn't expect

Rose to even leave the ship, let alone stick to Jon's side as he carried in barrels and trunks. She straightened her back and lifted her chin at the new attention.

"My name is Rose." She seemed to hold herself back from saying more, as if she teetered on the indecision of telling the truth or lying. Phantom had expressly requested that the villagers were kept in the dark about her identity. She didn't exactly have to lie to hold to that.

"Rose," Roger said, tasting the name on his tongue. The Minister's daughter was not well known enough to be recognized by a first name alone, but the curious gleam in Roger's eye said he suspected more. He reached down to grab her hand and placed a chaste kiss to the back of it. A pang of something bitter pinched low in Phantom's stomach. "It be a pleasure, sweet Rose. How'd ya end up wid this band of thieves?"

Her gold eyes shifted to Phantom. She clearly didn't know how to respond to the attention or the question. As much as he wanted to see how she would handle the situation further, he had a point to make.

Phantom crossed his arms in front of himself. A desperate attempt not to reach for her, or pull her away from Roger's attention. "She's my guest."

Roger's eyes glided to the Captain in question. The claim was clear. *She's mine.* Even if she wasn't. If it was made clear to the people of Kheli that harming Rose would be a personal offense to the Captain of the Eleven Devils, no one would risk the slight. Even if the cost was sharpened features from Rose. She clearly did not like Phantom laying claim to her.

But he'd deal with her retaliation later. Instead, he

focused on keeping his face straight and serious as Roger studied him. Roger broke their stare with a smile and a clap.

"Then she be our guest!" Roger announced with as much glee as he could muster. As if he wasn't staring down the Captain a second before. "Food and ale be on the house tonight lads." The devils cheered and whooped in response. "Mi 'lady," he said, turning to wink at her before swaggering off to the Wench's Tavern. The only tavern in Kheli.

Phantom held an arm out for Rose to take.

She hesitated, but the prying eyes of Kheli had come to see what Roger was bellowing about. There was a crowd to witness Phantom claim her. Her rejection now would only put herself in danger. After all, tonight she wasn't Rose Davenport, the songbird of Samsara. She was whoever she damn well pleased.

She hesitated for a second before she accepted his arm. They were a strange pair. He was dressed in full black leather pirate glory and she was in trousers, a puffy shirt, and long coat. Only those slippers were upsetting her look. The delicate things were already covered in mud. It was a rainy island after all.

He ignored the way her grip on his arm made his heart stutter as she whispered, "This isn't permission."

A single chuckle escaped his throat before he leaned in to whisper in her ear. "I don't see you begging." Her answering glare was muted, but still deadly.

"Don't hold your breath," she said in near resignation before an idea lit her face. "Or maybe do."

This time he couldn't control his laugh as it rolled from his belly. He had retorts. All sorts of things to make that small blush on her skin grow into blooming red, but he thought it best to leave her alone. It was too easy to want with this woman. Want every reaction from her. All the scoffs, rejections, and shuns, because it would be that much sweeter when she—

That's why he didn't respond and he didn't let the small victory of her arm in his distract him from the fact that she would return to Samsara. He'd have to give her back. For the same reason he risked his life pillaging, the people that stood around them now.

"My people," Roger shouted above the bustling and whispers. Even more joined the ever growing crowd. They silenced immediately.

Phantom leaned in to whisper in Rose's ear again. "That's the leader of Kheli. When this island is free and I'm sailing the sea, following stars, he'll be the one governing the people."

She snapped her attention to Phantom's eyes. There was only a breaths distance between their faces. A fact she didn't blanch at. The disbelief drained from her eyes.

Phantom was the one to lean away, narrowing his eyes at her. "So unexpected," he said so softly that he thought she missed it until her eyes softened.

She opened her mouth, but before she could speak, Roger bellowed. "Tonight, we be feastin', honorin' the devils and their Captain. And to the Goddess of Life who be giftin' our island wid beauty and prosperity."

"Macha Rithe!" The crowd shouted in unison.

When Rose's brows knocked together Phantom leaned in again. "It means "Macha Reigns" in old Brettanian. That's the Goddess they serve here. Another reason they would never follow a servant of Nemain."

This time she didn't turn, only blinked as Roger shouted

again. "And to our guest of honor, Rose who sails wid the devils." If there was ever stunned silence, it was the picture of Rose in this moment. Her eyes widened and her jaw dropped.

Luckily, Roger wasn't expecting her to respond. He hopped off the dais, the crowd resuming their daily tasks. Then he glided back to Phantom.

"A word, Captain," he said with a hushed tone. The man seemed to only have two volumes of speech.

Since he didn't specify if Rose could not be privy to the information Phantom inclined his head. "Lead the way."

Roger nodded before leading them away to the tavern he had originally been headed for. Rose was still latched to Phantom's arm in stunned silence. Somehow her grip had gone tighter. Not that he minded.

The tavern was mostly empty with the exception of a few old men exchanging laughs together and a couple barmaids tending to them and the counter spaces. The old men didn't bother checking who entered the tavern, but Phantom suspected they had resided at that table all night. He wondered if they would care about the two powerful men entering or the beautiful blonde on his arm.

Roger led them to an alcove of the tavern, slightly set apart from the rest of the room.

As he sat, a golden brown haired barmaid approached with three mugs of ale. Roger's favorite. The ale and the bar maid. He slapped her on the ass the moment the mug left her clutches. Rose flinched beside Phantom.

The barmaid was more than capable of handling Roger though. She turned on her heel and swiped a firm hand against his cheek. There were small lines caravanning across her face, but the age only seemed to make her more beautiful. Yet that line between her brow, was caused solely by the man below her.

He stuck a hairy arm out around her waist, bringing her down on his lap. She protested, "Ya big ol' hairy oaf. Keep ya hog skat caked hands off me. You're gettin' soot all over my new dress." Slapping his arms away, she clamored to her feet and attempted to wipe off the marks on her cream colored dress.

Phantom laughed. "Still no match for your wife, are you Roger?"

Rose relaxed beside him.

Roger raised a mug to Phantom in camaraderie. "May I never be," he said wistfully with a broad smile plastered to his face.

Phantom picked up his own mug, the liquid sloshing inside, nearly full to the brim as he claimed the seat next to the big man. "Ey. I'll drink to that mate." Their mugs knocked together before the liquid ran down his throat. It was this moment that he realized he hadn't eaten today yet. The answering warmth in his belly confirmed the fact.

Rose tentatively sat beside them. She had released his arm rather reluctantly. The situation was new and unfamiliar to her. He tried not to let the flutter of pride fill his chest that to her, he felt familiar enough to cling to.

Her mug remained untouched for a moment before Roger's wife shuffled across the floor. "No need to fret, lass. Ya mug got only water. If ya wish to join these day drinkers," she spat, earning a booing sound from her merry husband. "Then give me a shout, sweetie." She made a small curtsy before saying, "Ya call me Darla. What should I call ya by?"

The question seemed to startle Rose, but Phantom only

studied her. Curious why she seem so sure footed upon the ship, but a fish out of water here.

"Rose," she barely got out.

"Well Rose, let me know if there be anythin' I can get for ya."

The barmaid was about to walk back to the old men in the middle of the tavern when Phantom called out, "Do you happen to have a spare pair of boots?" Darla stopped and turned to the Captain, blinking at the request. "She did not plan for the journey as well as I had hoped."

Planting one hand on her considerable hips, Darla surveyed Rose's slippers with a *tsk tsk* on her tongue. "That'd be an understatement if I ever heard one, Captain. Ya poor darlin', trottin' around Kheli in those?" Her head swayed back and forth with the notion. "I be findin' ya some stompin' boots before you leave." Rose opened her mouth to protest. "I won't be hearin' a word of it lass. Ya not be leavin' my tavern wearin' those."

Darla shuttled off before Rose could say a word against it.

Phantom leaned in enough to whisper, "That would be Kheli's queen." There it was. In her eyes, the disbelief finally drained. Good. He wouldn't have stayed to rule these people if they begged. Freedom was the only motivator getting him through these years. Leadership over a country was as good a chain as any.

Roger gulped down his drink in a matter of seconds. Something was wrong. The man didn't normally drink so vehemently. Phantom cursed himself for not recognizing it sooner. That's what that staring contest was about earlier. It was a warning not to claim Rose. To not make her a target. There was danger.

"What's wrong?" Phantom spilled before Roger could set down his mug.

Shadows cast in his eyes. There were purple circles under them too. Roger leaned in closer to Phantom, his beard dragging against the table. "There be a camp set up on the East side of the island." A pang of worry shot through him. That was never a good sign. "Some of the farmers have reported missin' livestock and trinkets."

"Have they attacked yet?" Phantom asked, his voice lower than intended.

Roger eyes shot downcast to Phantom's pistol. "No," he said carefully. "But they could and we haven't the men to stop them."

"How many?"

"There be a few dozen."

"Bloody hell," Phantom swore. It was too many to drive out quietly. Too many for them to remain there silently. They would attack for the chance to use the land. The people of Kheli learned over the last few decades that it was not a land that could be shared. Not when greedy and coveting people existed in the world.

Darla filled Roger's cup. The burning liquid lapped over the edges. When she offered Phantom more, he held up a hand to refuse her. He couldn't let the ale take his better judgement, not when danger was nearby, not with his ticket to freedom by his side. *Everyone's ticket to freedom.*

He was both pleased with himself for hiding her identity and frustrated for not keeping her locked away on the ship. With Jon and Black standing guard, no soul could hope to grab her. But then, it would have been a burning beacon to something valuable in his possession. He cursed himself for buying time. Every second that passed by was another he could lose her and consequentially, everything.

All those thoughts must have been visible in his gaze because she shrunk under it. He hoped she was unfamiliar and scared enough not to do something foolish. It was not safe on Kheli.

"Perhaps, ya devils could take care of it," Roger suggested, glancing down to Phantom's pistol.

"Unfortunately, we are on a deadline." Roger's eyes shifted to Rose. He had to know it was about her. He'd never left in a rush before. "We have to leave before daybreak."

"Macha's tits," Roger swore. Phantom had never heard him swear against his own Goddess. He leaned back to guzzle the ale again. When he pounded it to the table a new idea sprang forth. "Can ya take care of them before tomorrow morn?"

Phantom inhaled. "Even if we manage to run them off before the morning, I cannot be sure they wouldn't come back to retaliate once we are gone. You know we always stay after to be sure."

Roger's eyes darkened. "There's another way we can be sure they don't come back." He said it softly. So softly, Phantom wasn't sure he heard him correctly.

He leaned back in his chair. "No."

"Ya know it be the only option."

"No," Phantom said firmly. "I'm not going to murder three dozen strangers. Men, women, and children. You know it's not just an army sitting on your island. It's families with no where else to go."

Roger steeled himself. "But they are not my family. And they will attack."

"But they haven't. They have not made a single move against you." Phantom's voice was less fierce now. It sounded more like pleading.

"They stole from us."

"And that deserves a death sentence for three dozen people?"

Roger's hardness melted away. The silence deafened. Phantom glanced over to Rose who sat as still as a rod, but her eyes glistened ever so slightly. She should not have been here for this. Or maybe it was exactly what she needed to hear. Maybe she could get her father to sanction patrols around Kheli. That only would matter if they failed. If he failed to earn Kheli's freedom.

No, her safe return to her father meant freedom for Kheli. Maybe then they could trade goods for protection.

"If ya do not do this," Roger started, his voice soft. "Ya have doomed us all."

Phantom stood suddenly, shaking and sloshing ale onto the table. He stepped away from the table and extended a hand to Rose.

"Good day, Roger," was all he said as Rose slipped her hand into his. They cantered out of the tavern as fast as they could. It took him a moment too long to realize how easily she had slipped her hand into his. Or the warmth of her skin against his. He shoved that thought away as they crossed the threshold into the brightly burning light. Something akin to the burning rage inside him.

"Sweetie!" Darla called after them, a pair of long brown boots in hand. She had a hand on Rose's shoulder before Phantom could stop her. Rose didn't flinch though. Nor did she release his hand.

Darla halted to a stop before them, bending over to

place the boots next to her slippers. "Right, these would fit ya delicate toes, lass." Rose let his hand go to pick up the new clothing. He missed the warmth immediately.

Darla's hand landed on his shoulder. She was several inches shorter than him, but her presence was large enough to make him feel small sometimes. "Don't be ragin' after my buffet of a husband, Captain. Roger only be doin' what he deem best for the people. On that, don't be blamin' him." A pause for breath and a smile before she continued. "But we not all be as defenseless as he believes."

She pulled a dagger from her boot and tossed it around in her hand, showing proper form and an acuteness for the way it sat in her hand.

"We ladies have been trainin' together for quite some time now," she stated. "My husband won't believe that it be enough, but we may be able to hold out long enough for ya and ya devilish crew to return."

Phantom let the tension drain from his shoulders slightly. A sad smile split his lips. "This is why he needs you, Darla."

She shot him back a crooked smile. "I know." Phantom feared it would not be enough either. There were maybe a dozen women in the village who could handle a weapon and their training likely didn't contain much more than self defense, yet Phantom had learned never to underestimate a mother bear protecting her young. Mama Owen taught him that.

"More weapons would be most welcome," she tacked on.

"I'll see what I can do," Phantom said with a small smile, before turning his attention to Rose. She had strapped on the boots. They hugged her legs all the way up to her thighs and Nemain damn him if it wasn't an attractive sight.

He blinked at Rose before turning to Darla again. "Assemble these ladies. I'd like to see them for myself."

A small curt nod and she was gone.

CHAPTER 11
ANGELS

Phantom stomped back to the ship with Rose in tow. The waves crashed against the pillars of the landing as gulls laughed at him from above. Were they minions of Nemain, reveling in his turmoil? He could practically hear Mama Owen. *Don't be dramatic, mijo.*

The moment he was about to climb the ramp to the ship, Rose's lips parted. "How can you just leave them?"

Phantom blinked. He would think a prisoner should act with a bit more self preservation. Then again, they didn't exactly treat her like a prisoner. Or even a stow away.

"You trade me for this island, then you come back to find the island has been claimed and your people are gone. What then?" Her voice was rough, nothing like the melodic tone he'd grown fond of.

He blinked again, trying to work out exactly who she thought she was talking to.

"These are not my people," he said softly. He put a hand out to the ship where Hyne, Tick, and Robin scurried about. "These are my people." He took a step toward her with narrowed eyes. "In fact, these are more your people than mine." The jab hit her harder than he expected. She didn't deserve it. Her father did.

"We can wait," she started, but Phantom scoffed before she could finish. "Take care of these people. Then take me back. You can still get your precious ransom."

Phantom took two more steps so they were only a breath's distance apart. "If we don't show up on time, what do you think your father will do?" He gave her a small frown. "Wait around for pirates to give his daughter back." Her back was taut, but her eyes wavered. "No, he will descend on Kheli and the wrath that he will ensue will be far greater than a pack of strangers."

Her eyes locked on his. Rose whispered, "If you leave, they could die anyway."

His arms were out before he could stop them. "Tell me, love." She flinched at the nickname. "What do you propose I do?" A beat of silence later, he added. "I'm listening intently."

She opened her mouth to respond, but promptly closed it. Phantom stared at her in wonder. This woman stood up for people she only just met. Then again, had he not done the same years ago when he first docked in Kheli?

"Black," Phantom commanded without taking his eyes off the songbird.

A mass of black clothing and triangular hat appeared in his peripheral. "Yes, Captain."

Only then did he break their stare. "Darla is assembling a group of women she has trained to fight." Black's eyes went wide. "I want you to test them. See what their strengths are, where their weakness lies. Jon and I will be along with spare weapons for them shortly. They'll be waiting near the Tavern."

No response followed. Only obedience. Black turned on his heels and cantered straight for the Tavern. Seagulls laughed above them as the waves lapped against the wooden deck and rocked the ship.

Phantom inhaled the salty air, gathering strength. "Your two options are these." Rose's eyes trailed Black before returning to her glower. "You can remain on the ship. My men will protect you. Or you can come with me, but you can never leave my side. Is that understood?"

Those gold coin eyes focused. "You said I was free to move about Kheli. As long as I didn't wander off?" Her words were sharp, bitter.

His brow lifted. She was there for the conversation with Roger same as him. "Whatever the outcome of us staying or leaving this night," he said softly, deadly. "It would be infinitely worse if those strangers captured you."

She grimaced. "I'm already captured by strangers. They don't know who I am."

"For your sake, you better pray they do. Then you will have value to them and they can take you to your father," he spat. "But if they don't know, rest assured they *do* know who I am, they will use you against me. I publicly claimed you. There could very well have been the wrong ears listening."

"Then you shouldn't have claimed me—"

Phantom scoffed. He regretted it the moment Roger gave him that uneasy stare. He lowered his voice. "It doesn't matter now." Then his head dipped. "It's your life, Rose." She flinched as if he had slapped her with her own name. "That's what is at stake if you don't stay close to us."

She nodded and he prayed to Nemain that she had at least enough self preservation to do that much.

The songbird looked to the ship and then Phantom, contemplating. He must have irritated her enough if she was even considering confinement.

Finally, she said, "I will go with you."

Jon and Phantom carried the spare weapons to the courtyard before the Wench's Tavern. Though if Phantom was being honest, Jon was doing most of the work.

The sight awaiting them was grander than Phantom could have imagined. There were a dozen women standing in two rows of six. Black stood before them with his arms crossed over his chest.

Both Darla and Angelica were among the fighters. No surprise there. They both had a considerable amount to lose. There wasn't a single dress in sight. Instead, every girl was dressed in tight trousers, shirts, and leather vests. Phantom had wondered why they requested leather from Samsara months ago. If he had known this was the purpose, he would have brought more.

They held a long wooden staff. The kind of weapon Wilson, a fellow devil and chef, always carried. The weapon was easily made and could act as a weapon or a shield. Plus, it was a good training tool that would cause minimal accidental damage.

Jon laid his impressive armful of weapons to the dirt and Phantom followed.

Phantom stole a glance to his right, Rose gaped. It was doubtful that she'd even seen a woman hold a weapon in

Samsara, let alone a squadron of them. He let the side of his mouth kick up.

The women yelled as they jabbed and blocked the air.

Black seemed unimpressed as he stood before one woman in particular. Her raven black hair was tied away from her face and braided along the top of her head. It was another barmaid from the Tavern. Phantom had seen her many times, yet usually in a dress of red. But today, her dresses were no where to be seen and freckles prickled her cheeks and nose. She was a fierce beauty with dark sultry eyes, but small soft features.

"This should be good," Jon whispered down to Phantom.

His earlier smile spread to a full grin. "My money's on the barmaid."

Phantom felt Rose's attention at the words.

Black spoke like a general. "Miss Clare." He put a hand out to the weapons behind him. "What is your weapon of choice?"

A sneer climbed up Clare's nose, but she stifled it. Apparently, her distaste of Black wasn't enough to deter her desire to prove herself.

When she spoke, it was with the urgency of a solider. "The long bow, sir."

Black got right into her face. Phantom was surprised she didn't flinch, but she did look up.

"Then show me."

Clare reacted immediately, as well as the other women. Darla ran to the back of the Tavern where a target hid. It was only a scarecrow with a red circle painted on its chest, but it had several holes littering its hay filled body.

Angelica grabbed a longbow from the back as well,

along with homemade arrows in a quiver. Right before Clare could take them, Black snatched them up. Angelica was fierce in the right circumstance, but she currently had more to gain from Black, so she allowed it.

Black sucked in a smile as he extended the longbow and quiver to Clare. Tentatively, she accepted it and positioned herself to shoot.

"Wait," Black started. "Move the target back ten paces." Darla ran out to the scarecrow and moved it back. Clare showed no reaction. Phantom agreed with the choice. Distance would be important in protecting the village, specially if they did have a skilled archer in their mix. Although, a lowered look from Black told Phantom that this was to get under Clare's skin.

Phantom leaned down to Rose, whispering, "Black has been advancing on Clare for months. She occasionally banters with him, but ultimately rejects him every time we come to visit. Black has yet to take the hint."

Rose whispered back, "Much like someone else I know."

Phantom jerked back as Jon coughed out a laugh.

Just as Clare was ready to release an arrow, Black came up behind her to change the positioning on her elbow. "Keep the bowstring right next to your mouth—"

Clare used that elbow to shrug him off her, forcing him to take a step back. "I don't need your help."

Black raised his hands in surrender. "Alright, then show me—"

Before the words were off his tongue, her arrow flew. It zipped through the air and straight into the center of the scarecrow's chest. Air left Phantom's lungs. Beside him, Rose's mouth dropped again.

Clare lowered the bow. It was not pride coating her eyes.

No, it was something much colder. A cool sort of rage spiraled off her and slammed into Black.

Black narrowed his eyes only a fraction before shouting, "Again."

Within seconds, she knocked another arrow and let it fly. It hit the target right next to her first arrow.

Black yelled again, "Darla, move it back another ten paces." Then he stared at Clare again. "Shoot its head this time."

Darla wasn't even finished moving the target back before Clare's arrow stuck out of the scarecrows straw brain. The woman had something to prove or she was letting Black know exactly what she was capable of. Knowing the swordsman, it would only draw him in more.

Black moved closer to her. Brave of him, considering how lethal she proved herself to be. "In the eye."

A heartbeat passed and Clare's arrow stuck out of the button eye of the scarecrow. Phantom wanted to clap and offer her a job on *Nemain's Revenge*. He could use a devil who could shoot like that.

Perhaps Black thought the same, because a tiny smile kicked up on one edge before he smothered it, turning to the other women.

"Can anyone else shoot?"

A couple hands raised, almost sheepishly. Phantom recognized the girls, but couldn't place a name to their faces. He had worked hard to ensure the people did not know him well. It would be safer for them and easier for him to leave. One girl was no older than fifteen.

"Good," Black started. "Go shoot with Clare."

The two girls ran off to Clare. Both of them younger

than her, clearly admirers of the barmaid with a straight shot.

Honing the archer was this group's greatest advantage. Strength would not be their ally, so avoiding a melee fight would be preferable. It would be especially intimidating if all dozen of them shot as well as Clare. Even the appearance of—

"Black," Phantom commanded and Black froze, letting his Captain walk toward the women. Black may be the best at weapons and assessing warriors, but no one was more cunning than Phantom. Who else could lead devils?

"How many of you at least know how to hold a bow?"

The women passed each other glances before turning their heads to Darla, who was staring him down. "They be havin' lessons, Captain. Clare's mother was a huntress. Trained the girl to shoot since she be ol' enough to be holdin' a bow."

Phantom tossed a look back at the barmaid, who was straightening the girls' stances. They were holding the weapons expertly enough to pass as good shots. With Clare before them, who was to say they weren't?

"And you?" Phantom asked. "Weapon of choice?"

Darla pulled a dagger he barely saw, but she was slow enough for him to adjust. He used the heel of his hand to bat her wrist away. The weapon dropped to the dirt without another sound.

Phantom leaned back with his arms crossed again. "I'm afraid you'll have to do better than—"

Another knife was on him before the words left his mouth. He looked down at a woman nearly a whole foot shorter than him, with a knife to his throat.

"This is awfully familiar," Phantom purred, letting his

eyes catch Rose's. She bit her lip.

Was she holding back a smile?

The look on her face was nearly enough to distract him from the sharp woman before him. He almost missed the third knife. Almost.

In two fluid movements, he knocked the third knife from her hand and seized the wrist holding the knife to his throat. This time he paid attention to the movement of her other hand. The clever old girl had them tucked away at her back. The knives were small and lacked the craftsmanship Jon's knives did, but they were still pointed and blood thirsty.

He caught her other wrist before she could manage to pull from her caché at her back.

"Bloody hell Darla," Phantom managed to bite out. "Exactly how many knives do you have on you?"

A smug smile was his only answer. More— Defiantly more, but she wasn't telling.

"Fine," he snapped. "But your form and technique could use quite a bit of work. I should not have been able to disarm you so easily. Jon," Phantom called, a small part of his pride bruised for how many times this woman caught him off guard. He needed to focus and glancing at Rose was assured failure.

Jon stepped up immediately. Out of all the devils, knives was his specialty. Phantom had the scars to prove it. "Teach her the proper technique and how to not lose her knives."

"With pleasure," he growled.

Phantom didn't have to look to know Jon would go straight into helping Darla. Only a few hours of work with him and her technique could significantly improve.

"Any other hidden talents?" Phantom tossed out, his arms wide. Black surveyed the women too.

One woman rose an arm, though it was unnecessary. Her frame and build were large enough to rival both Black and Phantom. She had two long blonde braids down her shoulders and a steel axe in hand.

"The axe, I presume."

She nodded curtly. Clearly, not one for words.

Phantom narrowed his eyes. "Show me what you can do with that." He let his eyes point to the steel in her hand. A leather wrapping gripped the carved wooden handle. It was a well maintained axe.

Angelica rounded the Tavern again, taking out another scarecrow target. This time it was thicker and harder. With a squint, Phantom realized it was carved from wood rather than stuffed with hay, then covered in ratted clothing. Even a toothy smile and eyes were carved into the wooden statue.

The woman with the axe cried, but it was not delicate nor meek. It was a mighty roar, like one of a lioness. Her arms flexed and Phantom watched her muscles peak and roll. Clearly, a force to be reckoned with. She plunged her axe into the statue as if the thick sea air wasn't allowing her arm to move fast enough.

A thunderous crack pierced the air as her axe sliced straight through the statue, as if it wasn't made of anything more than hay.

He'd hire them all.

"What is your name?" Phantom blurted before every splinter of wood hit the dirt.

"Hlin," she intoned, so fast, he nearly missed it.

"Do you have a shield, Hlin?" Her only response was a confused line creasing between her light eyebrows. "Hyne, shield please."

Hyne and Tick had only shortly joined. Just in time to

witness the statue's untimely demise. Hyne ran toward his Captain, shield in hand. The wood on these shields was thicker and stronger than the statue's, but it was the iron bars lacing it that really kept it together.

He began handing the shield to his Captain when Phantom shook his head. A cruel smile tipped his lips.

With Hyne still holding the shield, Phantom's eyes pinned Hlin.

"Try to kill him," he said dryly. Her focus honed in on Hyne while his eyes grew incredibly wide.

"Cap—"

Her axe pounded on the shield before the word could fully leave his lips, but it didn't even crack the wood. Soon she stepped into him to over power him. He backed up with the movement, scattering the other women behind him.

"Is this—" *Thunk.* "—some kind of—" *Thwack.* "—punishment?" He managed to get out. When he glanced at Tick, the man struggled to hold back a laugh. The axe drove into a tender piece of wood without fully diving through. Phantom let a chuckle roll from him.

"Come now Hyne," he said joyfully, as if it were a simple game. "Stop toying with her."

As if the words summoned some part of Hyne's memory, he lifted the shield against Hlin, tossing her to the ground. He drew his sword fast enough to place the tip at the base of her neck before she could stand.

Phantom was upon them before Hlin let the defeat fully settle in her. Hyne backed away in the same moment Phantom seized the shield from him.

"If you're going to wield an axe," he started, turning the underside of the shield to Hlin, who promptly stood, shaking off her defeat. "You will need a shield." He handed her the shield, gripping the edge of it. "This— is just as important as that axe. It will not only keep you from dying, but it can be used to take your opponent off balance, gaining you the advantage." He stepped back, letting Hlin take in the feel of the shield in her hand. The blue of Samsara complimenting her light features. He imagined red staining that shield. The blood of all those who dared to stand in her way.

"Hyne, teach her how to use the shield."

The devil inched on the woman with his hands raised. "As long as you promise not to hack my head off."

Hlin curved a smile, as if she considered it. "No promise, pirate." Hyne scrunched his nose.

Phantom stepped back further, taking in the rest of the women. They still gripped those wooden staffs. "I want every woman in this group to have a bow and arrow by the end of the day." He pointed to Clare. "Clare. Darla. Hlin. These are your generals. Listen to their every word as if you have vowed to. As if you have made an oath to obey them." He snatched a discarded staff from the ground. "I want spearheads on each of these as well." This command was pointed to Angelica.

She was the resident blacksmith of Kheli. Earhart trained her in the art.

She nodded. "I'll have six spearheads ready by the end of the day, sir."

"Good," he stated then turned to the remaining six women. "I will have Wilson come to train the rest of you," he announced. "By the end of the day, you'll be able to kill a man with those sticks alone. But we'll add the spearheads to make the weapons more deadly."

They all straightened, eager to prove themselves.

Now he'd only have to convince Wilson to train them.

"What do you call yourselves?"

Clare blinked for a moment, stealing a look to Darla before she shook her head. "We have no name."

It occurred to Phantom that they needed a name. He had his devils. There needed to be a name that would encompass the brave mothers, sisters, wives, and friends who came prepared to lay their lives down for the ones they loved. It had to be a name that sounded strong, but nothing like the dark glint "devils" held. No, a name befitting pirates couldn't possibly do for these women.

They needed something noble. Something that would not strike fear into their enemies, but rather provided hope to the ones they sought to protect. Something—

"Angels," the young girl next to Clare said, lifting her chin with an air of pride. She couldn't have been more than fifteen with a pink blush flaring her cheeks and fire orange hair cascading down her back. The other women seemed to ponder the name, letting it settle on them like a wave over bare feet.

Phantom lifted his brows then turned his head to Darla. She was having a silent conversation with the huntress across the courtyard from her. Clare nodded, accepting the name like a brand on her arm.

As Phantom's gaze traveled over the women, they each nodded their heads in turn as if hearing the name itself gave them their purpose, helped them understand exactly what it meant for them to be here today and to keep being here every day following.

Darla's face was stern. Impassive. "We are the Angels."

His smile was broad. Proud. The devils were training angels. Hell was freezing over.

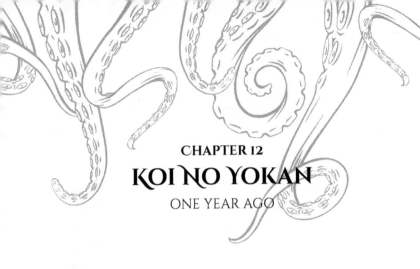

CHAPTER 12
KOI NO YOKAN
ONE YEAR AGO

K oi No Yokan was the single most beautiful place Phantom had ever seen. It felt wrong, dragging his dirty boots and creating trails of mud on the pristine stones. His crew of misfit devils, just as filthy, surrounded by the vibrant greens, pinks, oranges, and purples of the magnificent garden.

But it wasn't the waterfall streaming down the cliff edge before them that made Phantom's heart stop. It wasn't the large colorful fish swimming peacefully in the stream that made his mind flood with inspiration. It wasn't that floral aroma that surrounded them that made a piece of his soul transcend.

It was the people on the landing of the waterfall, moving their hands slowly before them in a pattern that felt similar to that water flowing behind them. They had staffs in their hands, using the object in tandem with their movements as if it were an extension of themselves. There was a peace that emulated from them, carrying to the pirates who stood on the other side of the garden.

A pained grunt made Phantom turn his head back. Three of his devils were face down in the stones. Hyne, Tick, and Jon. The two sea rats were out cold, but Jon was barely hanging on to consciousness, attempting to warn them of the danger.

Earhart drew his sword, a short broad thing as Phantom unsheathed his cutlass. There was no threat in immediate sight, so Earhart assumed position, putting his back to the Captain's. Jon's head dropped to the stones a second later.

Over the years, the two of them had found themselves in this position more times than they could count. It always did come down to the two of them against the world. At least ever since Ashby became the Commodore.

"Any sightings?"

"Nope," the first mate declared. "But those people at the waterfall are gone."

A sharp glance confirmed what Earhart said. The landing near the waterfall was empty, only a grass patch remained. It wasn't a good sign.

Phantom resumed his position looking the other way just to come face to face with a raised staff. With a grunt, Phantom used his blade to block the blow. He wouldn't have considered the staff even a weapon, but his men were not easily taken down. If that staff was the weapon used to knock them out, it must have been effective.

He pushed the staff away, examining his attacker more fully. It was a lean man with a firm face and upturned eyes. He was in a crouched stance with staff positioned delicately along his body, similar to how those people had moved with their staffs. His hair was black and long, braided down his back in a magnificent plait.

The air about the man was something akin to peaceful

resolution as if he were so completely in-tune with himself that he could do anything. Phantom was so stunned, so taken with the man that he failed to recognize the others that had surrounded them.

"Captain," Earhart grumbled from behind him, still pressed to his back.

But Phantom was too focused.

He had begun to understand when men were to become a devil. Perhaps it was the only time he felt the hand of Davina, drawing lines of destiny in the sand like the symbols they drew in their gardens.

All he knew was he had an understanding when someone was meant to be a devil. He didn't yet know if the feeling was simply him wanting the devil on his side, or the devil needing the adventure and freedom Phantom had to offer, or if it was something altogether bigger. But he didn't care.

When he got the feeling, someone became a devil.

"*Anatahadare*," the man spit out. A clear hostile reaction. Phantom was dazed enough to forget why the man wasn't speaking Brettanian.

"Pardon?"

The man jerked at him and Phantom flinched. Finally, Phantom noticed the other figures encroaching on the small spit of land they occupied. There were six people with staffs, mostly women to Phantom's surprise. He shouldn't have been so surprised though. Only the pathetic Samsarans believed women incapable of fighting.

Earhart nudged him. "Any great escape plans?"

"*Anatahadare!*" The man repeated, forcefully.

"Uh." Phantom glanced around for an idea to spring on him. Since they didn't share a common language, reasoning with them seemed ridiculous. Being outnumbered would prevent a proper fight, so escape it was, but how.

"Captain," Earhart prompted.

"Uh." What did he have? He had Earhart and... *Bloody Hell* his head worked too slowly. The people crouched forward, gaining proximity. He was running out of time.

Phantom felt more than saw Earhart push off an attack. "Captain! We could really use a brilliant plan."

The idea sprung in his head and he didn't have time to consider it fully, so he acted.

He reached back, finding Earhart's belt loop and tying the end of a thin rope there, then tying it to himself. Phantom's hand were swift from his days as a pick pocket on the streets of Samsara, so he doubted Earhart even noticed. He'd have to apologize to his first mate later.

"Walk forward."

Earhart hesitated. "I'm not sure if you've noticed, but there's no where to walk to." Earhart stood only a few paces from the edge of the waterfall.

"Just do it," Phantom commanded, never taking his eyes of his new devil, even if the man didn't know it yet.

Finally, Earhart stalked forward and Phantom was careful to keep his steps in pace. When the man stopped, Phantom didn't wait for his first mate to argue. He raised a foot behind him, placing his heel into the man's ass and shoving him forward.

Earhart screamed from the force and fall. Phantom winked at his new devil, who scrunched his brows curiously as Phantom was jerked backwards to join his first mate down the waterfall.

Just as he brushed the edge, Phantom threw out his knife, coiled with the rope, jamming it into the compacted earth next to the waterfall. He prayed to Nemain that it would hold. They jerked on the top as the knife held and swung them forward. The swing brought them to a cave below the waterfall, raining water down on their heads before depositing them on the rock.

Earhart rolled on the ground, Phantom following. He breathed heavily, attempting to stand.

"Bastard!" But Phantom was already hysterical. It actually worked. "That was your plan?"

Earhart's anger made him laugh harder. "Never say I didn't kick your ass."

Earhart grumbled, but began cantering down the cave. Those warriors with staffs would find them soon. Phantom climbed to his feet and ran after his first mate.

"We'll have to find a way to get the others back. Do you have a plan that doesn't involve kicking my ass?" When Phantom caught up to his first mate he was grinning from ear to ear. He knew the look too well. "Oh no." He walked on as if he could unsee or expel what that look meant, but soon he stopped to glare at his Captain. "You got the feeling?"

Phantom's grin couldn't fade even if he wanted it to. "I got the feeling."

CHAPTER 13
WILSON

Rose strode at Phantom's side in silence as they approached the ship again.

Phantom left Black, Jon, Hyne, and Tick to the angel's training. The name had grown on him like a blossoming flower bud. The cool irony enough to throw and enchant him. It described perfectly why he didn't feel comfortable in Kheli. He was a devil, surrounded by angels. The metaphor was too perfect to ignore.

"What do you think of the Angels, love?" Phantom managed to get out before they reached the ship.

She pressed her lips together, her arms folding before her. Her eyes flicked up to him, sparkling in the sunlight. "Who are those strangers on the other side of the island?"

Not a question he expected, but he should have. "We don't know. I sent Ramirez and Earhart to scout. Maybe they will have a better answer for us."

Rose bit her lip again. A habit he hadn't seen her do until she was faced with the newly minted warrior women.

He hadn't quite placed what emotion it was connected to, but he knew what emotion he wished it was linked to.

"If—" she started, taking a steadying breath. As if she had to examine every word perfectly before it rolled from her lips. "If we leave here, those women are going to die."

Phantom let a crease form between his eyes. "You don't have faith in the angels." He definitely didn't. He wasn't sure why he expected her to.

"I respect them for wanting to protect the village, but they are novices at best." The skin around her eyes creased with worry. "But if we stay—"

"No."

"But you could—"

"Let me make something perfectly clear, love." She flinched under his gaze. Phantom drew up a decorated hand, pulling a finger up with each point. "If we are late to meet with your father, they die. If we run out the strangers without staying back to defend against a retaliation, they die. If you get kidnapped or die during any of that, they die." She flinched again. He felt a pang of guilt but quickly smashed it under a mountain of responsibility. These people were directly effected by his actions, especially in this moment. He couldn't afford to listen to his heart.

Under his gaze, she steeled herself, ready to take whatever hits he could throw at her. He exhaled, lowering his voice. "Their best chance is to wait for our return. To be defensive until the devils can drive them out. I'm giving them the best chance by using the time we do have to prepare them."

She let a breath go, some of her fight exhaling with it.

Maybe it was the fact that he hadn't entertained a woman in some time. Maybe it was the fact that he was a

Captain that answered to no one. Maybe it was because he spent too much time at sea, but he gathered this moment to be the right one to bring bad news.

"I will have to seal you into my quarters for the night."

Her head snapped up, pinning him on the dock right there. "What?" A beat of silence. By her narrowing glare, this was her giving him a chance to take it back.

He would not.

"You said you weren't going to lock me away."

He blinked, long. "In truth, I should have all along. As a prisoner or a stowaway. Either role would have you suited for the brig. But it is not to contain you, love."

Her temper flared beneath her eyes, threatening to boil over and erupt. He hoped he'd be there when she did.

Phantom spread his arms wide. "It is to protect you and only for one night. As soon as we're off the island, you can move about the ship to your heart's content."

Rose's face shifted and she bit her lip again.

He took a heavy breath. He didn't have to reassure her. He was the captain. He never took orders lightly. He shouldn't have to try to convince the antsy songbird to behave for the night.

But his fingers were closed around the Stone before his head could fully convince him out of it. When he pulled it out of his coat pocket, she stared at it, the glimmering specks reflecting in her eyes. They created stars in the pools of molten gold.

"If you stay in the cabin tonight, locked and guarded, I will give you the Stone." Rose's eyes fixed on him again, searching for the trick in his words, but there was no such thing. She was worth more than the glittering rock. *Infinitely more.*

She bit her lip again. He still couldn't quite place what that meant. "Deal." She reached for the Stone, but he drew back. Her face grew irritated. "Am I supposed to take your word as a *pirate*?" She said, spitting out the last word.

He narrowed his eyes, letting his mouth form a small round shape. As if he were wounded by her insult. "No, love. You should take my word as a gentleman." He let the smile slip then. "After all, am I supposed to expect you to sit pretty just because I give you the Stone?" *Tsk tsk tsk.* "You know better than that, love."

Rose's steaming was lethal now, but she already made the deal.

"Robin. Russet." Phantom called.

"Yes, Captain," they both said in unison from the ship, too close to feign ignorance. Phantom shot the powder monkey and drunkard a scolding look. Sometimes he felt more like a mother than a captain. This was why he needed Earhart's patience.

"Take our guest to my quarters." He steeled his face as much as possible. "Don't let her leave unless you want to be dragged along behind the ship for our journey back. Do I make myself clear?"

"Yes, Captain," they said again, scrambling to the dock to escort her, but they were careful not to touch her.

With the last bit of defiance in her eyes, Phantom added, looking to Rose, "Do I make myself clear?"

She straightened, whatever high born demeanor she learned from the Prime Minister settled on her features. "Crystal, Captain." The last word was said without an ounce of disrespect, which had Phantom's head raging with alarms.

With one more warning glance to his devils he added,

"Watch her." Then he jumped onto the ramp of his ship and strode for the main cabin.

The kitchen was located under his own quarters. The room was small, but lined with tin to prevent the hot coals from setting the planks of wood on fire. Steam fumigated the kitchen indicating the devil was hard at work. He must have been cleaning up from lunch.

His black hair was shortly cropped to his head, nearly bald, but his beard hung in a slim line down his chin. His eyes were dark and upturned, common to the people of Koi No Yokan. He smiled with the memory of first meeting the man and the staff he used to fight Phantom off.

Though the devils called him Wilson, that was not his true name. The man preferred to never reveal his identity, but Phantom didn't care what they preferred to call themselves. He cared that they were loyal. Despite his cold demeanor and scary gaze, Wilson was loyal. He was grateful to Phantom for bothering to save the man's life.

He wasn't an easy man to save.

"You can't fight the dead, mate," Phantom had once said to him.

Once his reasons ran out, Phantom was there to lift him onto *Nemain's Revenge* and call him a devil. He always knew who would stay.

Near the entrance to the kitchen, Wilson's staff leaned against the wall. He'd never seen the man without it. The staff was sacred to the people of Koi No Yokan. It was an underestimated weapon that gave its wielder the grace and balance of a seasoned warrior. Exactly what he needed for a flock of angels.

"No," Wilson's graveled voice interrupted his thoughts.

"I haven't said anything yet."

Wilson turned, rag in hand, wiping away the water on his palms. "I should know better than to listen to *enu hyeo tashin.*" Wilson would often slip into his native tongue, the use of Brettanian still fresh in his mind.

Phantom let himself smile, lifting his hands in surrender. "Wilson truly. If you hate me so much, why are you still cooking for my devils?"

Wilson scrunched his nose then let a firm *tsk* escape his lips. The man used sounds to communicate more than words sometimes. He threw the rag over his shoulder, its usual resting place.

The Captain approached slowly, taking Wilson's staff in his own hands. "I have a job for you that doesn't involve feeding people."

Before he could blink, Wilson was on him, snapping the staff out of his hand and shoving Phantom away. Phantom lifted his hands again in surrender.

Wilson's eyes were hard, but his breathing was even.

"There is a group of women on the island, who need your help."

The man's eyes narrowed.

"We can't stay to defend them and we have a day to teach them how to protect their families. Surely, you can understand that." Wilson lowered his staff by a fraction. "They already have their own staffs. They just need your guidance."

He released a distressed noise. "The rest of the day?"

"Yes," he stated. "I ordered for some spearheads to be made." His eyes glazed over and Phantom couldn't tell if it was the steam from the kitchen or his ears. He set his hands before him. Of all the devils, Wilson was the only one who could scare him. "They need a sharp end as novices, you know that."

One side of Wilson's lip went up before he let out, "*Ey ah.*"

Phantom took that noise as reluctant resignation. That was as good as agreement. He knew that Wilson would never refuse to teach someone how to defend their families. Especially since he could not. His own stubbornness saw to that. It would never be something Phantom would hold over him, but the man could do it ten fold to himself.

"Do we have an accord?"

Wilson gave a light grunt, setting down his pots and wiping his hands on the rag again. He palmed that deadly staff in his capable hand, his eyebrows rising in impatience for his Captain to lead the way.

CHAPTER 14

LANGUAGE

EIGHT MONTHS AGO

"M*izu kata.*" *Water stance.* Wilson waved his staff in the air as he did the first day Phantom met him, tucking the wood to his back as if he were one with the weapon. Phantom moved his own staff, ridges rubbing over his callused hands as he spun the staff to his back.

"*Kuki kata.*" *Air stance.* Wilson moved slowly, treating the exercise as more of a dance than training, the staff landing outwards from his body, but still tucked behind him. Phantom mimicked the movement, the flow becoming more natural to him. He'd stumbled on his feet more times than he would admit to his devils when he first began learning Yokan *kata.*

"*Jigu kata.*" *Earth stance.* Wilson hardened, tensing his muscles as he pounded the staff into the air before him. This *kata* was more rigid than the others, requiring strength and a sense of firmness. Phantom moved with him, thinking he would resonate with this stance more, but it didn't agree with him as *mizu kata* did. He blamed the sea for that.

They repeated the *kata* cycle, over and over again until the movements felt as natural as breathing and existing in the beautiful garden with a waterfall splashing behind them. Phantom found himself unaware of when he began to sweat. The movement seemed to free his mind from the weight of time, from existing at all. There was a peace to it.

He wondered if his inner beast would respond similarly to the movement.

Wilson patted Phantom's shoulder which usually meant an end to the training. The man didn't usually break the *kata* cycle until his stomach growled, an offense he did not take lightly. He ushered Phantom into a large red roofed building with intricate design. It seemed Yokans took creativity and care into everything they did. Nothing was spared from beauty.

Phantom visited as often as he could over the next few months. Jon, Hyne, and Tick were returned to Phantom's ship before him and Earhart could make it back to regroup, but Phantom couldn't forget the man with the staff and the long black braid. So he continued to visit, choosing to come alone more often than not and finding the warriors of the village took more kindly toward one stranger than several.

After many interactions with the man, Phantom began to pick up on his language as did the man to Brettanian. Although, Phantom was not too proud to admit the man far surpassed him in learning.

"Wilson," Phantom parried over the steaming cup of blossom tea the man had poured him. A dish of soup Wilson called *suki* was laid out before him, still cooking it's raw ingredients. Although Wilson was not the man's name, Phantom had taken to calling him that. "Join me on my ship. The devils could use a cook as good as you."

He'd been trying to convince Wilson to join them ever since they could understand each other to some degree of success. The man always rejected, for the same reason he never told Phantom his true name. The man shook his head with a grumbled "*Ey ah.*"

"Is not thing I do." Wilson struggled with the words, but managed them all the same. Over the months, the two had gained respect for one another, showing each other fighting styles like the *kata*, or parlor tricks, or hacks to catch fish. Most of the time Phantom felt like he was on the receiving end, but Wilson seemed to enjoy having someone to teach. "Family." He found the word he searched for. "Family I stay." He grunted with finality.

"Bring them with you. There's an island I can bring them to—"

Wilson brush him off with a wave of his hand. "*Bah.*"

But Phantom knew the signs. He watched many kingdoms fall due to the necromites and Koi No Yokan was not far from destruction. "They're coming Wilson. Your family isn't safe here."

The man seemed to contemplate this, but Phantom wasn't sure if it was the words themselves or the meaning behind them. He'd come to find the villagers here were a stubborn breed, but they listened to Wilson. He must have been some authority figure for them, which made sense why he refused to leave.

It made Phantom question whether he meant blood when he mentioned family or duty. Word translations didn't always go as planned, so he couldn't always be sure.

Kheli wasn't ideal to send new people to with the Samsaran Navy porting and taking more than they should, but it was better than a land damned to Hell.

There were signs that Nemain sent before the necromites infected a land. Omens, but as a servant of Nemain, Phantom knew them to be as reliable as the tides themselves.

"Look." He held up a bit of dirt from under the tea cushions the two sat upon. When Phantom first visited, it was a moist and fertile land, now there was black rot littering the ground in specks.

Wilson looked up from his tea to glare at the rotten soil in Phantom's hand. "The ground is dying." He wasn't sure how else to say it so the man would understand. The dirt fell from his fingers so he pointed back at the once luscious waterfall garden Phantom first stumbled upon. Now, the large leaves were browned on the ends, flowers were wilted, even the colorful fish in the stream were beginning to come belly up. "This is death. It is coming for you and your family next."

Phantom wasn't even sure if the people of Koi No Yokan knew what a necromite was. From what Phantom could tell, there was nothing similar in their beliefs since they worshiped innocence or beautiful things. Like the fish in the stream were spirits to be honored and worshiped. Each season had a spirit they celebrated. Things that naturally occurred, as if the mere presence of humans was the only thing to disturb the peace.

The thinking bled out into their lives so easily. Especially in the way they fought, as if in complete harmony with the winds, rain, and earth. Even fire had a style of fighting, but they didn't often use it. Wilson had refused to teach him the *kata* associated with fire. Their fire spirit was the closest thing they had to a dark presence, one of destruction. At least that Phantom knew about.

Even then Wilson would explain it away, saying the fire spirit was there to cleanse the earth, to make way for the other spirits to flourish anew. It was never seen to destroy as only a means of destruction.

"Is Winter spirit," Wilson replied by way of explanation. "Every year she makes way for new." He still stumbled on a few words, but he hardly needed Phantom's help any longer. Phantom brought Ramirez with him a few times, since he was a scholarly man who had to learn Brettanian once to. The two got along extremely well. Wilson had even taken to watching the stars more closely after Ramirez visited.

"*Kyodai.*" A feminine voice called from upstairs, racing down the steps. She was a beautiful delicate thing that closed her eyes to take in the aroma of the *suki* once she reached the landing. The woman looked very similar to Wilson, same small nose and upturned eyes. Her long black hair fell in a sheet down her back and she was dressed in expertly stitched pink silk robes with small white blooms decorating the trim.

Wilson held a hand out for the woman, a sign of invitation. "*Jamae.*" The woman approached at the word eying Phantom with a hesitant gaze, but that was because he was already grinning.

Phantom stood placing a hand on his heart and bending at the waist. A greeting he had seem from other people in the village. "*Hinode.*" It seemed a typically greeting, but Phantom suppressed the urge to reach for her hand and place a kiss on her knuckles. He didn't think either would take well to that, but it was his usual response to beautiful women. Instead, he settled for the kind of eye contact he knew made women squirm.

He was too pleased with himself when she let out a

small gasp. Wilson was too busy trying to recall the right word to notice.

"How say family." He took her hand with a small pat. "With blood."

With that clue, plus the resemblance, it didn't take long for Phantom to work it out. "Sister." He felt even more eager to flirt with the woman. "She's your sister." Phantom used his hands to gesture his words so Wilson could easily pick them up.

"Sister." Wilson tasted the word, but seemed to find it displeasing. "Sister. *Jamae.*"

"*Jamae?*" Phantom tested the word himself, unsure if that was her name or the translation for sister.

Wilson seemed to understand the confusion, so he gestured to his sister. "Arita."

Phantom turned his eyes to her again. "Arita." He said her name slowly, intentionally, bringing a soft pink blush to her cheeks.

This time Wilson noticed, pointing an accusatory finger at Phantom. "No."

Phantom smiled, but nodded his respect to the man. Wilson narrowed his eyes suspiciously. A soft chuckle escaped Phantom at Wilson's swiftness to protect his sister, but the moment only soured his thoughts further. Arita was one more person in the path of monsters determined to drag everything in their path to Hell.

Phantom sighed. Wilson's small village didn't have enough time left.

CHAPTER 15
NEVER LET IT GO

T he angels were sweating bullets by the time the sun set behind them.

Black had put all his effort into the archers, although Clare had seen to most of the work. Each woman was fitted with a bow and arrow, even if they couldn't use it properly, Black made sure they at least looked like they could.

Hlin was drenched, sparing with Hyne or Tick for most of the day when she wasn't fitted for a bow. Hyne and Tick looked worse for wear as well, but Hyne got the tall woman to smile by the end of the day. A feat that alone exhausted him.

Jon and Darla were locked in a dance of thieves when Phantom returned to them. Her technique had improved dramatically. She held onto her knives with more steadfast gumption. Jon grunted proudly with her quick improvement.

Wilson was with the other six women. Their faces were

impassive if not fearful. No doubt Wilson had injected the fear of Nemain into these women. His face was shaped in a permanent snarl as he recited the *kata* to them.

"*Mizu kata.*"

"*Kuki kata.*"

"*Jigu kata.*"

The words brought peaceful memories of the waterfall garden. He nearly joined them to soak into that peace like the sea and let the motion wash over him.

Arita stood among the six woman Wilson trained. He was not happy to see his little sister amongst the women, but she was far from untrained. The village they had lived in taught the *kata* to all their younglings, even those would did not wish to fight would use the *kata* as a means of meditation.

Wilson's sister was at the forefront, teaching the moves right along with her brother, even if he continued to correct her, which often lead to a wrist slap from her. He seemed tense, yet unfeeling. A sense of unease trickled around the courtyard.

Times like these stood at such contrast with the man Phantom used to sip tea with in a garden. Wilson used to be a man of wisdom and learning. A man in perfect harmony with the world around him. One who would look for the good in everything, but that had changed when his country — his village fell.

Amidst their training, Phantom was hard at work positioning traps and illusions for the strangers, should they attempt to enter the village. A confined protective circle would give them the best chance of surviving. At least for the next few days, giving the devils time to return.

He promised himself hours ago that he would not

secure Kheli's freedom from Samsara, just to see it taken by a host of strangers. Just short of killing them all, this was the village's best chance.

He'd have to keep telling himself that if he was going to be able to sail away.

Sometime during the day, Roger had arrived to observe the training, his expression sour. Phantom's first reaction was to assume that his spoiled mood was due to his wife sparing with Jon. As handsome a devil as Jon is, Roger could keep a lid on his jealously easier than that.

No, it was the angels that gave Roger that crease between his brows and a resilience in his eyes. No doubt he hosted the same fears Rose expressed, that Phantom knew to be true. These girls were not ready for a fight. They needed this training a hundred times over before they were even close. It was exactly why he installed the traps. If luck would have it, the angels wouldn't need to pull a weapon.

Phantom sauntered over to where Roger pressed against the Wench's Tavern, leaning on it same as the chief.

"Any word from your men?" Roger asked, eyes drilled to the courtyard before him.

Earhart and Ramirez returned hours ago and assisted in the projects Phantom had busied himself with. The information causing him to work hard, more hurriedly. "The strangers seem to be Brettanian refugees." Since Brettania closed its borders thirty years ago, the refugees who weren't on their home island, became homeless.

Became bitter.

Became desperate.

Became dangerous.

"There are at least twenty fighters among them. They

have a stash of weaponry to rival our own, but they only have one ship."

Phantom let his eyes drop to the dirt. He kicked a pebble for good measure.

Roger turned to face him with eyes dangerously narrow. "I don't care if they be ridin' dolphins to get here. I want them off my island." Roger's face had turned red. His mood was not just sour. It was downright murderous.

Phantom widened his eyes and put out a calming hand. "When we get back, I swear."

Roger kissed his teeth and turned away, but Phantom continued. "My men also reported women and children. A pregnant woman, about to give birth. Elderly men who remember life before the war." The blood thirsty stare on the chief's face had not eased. "Bloody Hell Roger. I'll ferry them to Samsara myself if I have to."

"Ya know how we can protect *my* people without endangerin' the lives of *our* women." A sense of his responsibility fell from the chief. These were his people, not Phantom's. Even if they were the loved ones of his men, they weren't *his*. Before Phantom could protest, Roger added, "But I will be speakin' no more." He pointed out to the angels behind him. "Their blood be on your hands, Captain."

Roger stomped back into the tavern without another word. He did what he could to get his point across.

The exchange was not missed by the angels. A few of them turned their heads to Phantom, eyes wide, expressions gloomy. They wanted him to say something encouraging. Tell him how great they're doing. Tell them they aren't going to die.

He's a good liar, but no part of him could muster the words.

Beside him, steel clanged against steel as a heap fell to the dirt. Phantom snapped his attention— on Angelica. Earhart's perfect wife with her perfect children. She didn't even train with the others. She'd spent all day behind a blacksmith's fire. She worked tirelessly with soot staining her hands, face, and apron, just to see that the angels had the tools to defend the village.

Earhart slid up to her side, hooking an arm around her waist and placing his forehead against hers.

No, this was going to work. It had to.

"Angels," Phantom called out. The remaining women stopped and turned their attentions on Phantom. "This is not the end for you." He let his voice carry the truth to them. If he believed it in this moment, so would they. "You will survive this. Not because you trained hard. Not because you have the right arrows or the right bullets or even the right knives. You will survive and you will protect Kheli because you are fierce." He slammed a fist to his chest. "Because in your heart, you are the warriors who could turn the world upside down. And I will be proud to see what you all become one day. I will be proud to know that I helped the Angels become who they are."

Finally, they were with him, hope steaming back into those delicate eyes.

"All you have to remember, is who you are fighting for. Your sisters," Phantom suggested, pointedly looking at Clare and her two smaller shadows. "Your brothers." A glance to Arita and the brooding man beside her. "Your children." A look to Darla and the smaller versions of herself who had taken to Jon. Then he turned his gaze to Earhart's perfect family. "Your family." Silver lined Angelica's eyes right before it spilled over, running a spot of soot with it. Earhart wiped her tears away gingerly.

"Every single one of you has a reason for being here today. For training until you can't tell what part of your skin isn't sweating. For risking your life. Hold on to that. And never let it go."

Each angel nodded their heads in turn. Phantom let out a breath and forced his shoulders to relax. Perhaps one day, he'd find his reason.

After his speech, the angels dissipated, cleaning themselves up and preparing the rest of the weapons Angelica had made. The sky was dark when they found themselves in the tavern. Hyne, Tick, and Hlin had taken up guard duty on the border Phantom had provided for them. They already assembled a guard schedule for the angels to follow until *Nemain's Revenge* could darken their shores again.

For now, they celebrated. There wasn't really a reason, besides life and the fact that they were still living it. That was as good a reason as any.

He had to tell several sweet, wizened ladies that regrettably his "guest of honor" was predisposed and couldn't attend. The group of ladies had been haggling him for years to find a wife and settle down. Although he told them that it was the last thing he wanted to do, they persisted. Their glee at seeing him with Rose was incurable.

With a mug of water in his hand, he dodged them again, heading for the bar. With so many threats, he decided not take any chances with the chief's strong ale. He ordered his devils and the angels to do the same. Each one listened. The anticipation and nervous energy spun sticky webs with each of them.

The barmaid tonight was Clare. Or Sophia Clare more accurately. Phantom was used to calling people by their last names, it was odd to think some people called her Sophia. Like the ladies who insisted marriage upon them both.

Clare had donned her usual barmaid dress. A poppy bright red with black trimmings and bodice. It was a stark contrast to the huntress he'd grown accustomed to in the courtyard. Her raven hair was down flowing next to her generous bosum.

Not that he was looking.

"How are you fairing?" She asked. Her voice much smoother and sweeter without Black nearby.

"Worried," he answered honestly. "And you, my lady?" He said as one eyebrow shot up. He tried to flirt with her before, but it was like talking to a tree. She wouldn't even bait him with an insult like she often did with Black. Over time a mutual respect grew instead, a welcome replacement.

"Same," she intoned, filling his ale mug with more water. Her eyes were heavy, but not expressionless.

"Those girls seem to look up to you."

She sucked in a lip. "Their parents were killed by the Samsaran soldiers two winters ago." It wasn't uncommon knowledge. Most families in Kheli were broken due to the orders of the Commodore and Prime Minister. "I took them in. Taught them how to shoot. When I volunteered with Darla, I didn't expect them to follow me."

Her worry was for them, fighting along side her. He dumped the cool water to the back of his throat. "I could've told you they'd follow you."

Clare's eyes snapped to his. He thought of Robin. Of the things the boy had seen, of the dangers Phantom put him in by gaining his loyalty. He lowered his voice to a whisper and leaned in to the barmaid. "There are some places, I wish the devils wouldn't follow." The barmaid's eyelids grew heavy at the words, as if she could feel the very burden eleven had instead of two. "Do not blame them or yourself for their loyalty."

Instead of answering, she scrubbed aimlessly at the counter until her eyes flicked to a new addition to the conversation. Phantom didn't have to look to see who approached the bar. Clare's pupils widened, yet she glared in the same moment.

"Hello Miss Clare," Black all but purred. He learned it from his Captain. Black leaned against the bar, mere breaths away from her. "If I had known you were so talented with a bow, I would have watched my back."

Clare jerked back. "I don't need my bow to take care of you."

Black nearly leapt in excited, leaning further on the bar. "Really? How exactly would you have taken care of me, *señorita*?" His Quarencian accent slipped through. It was common in Samsara since most of the low-town consisted of Quarencians.

With a scolding glare, she slammed a new mug to the table and filled it with water, then she waited for the devil to bring the mug to his lips. "Poison would be easier," she mused, her tone light.

He stopped before the water hit his lips. Then a *tsk tsk* was on his tongue. "Such venom," he purred, finally getting the tone right. "Tell me what I did to deserve your bitterness?"

Instead of answering, she went right back to scrubbing at the bar.

Black rose to the challenge. "Come now, it can't have been that bad." He stared at her with his head tilted to one side.

Only cold dark eyes met his. "Good night, sir."

The clear dismissal was enough to sour Black's mood, taking every bit of lightheartedness he contained and snuffing it out. He took the mug again, gulping its contents then sauntering toward the door.

"Captain," he acknowledged.

Phantom offered him a curt nod. When the devil was clear out of earshot, he stared the barmaid down. "Why must you be so cold with him?"

On any normal occasion if one of his crew tried too hard with a woman who clearly wanted nothing to do with them, Phantom would put them in their place. However, Clare would, on occasion, flirt back. Her eyes followed Black as if she couldn't draw them away. Underneath all her posturing and masks, there was a hint of something *more*. Phantom recognized it like he was looking in a mirror. A sense of loneliness that only came from being in a crowd.

It was the only reason he asked.

She sighed. "When he's done lying to himself, perhaps *he* can be ready for me."

The ring of honesty in those words pulled Phantom back, an eyebrow raising. He examined the barmaid. She meant it.

Before he could chew on her words for long, Robin came barreling into the tavern. The act alone spiking Phantom's nerves. The boy was supposed to be guarding Rose.

He panted, leaning his arms onto his knees near the entrance of the tavern.

"What is it, boy?" Roger called out, but Phantom had already crossed the room to stand before his powder monkey. He put a hand on the boy's shoulders to steady him as Robin drew in heavy breaths.

Robin whispered, "Rose escaped. She's on the island."

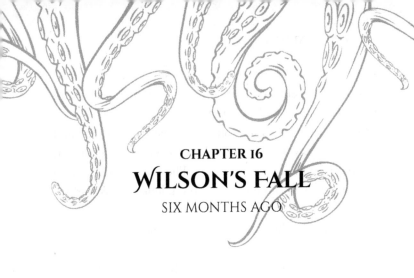

CHAPTER 16
WILSON'S FALL
SIX MONTHS AGO

I t was burning. All of it.

Phantom arrived to Koi No Yokan in time to watch a pillar of dark smoke rise into the air, barreling into the otherwise clear and beautiful day. A day that offered no rain or remorse from the sky. It was no matter anyway.

This was a matter of Nemain's. Not Macha. Not Davina.

There would be no mercy.

Serena screeched from the winds barreling through the sails. She tipped and bowed with the effort. It was an awfully windy day which made the impromptu inferno worse. Wilson was in there along with his sister and the rest of the villagers.

"I'm going," Phantom declared, but he was quickly cut off by his first mate.

"Like Hell you are." Earhart stood between him and the longboat dangling off the side of the ship. Soon other devils stood between Phantom and his way to the village. Jon crossed his arms and puffed out his chest. Black had a hand on his blade. There wasn't a single one of them willing to risk their Captain for a lost cause.

But it wasn't lost. Phantom could see that the fire had not been burning long, but he knew what the fire meant. The hoards had at last arrived. The battle could have already waged with no escape for the talented cook and his people.

Still, Phantom knew there was a chance he could save them.

The winds blew strongly, tossing his hair violently and causing the devils to place a hand on their hats.

"Out of my way," Phantom seethed. He had the respect and loyalty of his crew members. This was the first time they so openly defied him. There was no standing for it even if their intentions were honorable.

"Can't do that, Captain," Black's light voice carried. He wore stubbled coal on his chin to make up for the lack of beard.

Earhart planted a hand on Phantom's shoulder as if wanting to shake his Captain. "They're gone. It's too late. We're too late."

Phantom refused to accept that, but he was running out of time. There was no use convincing his crew. The more time he wasted, the more likely they would be right.

Fine, the devils refused to let him board his own longboat, he'd find another way. A glance in his peripheral told Phantom there was one devil who believed in him enough.

"Fine." Phantom let his shoulders drop and his head bow slightly, the posture of a defeated man. This seemed to calm his devils. Sometimes, they were just too gullible.

He turned from them to the where the helm held the wheel on the quarterdeck. It was the highest portion of the ship. Perfect. They had a pile of old sails lounging in the back. As if reminiscent, Phantom picked up the staff he obtained from his training with Wilson. A solid dark wood with small rivets for grip. The *kata* begged to be used in the back of his head. To roll with his muscles as easily as the wind, water, and earth.

Again, Phantom found himself wishing he had learned whatever *kata* fire dominated. He couldn't imagine a better time for its use.

His crew had not retreated from their spot near the longboat, clearly learning *something* from their time with the Captain. Not enough it would appear. However, Ramirez stood on the quarterdeck gazing at Phantom with equal parts horror and determination. He had grown fond of the man with the staff, too. A willing student to learn the stars and perhaps the man reminded Ramirez of himself. Of who he was to his own people.

The wind blew furiously towards land. Phantom tossed his eyes to the back of the quarterdeck then back to Ramirez. With a nod, the old man understood, descending the steps.

Phantom broke into a run, unwilling to waste anymore precious time. His devils chased after him, but Ramirez kicked a bucket of soapy deck water into their path, too unexpected for them to adjust in time.

Phantom reached the quarterdeck and dove for the sails. He tied off two ends of the sail to one end of his staff and the other two to the other end. He'd had crazier ideas that had worked, why not this one?

Before the devils could reach him, he jumped onto the

railing throwing the middle of the sail out. It caught the wind easily, sailing freely as Phantom gripped the middle of the staff. The sail lifted him over the sea toward the shore. He narrowly avoided Jon's grasp before sailing over water. Serena screeched with the commotion as Phantom felt empty air beneath his boots. The wind retreated, making the sail dip, but it caught again, pushing him through the air and to the shore.

His arms strained with the pressure of holding all his weight to such an unsteady force, but the shore wasn't far. A few more gusts and Phantom tumbled to the mossy ground with a roll. The sail fanned to the ground then ripped against the wind since the staff was still firmly in his grasp. Phantom palmed his knife, freeing the wood from the sail.

If he'd learned anything from his time with Wilson, it was to not lose the bloody stick.

Phantom scanned the area around him. The fire burned the buildings nearby, but the garden wasn't overtaken yet. It would be soon though, the ground and plants had dried significantly over the last few months. The fire would spread quickly.

He went to the building first, the part that was the least scorched, looking for survivors, instead there were bodies. Dead bodies walking around like a ghost of the life they once held. Some were new, only ashen in skin with opened wounds from where they had been bit. Others were old, skin falling and rotting off the body, hair balding, and fangs growing. But all of them were once from Koi No Yokan. It was apparent in their upturned eyes and dark hair.

The outbreak had been happening for a long time. Wilson's village must have been one of the last to be taken.

The necromites growled and groaned as they shuffled

through the house and around the building. Some were old enough to walk with a stumbled gait. None were old enough to run, at least not any that Phantom could see. It was an advantage. They could outrun these creatures.

He searched the grounds coming to the waterfall, there at its base, Wilson stood with his staff tucked at his back in *mizu kata*, a group of six huddled behind him. That fighting style was Wilson's favorite, full of grace and ease. A tricky one, Phantom had come to realize, but it was unfit for the surroundings. Hell was descending upon the man, he needed fire stance to counteract it.

Arita clutched a child, a village boy Phantom had come to know, but in her other hand, she held a staff of her own. He'd never seen her fight, although it was clear many of the villagers knew how.

The others weren't armed and seemed petrified with good reason. These people didn't even have a word for the monstrous creatures before them. A hoard of necromites shuffled toward where Wilson and his people were trapped. There were twelve necromites hissing at them. He'd have to kill everyone of them. And with a staff?

Phantom broke into a run, heading for the group.

Just as the necromites drew close enough for Wilson to raise his staff Phantom jumped off a nearby ledge, using the staff in his hand to knock back a reaching necromite. He got it straight in the head, but the body was rotted enough to crumble under the pressure. The head caved in and the body fell.

Wilson stepped in beside him, swinging his own staff and downing another necromite just the same. The man's face was straight forward, not honing in on another necromite, just still, waiting for one to come to him.

Phantom hadn't quite mastered that level of control, so he whipped out his staff again and again.

Together they dropped every necromite to the landing or into the water, black blood flowing with the stream and twining with the remaining fish bodies. It was a shame this place was ruined so thoroughly, but that was the world. Everything would eventually be ruined.

Death is what remains.

More necromites came, but Wilson ushered the group along, taking them in the opposite direction, towards the shore. Phantom's arrival had provided them with an escape. He'd fit everyone he could on the ship and sail them to Kheli.

"*Isogashi!*" Wilson yelled at them and they hurried along, climbing the stream's ledge to where the garden stretched out. The boy clung to Arita's hand, running with her when they reached the top. He held onto a small doll in the shape of a dragon.

A cry drew Phantom's attention. A stray necromite had emerged from the brush and swiped an older man in the group sinking its teeth into the man's shoulder. Arita reached for the man, dropping her staff and trying to pry him away from the monster, but Phantom lunged for her.

"It's too late for him." She continued to pull so he searched the words he had learned. "*Kare yijing shi.*" *He's already dead.*

She blinked at him, seeming to understand and not understand all at once. There was no saving the man. Phantom knew it so strongly that he pulled them away from the man, the necromite devouring him. He continued to scream and Arita closed her eyes against his pleading. Phantom grabbed her hand and tugged her toward the shore, but the boy on her other hand began to cry, clutching his dragon doll in a death grip.

Arita bent down to comfort the child and some of the others in the group started complaining at the disruption, speaking too quickly for Phantom to make out the words.

Phantom bent down to the child, a hand on his bent knee. He'd come to know the child as Karasu, which is also what they called several of the squawking birds around the village. The boy stopped being afraid of Phantom a couple months ago.

"*Yukan ni naru toki ga kita.*" *It's time to be brave.* Phantom knew the words well. Karasu loved to speak of being brave. Of traveling the seas as Phantom did. He'd grown used to the boy running up to him, asking about what adventures he'd crossed recently. "*Sekai o mi ni ikou.*" *Let's go see that world.*

This seemed to stop the boy's crying. He puffed up his chest and wiped tears from his face. Phantom nodded at him then turned to check the surroundings for anymore surprise attacks. He felt a tiny hand grasp his free hand. Karasu seemed to pick Phantom to run with. He'd have to hand the boy off to Arita if he needed to fight, but he could do this for now.

"*Isogashi!*" Wilson yelled again, spotting the necromite hoard heading for them. The villagers jumped and scrambled to get as far away as they could. Phantom stumbled to stay ahead of them, Karasu lagging behind. He gripped the boy, hoisting the small body into his arms. He barely weighed more than a sack of apples, so it made the running easier.

Until a couple of rotting corpses came groaning into their path, halting the group completely. Phantom scrambled to hand the boy to Arita, but before he could fully turn, Arita had swiped Phantom's staff and barreled into the creatures. She waved the staff firmly in her hand smashing the end into each necromite's head as she had watched Phantom and her brother do.

The two bodies fell to the ground in a splat.

"Right," Phantom managed to get out as she grinned. Wilson yelled something too fast for Phantom to make sense of, clearly chastising her for putting herself in danger. Ever the protective brother. Her shoulders sagged for a moment, but the groans of the necromites from the trees urged them onward.

The fire was stronger in this area, coating the air in a thick cloud of smoke. The villagers began coughing at the invasion in their lungs. Phantom had smoked a cigar or two of Ramirez's so the burn was familiar, but he'd be coughing with the rest of them soon.

The edge has to be here somewhere.

Phantom knew this part of the garden backed up to a cliff that dipped off into a deep section of the sea. His ship would be nearby, but with the smoke this thick, he'd scarcely be able to signal for help. Unless—

He whistled in a high pitched staccato tone. A noise he used to call the little beastie. The answering screech was too far away, but he'd gotten them a signal to follow. Serena would fly out ahead and search for him. He whistled again to solidify it.

He reached out his booted foot, tapping the ground in search of the cliff's edge. The little boy coughed violently in his ear and he considered turning back to where the air was clearer, but the sound of shuffling feet and moans told him there was no where else to go.

Finally, his foot dipped off the edge. He handed Karasu

to Arita so he could kneel at the edge and grasp for a rope he had left there months ago. Flames licked up the cliff face, reaching for them.

The ground creaked and rattled. It was too unstable after the assault of the fire and the weight of villagers. It crumbled.

Screams pierced the air as several of the villagers fell from the cliff's edge to their deaths below. The fall might have been survivable under better circumstances, but they were coughing forcefully when they fell, hardly able to get enough oxygen into their lungs. It wasn't likely.

The smoke cleared enough to see Wilson hunched over the edge, watching his people fall to their deaths, uncaring about the precarious state of the ledge. Phantom stole a glance behind him to see Arita coughing with Karasu, but no one else.

Phantom felt the ground move as he grasped the rope in his hand. He reached out a hand for anyone to take. A thick, stove weathered hand clutched at his wrist in a tight hold as the ground fell out from beneath him.

Everyone dropped and Arita screamed as she continued to fall, but he could do nothing to stop it. Wilson however, wouldn't allow it. He grasped the staff still in her hand and held tight, the ridges giving enough grip for him to hold on. She dangled from the staff, one arm around Karasu, who shook violently. The shock enough to keep him from coughing. It wasn't a good thing. He needed to get the poison out of his lungs.

Arita clutched onto the boy, but he grew limp in her arms.

"Arita!" Phantom shouted just before Karasu lost

consciousness and fell out of Arita's arms. She reached for him, but he was too far already.

"*Na!*" Arita shouted at the air as if her protest would stop the inevitable. There wasn't a way he would survive the fall.

Phantom closed his eyes, refusing to acknowledge the splash of water his body would make upon reaching the surface. Karasu was a heavy loss, heavier as he heard Arita's pleas turn more desperate, sobbing.

But the splash never came.

A screech flew through the air, then a trill as Serena swirled in the air around them, unbothered by the smoke, but her presence meant one thing.

Sure enough, the smoke began to clear as the wind picked up again and the ship below them came into view. He'd never been so relieved to see the love of his life.

Jon stood with a limp boy in his arms. Smith came with a bag of his supplies to inspect the boy. Phantom let out a sigh of relief.

He survived. Phantom relaxed, careful to not loosen his grip.

Arita seemed hesitant, but Phantom couldn't hold out much longer. The beast stirred under his skin, lending him the strength to hold on.

Russet rushed to position himself below the chain of bodies, ready to catch Arita. Although she wasn't prepared, Wilson let go of the staff and she screamed all the way down, landing in Russet's arms.

Wilson jumped next, landing on his feet like a thrown cat. He immediately picked up the staff that landed on the deck.

Jon stepped out, prepared to catch his Captain, so Phantom let the rope go.

The air rushed through his hair and cleared his lungs of smoke as barrel arms caught him by the back and legs. Phantom let a sly smile grow on his face, throwing his arms around the brute's neck.

"I always knew you'd warm up to me," he teased, but Jon's nose wrinkled up in disgust. He tossed his Captain to the deck without a second thought. Phantom laughed as he hit the deck with a great thud, a small cough accompanying the strain on his lungs.

Arita was still in Russet's hairy orange arms. Her arms clutched at his neck, staring at him with shock, but his eyes were struck dumb. Phantom never did mention to his crew how pretty Arita was and after her display with the staff, he was convinced she'd make a good devil.

Eventually, he seemed to remember himself and set the beauty firmly on her feet. She swayed a bit then trotted off to the boy laid out on the deck floor.

Smith gave his Captain a nod, signaling that the boy was fine, just shaken. Phantom found himself excited to see the boy's reaction to the beastie landing on his shoulders. Serena trilled and rubbed her head against his. She was clearly worried about him.

Good, at least one of his devils was.

The ship sailed away from the smoke, Earhart at the helm with a sour expression on his face, but he'd deal with Earhart later. It was Wilson who drew his attention. The man stood watching the village and garden before him burn.

Phantom made his way up the stairs to Wilson's side. The man had tears streaking his soot covered face. As he scanned the flames, a scream erupted from the hellscape. He closed his eyes against the sound. Phantom recognized it as both rejecting its reality and memorizing it.

"Your sister is alive." He hoped to reassure the man with the thought, but that seemed to hurt him further. His sister and the boy against countless others. "So is the boy."

Wilson didn't reply, instead he reached for the knife tucked away at Phantom's boot. Wilson never carried weaponry other than his staff. It wasn't needed— until now.

Phantom flinched at he brought the blade to his neck, but it didn't touch his skin. Instead he sawed off the braid at his nape. The strands released reluctantly. He held the cut braid in his hand like a dead animal. He discarded it into the ocean, content to release himself of his pride.

The long hair meant a lot to the people of Koi No Yokan. It meant success and honor. Things he lost, along with an entire village of people he was meant to protect.

His cut hair would serve as a reminder of his failure. Phantom knew in that moment, he was a devil, the same as any of them. Just the same as he knew those necromites were coming to wreak havoc on the land.

He'd never been so sad to be right.

CHAPTER 17
HEAVEN AND HELL

F ury.
Phantom's vision had turned red the moment
Robin spoke.

Damned monster. Damned songbird.

He was angry for so many reasons.

Angry at Russet and Robin for letting her escape.
Although, the question of how was something he wanted
every detail to. He'd see to punishing them for it later.

Angry at the strangers, for finding now a good time to
land on an occupied island with no sign of leaving.

Angry at Roger and the words that have been on repeat
in his head since the morning.

You know it's the only option. A statement that was
becoming truer by the second.

There was only one offender that made his blood boil
from anger to ferocity and that was Rose Davenport.

He turned back to the tavern that was now shrouded in
silence, a thick and heady thing, but Phantom saw it in only
a blur as he shouted commands. "Devils! Move out, bring

175

every weapon you can. There may be war tonight." His gaze sharpened on Smith. "Bring your supplies, doctor. If she's not dead, I'll kill her myself."

He wasn't sure how that statement was going to prepare the doctor. Perhaps he needed someone to convince him to stop when she stood before him.

Every muscle in Phantom's body tensed and pushed at him, urging him into action. Urging him to battle. Even the voices in his head grew to an unbearable level, but the steady voice that seated itself between his eyes whispered to think. To be smart.

With any luck, she had not been seen yet. They could steal her back before the Brettanian strangers knew she was close. Perhaps, they could still avoid war.

Once in the courtyard, every devil stood in a circle around him, grounding him. The looks on their faces were vengeful. They'd been waiting for a fight, same as him.

Phantom forced his voice to cool. "We will move quietly. Avoid detection, but do not let the strangers get their hands on our prize." The last word seethed through his teeth.

The devils called out their agreements and grunts.

"She is our ticket to freedom. Not theirs!"

Their calls were louder, grander. He could rile them to war with only a few more words. He'd done it before.

You know it's the only option.

He'd lead them to that before. They would do it again. They would kill everyone in that camp if it meant protecting the people of Kheli.

Phantom looked to the old stargazer and saw sorrow in Ramirez's eyes. He wouldn't want to, but he would do it. Phantom wondered how he acquired such loyalty. This type of loyalty stung. He didn't want it.

He let his breathing slow. Let the fire douse enough to look at his devils again.

"Avoid detection. Avoid a fight. Find Rose."

The words were final, so the men dispersed, everyone of them heading East. Straight into the jungle of Kheli.

Whether it was minutes or hours that passed, Phantom did not know. Only the cover of darkness and the mockery light of the moons told him it was still the same night.

The devils were near silent scurrying through the trees and dense foliage. All searching for a head of golden blonde hair.

Phantom should have known she would escape. He knew her to take advantage of other's underestimation of her. It was a quality he admired, even if she seemed determined to undermine him.

A low whistle. Earhart.

They were approaching the stranger's camp. No one had sights on her yet.

Over the next ridge, smoke trailed up to the stars at a lazy pace. Its origin a large bonfire with several occupants surrounding it. They passed food to each other. Likely, a livestock that belonged to one of the farmers of Kheli.

He had made a bet to himself and sure enough. There she was.

Rose Davenport was crouched behind a large tree, unnervingly close to the bonfire and its caretakers. She looked on at the strangers with something akin to curiosity. He half expected her to turn around, sneak right back onto *Nemain's Revenge* and pretend that she never left. The other half expected her to walk straight up to them as if they would be her saviors sent to take her back to Samsara on a golden pillow.

Phantom was tempted to find out which side was right, but too much was at risk. He put up a hand to signal his devils in place. They would not move to her. Not yet.

He crouched low and inched until he was right behind her. Foolish girl heard nothing. Suspected nothing.

Still, he was tempted to see how this would play out. Watch her expectation fall as she realized they were only to be her new captors. If he didn't have so much riding on her, he probably would let her understand the consequences.

She moved to reveal herself from the tree, but he was quicker.

Phantom wrapped one arm around her waist and the other hand clamped around her mouth. He pulled her to himself, crushing her to his chest. She struggled against him and hummed against his mouth.

The sound was too much. He slammed his back into the tree, to erase them from view. "Shh," he snapped into her ear. She must have recognized the voice or the silver and black rings decorating his hands because she went quiet and stopped struggling. An action he didn't quite understand, but he couldn't think on it long.

"Did you hear that?" A male voice said, alarm lacing his tone.

"Nah," another voice responded. "Some animal in the jungle."

The first man seemed satisfied, because Phantom could see Black in the distant tree line. He nodded his head. All clear.

Phantom pushed her forward with his body. The most silent gesture he could use. She obeyed, but he didn't trust it. He spun her around and forced her against the tree, careful to keep the tree from giving them away. His body crushed hers, but he only let up the pressure when he saw her wince.

With his senses so heightened he felt every pull of her breath, every beat of her heart. Both of which were rapid and hard, but not due to what she was about to do, the danger, but to him. Was it fear of him that drove her to this? He searched her eyes, but found them dry and staring, gold glittering under the light of the moons.

Phantom didn't risk speaking, not so close to the enemy, but he wanted to remove his hand. Ask her why and what he had done to make her so afraid. But more than anything, he wanted to know if he was alone in the stirring feeling in his gut. If he was alone in enjoying the closeness, the warmth—

The promise. He had told her he wouldn't touch her, yet here he was. Maybe that was the fear in her eyes. He'd allow himself to break it to retrieve a runaway, but beyond that— Besides he was furious with her.

He kept a hand on her waist and the other on her mouth as he pushed off the tree. They staggered back to a dense point in the jungle. To the line his devils had formed out of sight of the Brettanians.

He released her and she whirled on him.

"Are you crazy?" The words spilled from him before he could catch them.

Whatever fight she had. Whatever she was about to say, died on her lips.

"Those men could've done so much worse to you than ransom you to your father. They are *not* from Samsara." The words continued to spill. He couldn't help it. He needed a battle. She would have to do. "They have more to gain in hurting me than coming after your father. They could've killed you just out of spite."

She didn't blink. Not once.

Phantom tipped his head back, looking down at her with lowered lashes. "Do you have a death wish?" He whispered with genuine curiosity.

The hardness fell from her face, as if she couldn't answer that question.

"Hey, who's over there?"

Phantom blinked. Long.

When he opened his eyes and turned, there was a large Brettanian man only a few paces behind him. The man had examined the noise he heard. Good watch. Too bad he'd have to die for it.

He locked eyes on Phantom and recognition sung in them. Phantom did not know the man, but Captain Phantom was legendary among the Isles of Carriwitchet. Many people could easily recognize him. It was exactly as he feared, especially when the man narrowed his eyes and raised his sword.

As he suspected, these men would have killed Rose just because she was his.

Before the man could take any further steps, an arrow zipped into his eye and he collapsed backward.

Phantom raised a brow before turning back.

On a rock, one leg anchored as her bow was primed with another arrow was Miss Sophia Clare. Her dark hair had been braided back, her dress was wrapped through and around her legs to stay out of the way, boots climbing up past her knees.

Phantom stole a glance at his swordsman. Black was dumbstruck. Possibly lovestruck.

Clare stared down at the Captain. "The angels will fight with you. We end this tonight."

Seeing her on the rock, the shot she took lifted a burden off his shoulders. He no longer bore the weight of Kheli. The angels had Kheli now, but there was another burden. Men would die tonight.

Voices rose up from the shore, orders ringing out.

Phantom smiled and there was a cruel note to it. His primal side kept just under the surface.

"Let's bring Heaven and Hell upon them tonight."

Clare nodded. Phantom turned to Robin and Smith, who gaped at the huntress. "Take Rose back to the ship. Make sure she stays there."

Finally, he looked down at Rose. He wanted her to understand exactly what she forced them into, but he kept his mouth shut.

She stared up at him, but the fight left her and she sighed. Smith nudged her and they led her to safety. He watched until they were out of sight before turning to the devils and angels that surrounded him.

There was one last thing he could do. That he owed each of them before asking them to fight.

"Clare, I want you and your angels at the ready. Make sure everyone of them has a bow in hand. When I give the signal, I want your bows knocked and aimed at their heads. Let them to see you, how many there are of you."

Clare nodded and the angels prepared their bows and arrows.

"Black, be ready. They likely won't yield."

Black nodded, mirroring Clare. He seemed to be drawing strength from her now. Something he'd never see the swordsman do. With anyone.

Phantom exhaled and walked back over the ridge, dodging the fallen man.

He raised his arms as he descended. The men had swords and were there in an instant.

"Let me speak to your leader," Phantom demanded.

The men spat at him. Clearly, they harbored no love of pirates.

One aged man with the gait of a General prowled forward. "And if he doesn't wish to speak with you?" The man was adorned in the colors of Brettania, still loyal to a country that would never allow them reentry. Phantom glanced around him. The soldiers were old. Older than most who would serve in the Navy. Surely past their serving age, but they held experience like it was a treasure with clear keen eyes. They hadn't stepped on the soil of their homeland in thirty years. A battalion of soldiers, forced to survive.

Phantom narrowed his eyes at the man. The firelight from the men's torches showed grey lining his temples and beard. Lines and sun spots decorated the skin on his face. Phantom leaned forward, "Then you will regret it."

No smile or grin breached that cold face, only distrust and distain.

"Do you think I don't know who you are, boy?" Phantom let his arms cross as the man spoke. His cool, relaxed demeanor agitating the General all the more. "We've been in exile longer than you've been alive, but you've built a reputation on these seas."

Phantom let a smile curl his face. No amusement, but the way it made the General bristle was enjoyment enough. "Have I?"

The General narrowed his eyes again, his nose flaring.

"You've met your match Captain Phantom." He spat the name like it was miles beneath him.

Phantom let his smile curve higher and parroted his own words. "Have I?" He let his lips fall to a familiar position, a whistle low and long. It made the soldiers flinch, then hold their swords more firmly.

The next second, Clare stood on the ridge into the jungle, clearly visible, aiming her bow directly into the General's head. Her stance was fierce, cold, and unwavering. Phantom found himself in admiration of the barmaid.

But the General laughed. A breathy sound that ended in a cough. "A girl is your backup? Perhaps, the rumors about you were only a farce, Captain Phantom." Some of the soldiers chuckled back, some were still wise enough to be tense.

The rumors Phantom allowed to circulate served their purpose, such as this. Not all of it was true although much of it was. They'd have good reason to fear him.

Before the laughing could cease a zip sliced through the air. A grunt abruptly ended the laughing as Clare's arrow jutted from the General's shoulder. He seized the arrow in his hand, but the arrowhead had pierced through his back. Another seasoned solider snapped the end off so the General could pull it free. Blood poured from the wound, soaking his tattered red uniform in a darker shade of crimson.

Should have left it in.

The General tossed his head toward Clare. "She alone will not save you. Kill him."

The soldiers approached, but Phantom didn't flinch.

Didn't bother to reach for his blade. He had not made his move, but this was Clare's move.

Her voice, loud and mocking shocked the soldiers enough to slow their assault. "What makes you think I'm alone?"

Then the angels descended, eleven women with bows drawn crested over the ridge. Arita's eyes were steely in the light of the moons. Since only eight men stood with their General, they straightened, unwilling to see to Phantom's death.

The General hurriedly searched the ridge. He could see enough to tell that they were outnumbered and he had no reason to doubt every angel could shoot like Clare.

But his eyes settled on Phantom once again. There was a hatred there. Maybe not personal, but close. As if he refused to be bested by a band of pirates and women. This battalion survived on their own for thirty years. No small amount of pride glinted in those hate filled eyes.

"Kill them all," the General ordered and his men attacked. Phantom allowed himself one heartbeat for those words to settle. They were the wrong words. The exact wrong words. It was the only way the General could have secured his people's deaths. So Phantom used that heartbeat to steel himself. To let loose the monster of their legends, but it wasn't just Captain Phantom and the Eleven Devils who would eradicate them tonight. The Angel of Death was an archer and she brought her own garrison.

The second heartbeat and his sword was drawn.

CHAPTER 18
ANGELS AND DEVILS

Clare struck the soldier before Phantom could stick him with a blade. The arrow pierced the man's heart. He spurted blood as he fell to his knees.

Another man crossed Phantom's path, having a death wish. He said nothing, but his eyes promised pain along with death. Phantom let his eyes sparkle with the same sentiment. The man swung low and Phantom tipped his blade against it, clashing steel against steel.

Behind him the devils joined the fight. When Phantom drew his blade, he called them to the battlefield with him. He hoped the angels stayed back, even though he knew it was foolish to hope for.

In a blink, Black was at his side, taking the blade of another soldier. Now the solider would have to fight the best swordsman that ever boarded *Nemian's Revenge*. The man had enough wherewithal to look frightened.

The man before Phantom moved again, circling his blade around Phantom's cutlass. The blade in the soldier's hand was slimmer and lighter than Phantom's cutlass. It gave him the advantage of speed, but not strength. Phantom only needed to land one good blow.

He advanced on the man, forcing him back. The man must have been in his fifties, but he was lean. Although Phantom was no brute like Jon, overpowering him was too easy. He yielded, taking two steps back to take Phantom's advance, but he pushed off the Captain and swiped low again. Narrowly, Phantom dodged, sending him back a step, but the distance was enough.

With a quick movement under his coat, Phantom slipped his pistol free. Another fluid movement and he blocked the man's blade, aiming it away as he extended his arm. The barrel of the pistol pointed directly at the man's forehead. He sucked in a breath, but his eyes were still heavy laden with hatred.

"Pirate," he hissed at Phantom.

No smile cracked his face. No remorse either. Only cold determination.

He let the pistol crack and ring, ripping a hole between the soldier's eyes.

Before the man's back hit the jungle floor, a new wave of battalion soldiers rolled to the ridge, behind him screaming ensued. Not light and afraid, but loud and forceful like a mighty roar. Hlin, Hyne, and Tick held their shields out before them with their swords and axes in their opposite hands. They assumed the first line of defense.

Hlin's braids tossed in the air behind her as they slammed into the wave of soldiers. Had it only been them, they would have fallen, but a line of six angels came up behind them, Arita commanding them, spearing the men the shield line had crashed into. There was no hesitation in their brutal strikes like he expected to see, their resolve in protecting the island far surpassing natural morals. Like a mother bear, protecting her cubs. And there was an army of them.

From above, Clare and her two adoptive sisters rained arrows down on the men further back. The two girls were more impressive than he gave them credit for, but of course, Clare taught them.

The angels carried the brunt of the battle.

Phantom glanced to his sides. Black stood with blood splattering the front of his brown leather tailcoat. Jon was a mountain of muscle at his Captain's side. Wilson stood as still as death beside them, staff in hand, steady in water stance. These were his top three fighters and they were sidelined.

"Come on devils," he barked, waving them to follow as he jogged into the battle. "We can't let them have all the fun." His three best fighters jogged after him, Darla and the archers trailing behind. Darla joined in with Jon, the two of them seeming to bounce off one another.

Phantom held back as soon as he reached the battle, letting his devils and Darla into the thick. The object of his advance wasn't present, which was the most telling feat of all. The General had left his soldiers to fight for him. He didn't even return with the back up.

Rounding the fighting, Phantom crouched in the foliage to find his way to shore. Where the sand met the trees was where they had set up camp. A bonfire burned alone in the white sand. The women and children his men had reported were missing.

Phantom peeked in the tents surrounding the bonfire and each one was abandoned. It rang warning bells in Phantom's head, ripping through the haze of the monster. Through the haze of battle, grunts and screams echoed behind him as he crouched through the camp.

Finally, he spotted a pin where livestock would normally be kept. Instead it was people. Women and girls. Not a single boy in sight from what he could tell and they were not from Brettania. Their skin was slightly darker with rich brown hair, bold eyebrows, and light blue or grey eyes. They were from Kalon.

He squinted his eyes. They wore metal collars around their necks. There were not the families of the soldiers. These people were slaves. Phantom shook his head, the monster ebbing and flowing with the new found information. Sympathy sung in his head, but vengeance was more powerful.

With whatever he had left of his humanity he inched forward out of the shadows. A woman gasped and clutched onto her child as he approached. He froze at their fright, but he raised a single finger to his lips. "Shhhh," he whispered. "We will get you away from them."

That seemed to quell no fear from these slaves, but much like with Rose Davenport, he would have to earn their trust. The first step to that was destroying their masters.

Phantom pivoted, leaving the slaves behind him. He would come back for them. Sail them back to Kalon himself if there was anything left of the country.

One more scan around the camp and he spotted a ship anchored distantly off the shore. Several longboats decorated the shoreline and there was the General with two other men, smuggling bound Kalonite girls onto the longboat, gags preventing them from screaming. Vengeance burned hot in his core.

He wouldn't risk his pistol with the girls so close. He raced up to the first man, slicing open his belly before the man could draw his sword. The three girls were not only bound and gagged, but blinded too. He thanked Nemain for the blindfolds, even if the sight made him want to find new horrific ways to kill them.

The second man had drawn his sword, fending off Phantom with a flick of his thin blade. The coward General pushed off the shore. Once he was in the water, he'd never see the bastard or the girls again, so Phantom desperately lunged to severe the soldier's neck. Perhaps, take his head from his shoulders, but the man was nimble and swift. He was younger than the rest. A son to one of them perhaps.

Born after war, raised by men who never truly knew peace.

The General had his boots in the water, there was no time for this man. As if answering a prayer, an arrow zipped into the man's eyes, knocking him backward. Phantom didn't bother to look behind him. There was no luxury of time. He pulled his pistol and pointed it.

The coward froze in place. He wouldn't make it to his ship if he was dead. He lifted his hands as Darla and Jon came around him to seize the longboat.

Phantom's eyes narrowed on the man, who had the courage to fill his eyes with hate, when he was the smuggler of it.

"Is this what Brettania deals in?" Phantom called out because he had to know. He had to know if the slave trade had begun anew. "The lives of innocent people."

The General furrowed his brow. "If you do not know

what they are worth, *boy*, then you are more simple than I could have bet." When no emotion breached Phantom's impassive face, the General continued. "Brettania would not allow their own soldiers to cross the borders." He tossed a hand to the girls in the boat. "This was our ticket to finally return home."

Two things settled on Phantom in that moment, Kalonites were valuable in some way that was specific to the females. Or the men were too much trouble to transport. The other was that these soldiers had no intention to stay on Kheli. They likely never would have attacked the village, but every fiber of his being was ready to thank Rose Davenport for forcing his hand. Otherwise, something much worse than slaughter would have happened to these girls.

Without moving an inch, Phantom said slowly, "Walk back to the shore."

With hands raised in surrender, the General inched through the water, but his steady eyes still promised death.

Phantom recognized the look. There were only a few ways one reacts to sure death. He would like to think it would be the same look he would possess given the prospect of certain death. The General might have been too much a coward to stand with his soldiers, but in this, he was not.

He would go down fighting.

The man flinched, going for someone to Phantom's left, but the Captain let his pistol ring. In the near silent waters his boots were drenched in, the shot rang out and echoed against the land and through the sea.

The General was gone instantly, but his body fell forward and splashed into the waves. A ripple of red escaped around the corpse's head. Phantom regretted giving the vile man such a quick death. He deserved pain.

Finally, Phantom turned his attention to the left and let his ears absorb the world around him. In his desperate attempt, the General had plunged a knife into the belly of Angelica Earhart.

CHAPTER 19
WHAT'S BEEN DONE

T here would never be a woman more precious to the people of Kheli than Angelica Earhart. She was the heart of the island. The silent strength that never wavered. The woman who would come to each door and ask what help they needed. She taught her children to do the same. Earhart's children. Phantom's first mate and his beautiful, resilient wife.

Maybe that was why Phantom shouted orders before she could fall into the waves. Earhart caught her in his arms, but he did not dare to remove the knife at her belly. He had too many years as an officer to make such a mistake.

"Angelica," he whispered, but it came out shaky. "You'll be alright. Stay with me."

Her eyes were wide with shock one second, then drooping the next.

Phantom couched down to where Earhart held her above the waves. Blood coated her abdomen already, running down Earhart's arm. He didn't watch his Captain.

His eyes were firmly fixed on the love of his life. "We have to get her back to the village, mate. Smith is there."

Earhart's dark eyes snapped up. Phantom expected rage or worry, but a steely sort of determination washed over him. The island of distance between him and the doctor made no difference. If there was anything in his power he could do to save his wife he would.

He stood, her body limp in his arms, but she still breathed. He gazed at her face. "Stay with me," he whispered. "Don't you even *think* about leaving me."

Phantom shouted to his fastest devils. "Hyne, Tick, run ahead to the doctor. Tell him what happened. Make sure he is prepared for our arrival." The men nodded their heads then broke into sprints toward the jungle. They would get there as fast as their legs would carry them. For Angelica and for Earhart.

Earhart waded through the water, his pace altogether slower, but speed would only exhaust him and deepen her wound. Jon leaned down to retrieve Angelica and Earhart snapped his eyes up to the brute. Jon lifted his arms and backed away.

They walked back in near silence. Earhart's steady breathing was the only indication that he still lived as he trudged through the plants and mud to reach his wife's only chance at survival. Some of the angels had wrapped her wound as best they could with the knife still stuck in her belly.

These were the moments Phantom wished he prayed to the goddess of life or fate instead of death. All he could pray to Nemain was that she would pass over the woman. To not claim her soul for Heaven.

"Captain," Black's voice was still and sure. Someone

had to be. It wasn't him. He had begun shaking. The need for more action, more vengeance, more violence and blood was an overflowing cup. "Captain," he said again. Of course Black noticed.

"What?" Phantom snapped back to his swordsman. A man who could best him easily, but Phantom would not need his sword to tear into Black. Not with the bloodlust blooming in his very core and red swarming his vision like a bloody omen.

Black had the sense to shift backward. Not a retreat, only precautionary.

"You need to cool off," he stated dryly. Black had seen what Phantom was like if he let his monster have the reins for too long. The creature always demanded more. *Needed* more.

Phantom blinked away the roaring in his head, but the blackness only made it worse. His eyes strained. No doubt they were dilated enough that only a sliver of the blue could be seen, if that. He couldn't allow it to go on. There wasn't an enemy to fight off.

When he spoke again the words came out in a growl, "I will see her to Smith before I do anything else." He let his eyes drop on Black, who kept his face impassive. A void of worry, but only in appearance. "Is that clear," he bit out, "devil?"

Black only nodded, but he kept close as the minutes dragged on. If Phantom should act out of his bloodlust, out of the monster's bloodlust, Black would stand in the way of it reaching anyone. Jon arrived on his other side soon enough, with hands ready on his knives. He too, would stand in the way of Phantom and everyone else.

Just like they once promised him.

He spared a glance behind him. Ramirez, Wilson, and the other angels escorted the Kalonites yards behind everyone else. They clutched their arms close and held their daughters closer, an apprehension clung to them. He hated that look. It was a helpless look that only came from someone who learned to distrust everyone yet had accepted that they had no choice in where they would go. Or what they would do or who they would be.

Red licked at his peripherals. He forced himself to look away. There was too much to be vengeful about. With the beating in his head and the fire in his veins, the walk back to the village felt like hours. A vile nasty part of him didn't think Angelica would make it. Even with Earhart's whispered, *stay with me. Stay with me. Stay with me.*

Finally, when the lights of the village blinked into view, Smith stumbled into them. He moved remarkably well for a man with a wooden peg leg.

He spoke swiftly, "Get her into bed."

Earhart rushed ever so slightly to match Smith's pace.

Jon and Black stood as pillars beside Phantom. The doctor found Angelica, but with the beast still so close, he did not trust himself to enter the village, lest the beast surface.

"Go after them, make sure the doctor has everything he needs," he said, a rumble etching his tone.

Black nodded then trotted after them, with only a brief look back.

"You too, Jon. I will not be able to settle in your presence."

With a weary glance, Jon stepped away. "Captain," he said before tipping his head. Then he walked down to where Earhart and Smith disappeared.

All at once, everything needed to stop and start. The clothes on his back needed to be gone. Anyone within a hundred feet needed to cease existing. Even the stars and moons needed to disappear from the sky.

Phantom trotted north, away from the village.

This wasn't the first time he couldn't let the monster rest in his chest. It was too brutal, too swift to be controlled. In battle, the monster allowed him the ruthlessness to drown out his humanity and finish the job. Luckily, he had held onto enough of his humanity to not slaughter those Kalonite slaves. If he had let the monster take full control, he would have freed their souls, allowing Nemain to carry them home.

But his humanity was present enough to recognize those ashen faces as miserable. The knowledge of their slavery was enough to fuel the monster back to full power, but the anger he felt at seeing those slaves. At seeing the slavers try to escape with girls, *children*, was enough to enrage the monster beyond control. The leash growing closer to snapping with every passing second.

It was why Black and Jon caged him in.

Every time the monster was slipping the leash, Phantom made his way to the lake. The lake that stood before him now. It glistened in the moonlight of a near full silver moon and crescent lilac moon. The lilac moon belonged to the Goddess of the Kheli people, Macha. The Goddess of Life. The Goddess he wished he prayed to, then perhaps he would be of some use to Angelica.

The lake sat below a waterfall that spilled mountain run off from the island's volcano. The water it possessed was cooler than that of the ocean. The bite was perfect for stilling the beast inside, as long as he remained undisturbed.

Phantom pulled at his coat, shrugging it off behind him to settle on a rock. Unstrapping his belt, he laid his cutlass and pistol on the rock to join his coat. Soon his boots, shirt, and trousers followed. The mass of clothing on the rock was near solid black.

He dove under the cold surface, not bothering to pluck off his rings.

For a moment, he waded under the water, unwilling to resurface. Perhaps, if he stayed under the water until the last possible second, he could dismiss the monster faster and spare himself the pain.

His heart rate slowed, his head still bursting with bloodlust. His closed eyes summoned scenes he'd rather forget. Of the violent acts the monster was capable of. Red invaded his vision in spots of blood from severed heads, sliced innards, and torn throats.

Most of his victims were deserving of their fate, but the monster was less choosy than him. It seemed to be only a single minded vessel with a Nemain given mission to destroy.

He swung his head out of the water in a desperate need for air. The monster did not react well to being threatened. Of course, there would be no easy way out of this. There never was.

Every time he settled the beast, it started with the unquenchable bloodlust, until it shifted into crushing guilt. Only when the voice that spoke from that hollow place in his chest, soothing him with all the reasons why those deaths were necessary, would he be able to be Captain Phantom again.

The process took hours at best, days at worst. He didn't have days, it would have to be hours. Even sunrise was not far off. They'd have to bet on the tide to reach Samsara in time. He hardly had hours to do that.

Phantom rubbed at his eyes, wanting to expel the bloodlust images with stars.

Snap.

The monster reared its head and moved to the sound. He sensed her before he saw her. In his monster state, he could scent her. The smell was a harsh contradiction of campfire smoke and fresh flowers, but there was an undercurrent of something tangy. He'd come to know this scent as fear.

Phantom managed to jerk on the monster's reins before his waist crested the water's surface, but the monster did not seem angry, rather it seemed excited.

"Love, if you wish to see me naked, you could have chosen a more convenient moment," he purred.

Her scoff echoed as she spun around from the tree line. "I was not—"

She stopped in her tracks, seeming to only just understand that he was indeed naked beneath the dark waters. For a brief moment, she let her eyes drop to his chest then back up.

She straightened, as if punishing herself for looking.

A flicker of a smile etched the side of his mouth. For a moment, he nearly forgot the monster was still present. He steeled his features, possibly the first time he'd ever looked upon her with such stoicism, but she showed no reaction.

"You need to leave, Rose." She only narrowed her eyes. Nemain save him from stubborn women. "You could get hurt. Go back to the ship."

Her eyes flicked to the mass of clothes on the shore. To his coat. "Ah, you don't seek me. You seek the Stone." She flinched, ever so slightly. "You broke our deal, love. And if you intended to steal it tonight, you've run out of luck. I gave it to one of my devils for safe keeping."

"Which one?"

He let a chuckle leave his tense body, it nearly came out in a growl. "Like I'd tell you."

As soon as he let the words fall, that tangy scent filled the air again. Fear. The stubborn woman was afraid and yet she held her ground on the lake's shoreline. Then the events of the night that led up to him nearly unleashing the beast sprang forth.

She had run and he laid hands on her. A wash of both anger and regret washed over him. He must have been in the second phase of settling the monster because regret was stronger. Or maybe it was the fact that her recklessness saved the lives of slaves.

If he was being honest with himself, he stopped being angry with her the moment he saw those girls being loaded onto a longboat. His anger shifted to the General and his soldiers instead.

"Forgive me," he said in a hushed, low tone.

Rose's eyes shifted their attention from the pile of clothes to him. He wondered if she could see that his eyes had turned black with red swimming at the edges. He wondered if she could sense the change in him. If she could, she showed no sign of retreating from it.

Her brow furrowed. "For what?"

Phantom shifted under her gaze. He wasn't sure if she searched for a longer apology or if she genuinely didn't know.

"I promised I wouldn't touch you, yet I laid my hands on you when I had to stop you from entering their camp." It took every ounce of his strength to not say. *To save you from killing yourself.* "For that, I apologize. My promise remains intact for whatever that's worth."

He studied her as she contemplated the words. He expected her to call him a pirate in reprimand. To tell him that he broke what little trust he had built with her.

Instead, she walked toward him, water lapping at her boots then soaking them completely. Her borrowed trousers and waist belt were next. He urged— begged his body to retreat. To gain as much distance from the beautiful creature as possible, but it refused. Too much of the monster was still present. For the first time in his beast state, he was terrified.

Rose marched up to him with sharp, clear eyes. A reflection of Davina's moon spotted those gold irises. He noticed beads in her hair and little braids that created interest in her blonde locks. He resisted the urge to touch them. The realization of how close she was and how dangerous he was seemed to be the only thing to sober him.

He folded his hands together in front of his stomach in an attempt to hold himself back. Something about this moment was a hundred times more vulnerable or intimate than any dalliance he shared with a woman. The fact that she was completely clothed and he was not.

Rose Davenport lifted her hand, placing it on his arm. It wasn't the most intimate of places she could have touched, but the contact spread prickling shock throughout his body. It was entirely deliberate. He expected a wash of that tangy scent to overwhelm him, but the air was clear. The only indication that his monster still resided close by was the smokey sweetness of her scent.

"I do not fear your touch, Captain." The words were

not said with the sweet note of seduction or the bitter taste of challenge. They were said dryly. "You've had every opportunity to take advantage of the situation and you have not. As Captain, you would have no one to answer to. No one to question you." Although she did not intend the words to bite, they did anyway. "Yet, you allow me a weapon." Her eyes glittered brighter than any treasure he'd seen. She took a breath. "I do not fear you. So please, do not make promises you cannot keep." Those words jutted from her like daggers of ice. Not even a hint of warmth was present.

The words were not an invitation, so he did not take them as such. They were an understanding. An olive branch of trust he wasn't sure he earned.

But the words begged another question from him.

"Then why did you run?"

Her eyes averted from his, turning to the waterfall behind him.

Suddenly, absolutely nothing made sense. If she had enough trust in him as Captain to bring her back to her father without hurting her, what did she hope to gain from strangers?

"Angelica visited me while I was shut away in the ship," she breathed. This time, she did mean the words to bite, but a smile breached her lips and he forgot the aggression. "She brought her children with her." She reached up to her hair. "Maria wanted to tie beads in my hair and Ana wanted to braid it, so I let them. Angelica had her hands busy making arrows, but she was kind to me and spoke of what the crew has done for Kheli."

Phantom froze. Angelica should not have been so brave. As daughter to the Prime Minister, all of that information would now be his. If she had been anyone else, he would have to dispose of her in that lake. Allow the monster have one last kill then find somewhere else for it to settle.

But even as he thought it, he noticed the monster had settled. Not completely, but with Rose's hand on his arm, its presence seemed to curl around her. Like a feline wanting to nuzzle up her neck and nap there on her chest. His monster had never reacted this way to anyone.

"Interesting," he whispered.

She glanced back up to him and withdrew her hand. He did not expect the icy coolness to return to his arm so quickly. "I—I won't breath a word of it to my father." There was a weariness in her eyes. He couldn't tell if it was self-preservation that pushed her to say the words, or genuine concern. Her lashes fluttered down, but she seemed to realize she made a mistake and quickly righted her gaze back to his eyes, a blush forming on her cheeks.

Phantom nearly burst from laughter at the sight, but he settled for a cat-like grin. Or perhaps it was the monster who smiled.

He took in a breath. "You still haven't answered my question." A line formed between her brows so he repeated, "Why did you run?"

She blinked up at him. She even opened her mouth to reply, but the words fell short.

Phantom leaned his head back, reexamining her. "You did answer." At that, her jaw snapped shut. "You ran because Angelica visited you." He leaned down to her and she yielded a step. "You ran because your father's officers should be protecting Kheli, not me." She blinked rapidly. He was onto something. "It was not my hand you were trying to force. It was your father's."

She turned to walk back to shore, but he grabbed her hand, gently. She turned at the surprisingly light touch, meeting his eyes again. "You thought you could convince them to ransom you instead. They'd leave the island and you would have given us enough time to defend Kheli." Then her eyes weren't just cold. They were calculated. "No," he whispered. "You were counting on the Navy to wipe them out." He breathed out, she was very still under his touch. "All because Angelica visited you." His own brows knocked together. "Have you never had anything to fight for before?"

Phantom's earlier words snapped back to him. *Do you have a death wish?*

He was beginning to believe his accusation was not all that inaccurate.

"They are my people too," she bit out, but she still did not tear away from his hand.

The words startled him enough to shift. He had never heard the Prime Minister admit any responsibility to the people of Kheli. No more than those Brettanian soldiers held over the Kalonite slaves. He hadn't even heard it from the Commodore. Although, when Ashby was a new recruit, he saw the world much brighter, fuller. The Navy stole that optimism from him.

Yet here was Rose Davenport, willing to lay down her life for their safety and they may never know.

"Thank you," he found himself whispering. She flinched from the words, as if they were unfamiliar or all too familiar. "If you had not run, I would have left Kheli to bring you back to Samsara. And those *men*," he said with distain, without an ounce of respect. There was nothing human left in those Brettanian soldiers. "They would have returned to Brettania with slaves." Rose snapped her eyes to him. "They never would have attacked the village, but we would have never known about the Kalonite slaves. Even if you didn't mean to save them. There are a couple dozen women and girls who owe their lives to you."

A silver glisten added to her gold eyes. The facts seemed to drip from her and that tangy scent returned. "But at what cost?"

Finally, it registered where her fear was rooted. Her fear had nothing to do with him. It had everything to do with the near lifeless body Earhart carried into the village.

"Angelica," Phantom's whisper carried across the winds of the lake, prickling at his cool skin. To his surprise, the monster did not rear its head. It did not roar at the thought of losing Angelica. "Too high a price." He had little hope she would survive. If they had been closer to the village when she was struck, perhaps, but luck was not on her side. His first mate would lose his wife.

Phantom let her hand go, despair and guilt making every movement, every blink, an effort.

Her voice was soft, a kindling of warmth. "I can save her."

His eyes snapped up and he dared to let a trickle of hope into his heavy heart, then he narrowed his eyes. "How?"

She studied him. Wearily deciding if he was worthy of such information. He wasn't. He knew he wasn't, but he would drown in every bit of shame, guilt, and regret if there was even a small chance at saving Angelica.

She swallowed. "I need the Stone."

"The Stone can heal her?"

She hesitated. "Yes, but you have to know how to use it." It was worth a try. Anything was.

"Do you know how to use it?"

"Yes," she breathed.

He moved and she all but jumped out of the way, slamming her palms to her face. "Don't be shy now, love." Part of him wished to tease her further regarding their current predicament and the red blush he watched crawl up her neck. Oh she saw something, but he didn't have the luxury to tease her about it.

His skin was wet and sticky, but he got his clothing on as quickly as possible, flipping his soaked black hair back as he strapped his cutlass back to his hip.

When he turned back to see Rose's hand still covering her face he smiled. "I'm decent, love." She let her hands drop as he put a hand out for her. "Come now. We don't have much time."

She wrapped her hand around his and they ran.

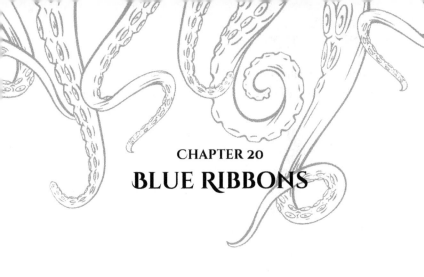

CHAPTER 20
BLUE RIBBONS

The jungle was dense, but the village was not far.

Hand in hand they ran and leapt through the foliage of the tropical forest. He would have swung on vines if he thought it would get them there any sooner.

Finally, they crossed into the threshold of the village. Phantom directed Rose's steps away from a trap he had set in anticipation of strangers. Her feet missed the pile of leaves that loosely sat above a six foot hole. He hoisted her into his chest, like before, but she faced him this time. An adorable yelp escaped her.

Her face was close. Too close for him to think properly. Her scent was too potent. He could pick out the distinct floral aromas, plumeria like the ones that used to grow in Reverie, but now resided in rich Samsaran gardens. There was also jasmine, a muskier night dwelling scent that thrived in Kheli. And of course, roses. "There was a trap there," he managed to breath.

Her lips parted. "Thank you."

Phantom shook his head, snapping the spell and setting

her down. She diligently followed him through the building to the one where the Earharts resided, but a coolness glided across his hand.

Jon stood guard outside the house. It was closer to a hut, but one of the biggest since Angelica ran her blacksmithing through it as well as cared for three children. Jon's shoulders tensed, rippling with tension upon spying Phantom.

"I thought you were cooling off." Jon's eyes shifted to the blonde in his shadow. The man was fully prepared to stop Phantom at any cost should the monster make an appearance. The monster was not fully settled. Phantom knew this by the tangy scent of fear and copper scent of blood. A lot of blood, but he could also hear heartbeats. Two strong ones and one weak one coming from inside the hut.

Phantom put his hands out to his sides. "Would I be here if I still needed cooling?"

Black, Jon, Ramirez, and Earhart were the only ones who knew the truth. At least enough of the truth to know that the monster was not simply recovering from battle or uncontrollable wrath. Some of the other devils suspected, but since there hadn't been an incident in years, no one had dared to question their Captain. This was why they spoke in code. Or, perhaps, it was the half-soaked blonde behind him and his own drenched state.

Jon furrowed his brows and glanced to Rose.

"Open the door, Jon."

Jon pressed his lips into a hard line, but he moved, opening the door. The scene was a wash of linens and blood. The Earhart's hut did not contain separate rooms aside from the blacksmithing area. The bed Angelica laid upon was to the side immediately upon entering the room.

The knife was gone from her stomach, replaced by wrappings that were already soaked through. Her eyes were closed and her breathing was soft, but Phantom could hear the too slow thrum of her heartbeat. The doctor knelt at her side, putting instruments away.

Earhart knelt on the other side, both of his hands entangled in one of hers. He held her hand to his mouth, pressing it against his lips.

Phantom stood at the threshold. Part of him didn't think he would be welcome. Although Earhart's gaze was steely, it was not unwelcoming.

"Smith," Phantom said. "How is she?"

The doctor blinked long as Earhart steadied his attention on him. Smith reached out to Earhart with a heavy expression. Before he could speak, Earhart was shaking his head. "No," he started. "No, Smith." A tear broke free from the first mate's eye. "Don't say it. Don't take away what hope I have."

Smith leaned in and put a firm hand on Earhart's large shoulder. "I cannot give you false hope, mate."

Earhart's head dipped, pressing his wife's hand into his forehead.

Smith released Earhart's shoulder and stood to face his Captain. "I would be surprised if she ever woke." Earhart jaw dropped, the final piece of hope he had melting away. "I'm sorry." Then, the doctor left. The doctor never leaves. There had always been grave patients, but he never left before the patient took their last breath. He did it for Earhart. Let the man have one moment more with his beloved wife and the mother of his children.

Phantom glanced back at Rose. Her own tears fell down her face now.

"Jon," Phantom ordered and there he was. "Do not let a soul cross into this house. Not until we leave, is that understood?"

Jon hesitated and studied his Captain. For the same reason he could hear heartbeats, he knew his eyes were still mostly black. Those dilated pupils taking up the irises completely. A tell tale sign of the beast.

When Jon didn't move Phantom snapped, "That is an order, mate."

Still weary, Jon nodded and closed the door.

Earhart cried into his wife's hand. He didn't have the heart to tell his first mate and best friend to leave his dying wife, especially since he wasn't sure it would work.

At Rose's hesitance, Phantom reassured, "I trust him with my life. He'll keep a secret if I tell him to." Earhart glanced up, his eyes red and dewy, but they lit up, the tiniest seed of hope sparking. Phantom would regret causing that hope if Rose couldn't do anything to help. Even if the Stone possessed some element of healing, it could already be too late for Angelica.

Swiftly, Phantom pulled at the smooth rock in his coat breast pocket, revealing its glittering surface from the dampening black velvet pouch. Rose's expression melted from weary to irritated. Her mouth forming a thin line and her brows dropping.

"Pirate," Phantom pointed out.

Earhart stared at the rock with furrowed brows then lifted his gaze to his Captain.

"Mate," Phantom started. "I don't know if this will work, but I would try anything to save her." Finally, he let his eyes drop to her face. Even her rich brown skin was ashen, as if her very life force was being drained. He stretched out his hand to Rose and lifted his gaze to her. "You will return this when you're finished."

Tentatively, she accepted the Stone, careful to only let her fingers touch the black velvet. This woman had been ready to steal it from him while he was in the lake. There was no way she would have been able to hold onto it, yet she risked the consequences at the chance to heal Angelica.

Rose knelt at Angelica's side, opposite from Earhart while Phantom took up a position at the end of the bed. She placed her left hand on the blood soaked bandage at Angelica's core. Once more, she glanced back to Phantom. The weariness was gone. Only a resigned determination crept over her features, like a wave lapping gently at the shore.

She withdrew the Stone from its pouch. The moment her delicate fingers glided over the smooth stone, blue glittered from within it. Blue like a clear sky after a storm. Blue like the sea in the lagoons near the Kalon ruins. Blue and bright and pulsing then mixing with the lilac glitter and silver streams.

The last thing Phantom expected was to hear Rose sing. There were no words, just a soft note she carried on a hum. The songbird stared at Angelica as she sung. At first, Phantom believed it to be a soothing melody, something to coax Angelica's sub-conscience into accepting her help.

Until the blue light grew, dancing across Rose's fingertips, then up her arm. It reacted to her voice and the beautiful melodic tone she carried. It ebbed and flowed; advanced and receded with the high and low notes resonating off Rose's tongue, crawling up her arm, bright even through the clothing. It snaked up her neck and the side of her face until it bled into her temple.

Rose's entire body straightened, tensing with the intruding blue light. Phantom almost flinched. He nearly ripped the offending Stone from her grasp, but there was no fight. Rose welcomed the light. Welcomed the essence of the Stone into her body.

Earhart stared with as much awe and fascination as was no doubt on Phantom's face.

She opened her eyes and they were no longer coins of gold. Instead, they glowed blue like the light. As if the Goddess Macha had replaced Rose and knelt before them now.

But Rose continued to sing, lyrics emerging from the sweet notes and tones.

> HEAVEN NEED NO MORE
> HELL CLOSE YOUR GATE
> HEAL ALL THAT WAS TORN
> BREAK THE LOOM OF FATE

The words came out as a choir, as if it wasn't one voice but many. Phantom remembered the conversation he won with her the night before. She had claimed the Stone stole the voices of the dead. That those voices could still be heard. Did they sing with her now?

> NEMAIN REST IN BLISS
> MACHA GIFT YOUR KISS
> DAVINA REWRITE THE STARS
> BUT LEAVE US WHAT IS OURS

As the words cascaded from her so did the light. A blue

hue radiated from Rose in tendrils of silky light. It wrapped around her in ribbons.

The verses repeated as the light thrummed around Rose. It pulsed it the air, on her arm and neck, and in her eyes. The verses repeated again and a heartbeat grew. For a moment, Phantom believed it to be his own, but a glance in Angelica's direction and he could see the evidence of it. Her face was no longer ashen. Earhart noticed in the same moment, a new wash of hope bleeding from him. He straightened with awe branding his face. He wouldn't look to Rose anymore or to the glowing blue light encasing her. He only stared at Angelica and kissed her knuckles firmly.

The verses repeated again. She sang the words like they were a chant, a spell. The magic that the Stone possessed needed someone who knew how to use it, because it required a song.

There were so very many questions he wanted answered, but not a single one could fully voice what was inside his head. There was a woman glowing blue only a few feet from him. He knew why Commodore Ashby looked at her with such possession. It had nothing to do with his feelings for her. It had everything to do with the Goddess magic pulsing through her.

But it didn't answer his other questions.

The song faded from Rose and so did the blue, crawling back into her like a tide washing out to sea, but the light in her eyes, neck, and arms still stayed.

Phantom inched toward Angelica's belly. Earhart stared at the bandage, body tense. As if he didn't want to know. Didn't want to lose the hope he clung to.

The Captain peeled the wrapping away from her skin and it slid away easily in the blood. With a small rag in hand, he wiped away the blood below the bandage to reveal perfect rich brown skin. Not even a scar marred the warm flesh.

An audible sigh of relief left Earhart as he sobbed anew. Not tears of despair anymore. The tangy scent left him completely, replaced by something sweet and clear like fresh morning air, relief.

Phantom let his eyes land on the songbird across the bed. Her back was as straight as a blade. No emotion or relief painted her features. Only cool calm and something blank, as if she wasn't present in her body at all. The blue still pulsed from the Stone in a line to her temple, illuminating her eyes.

He almost didn't want to disturb her, but that tangy scent was still in the air. It was radiating from Rose. She was afraid. He had the most overwhelming impulse to remove fear from her life.

Phantom whirled around the bed and knelt beside her. She didn't flinch. She didn't turn. She only stared at a distant spot on the wall and breathed. He reached for the Stone in her hand and she did nothing to stop him. He slipped the Stone from her hand and snuffed out the light with its velvet pouch. The light blinked out from her eyes, only briefly did he see the gold, before her eyes fluttered shut and she toppled over.

He caught her body, leaning her to land in his arms. In a couple grunted moments he lifted himself to his feet, carrying her limp body. Her head rolled onto his upper arm and he stared.

"She saved my *tresora*," Earhart breathed, barely audible.
My tresora. My treasure.

Phantom had never believed he would think of a person

in that way, but looking at Rose collapsed in his arms, he wasn't so sure.

He steeled his features. The mask of the Captain was difficult to place when he was so awestruck, but he thought of this information landing in the wrong hands and it was enough to sober him.

"Tell no one."

Earhart straightened the slightest bit and nodded. There were no questions. Earhart knew he wouldn't get answers. The information alone was a kindness to his wife that he was fortunate to have witnessed. The man still looked like he wanted to say more, but Angelica stirred beside him. His eyes lit with the final piece of hope lodging into place.

Phantom strode out of the room. The Earharts needed their privacy and Phantom needed to find a safe place for Rose to recover. He softly kicked at the door in a knock.

It opened slowly as Jon took in his Captain and the dead weight in his Captain's arms. He glanced further into the room. It was dark, but he could see the miracle behind them.

Angelica was awake enough to accept the desperate hugs and kisses from her husband. Jon's features softened and he looked back to the fallen girl in Phantom's arms.

"Jon," he started. "You mustn't breathe a word."

The brute nodded and allowed his Captain to pass.

Phantom strode from the hut, but it was not lost on him that the monster was still present in his body. Still awake, but soothed— settled. It had never done that before.

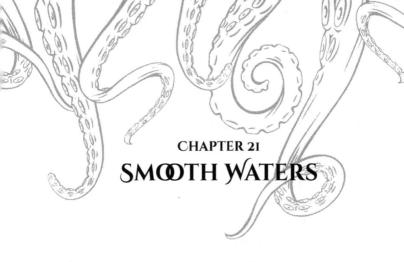

CHAPTER 21
SMOOTH WATERS

P hantom had carried her all the way back to the ship. He had considered asking Jon to carry her back, but he couldn't bare the thought of anyone touching her. Not by some enate desire to covet her or her healing magic. No, he was scared to death that she was fragile enough to fall apart at any moment. He felt like he owed her that. At least that.

He owed her a hell of a lot more than that. It was only one night and she managed to change everything by running away and forcing his hand. Those Kalonite slaves would likely be loaded onto that ship and sailed to Brettania on the next high tide. Without her action, he never would have known.

That fight felt like it was weeks ago. Months ago. Not hours.

He gently laid her in the red covers of his own bed. The bed that had been hers for the past two nights and would be hers one last night.

Phantom stood back examining her. He didn't know

how long she needed to sleep, but he wouldn't be able to leave the room for one moment of it. Who could he trust to stay with her now?

The voices that came from her echoed in his head. He'd never forget the sound in all his life. No, he'd remember it through all his lifetimes.

The minutes ticked by as Phantom sat on the chair at his desk. His arms draped over his knees as he watched her breathe, contemplating her entire existence. He wished she'd wake up and explain it all to him, but he knew she wouldn't. It was a gift that he even witnessed what she did.

The waves behind him shined with the newfound sunrise. They'd have to leave port soon if they were to make it to Samsara in time.

The scent of woldenberries and citrus wafted from the door entrance. The woldenberries were native only to Kalon, but Ramirez always did smell like his home. A soft knock ticked against the wood of his door, soft enough to discourage waking its inhabitants.

He sighed, he could not neglect his devils for long. Not if they were ready to set sail. "Enter," Phantom ordered.

In strode a silver haired man with a large feathered hat firmly placed on his head. Ramirez tipped his head, "Long night, Captain." It wasn't a question. Everyone was exhausted from the eventful night.

Phantom pressed his lips together. "Indeed." His eyes never left the bed, but his hand crossed his body, resting against a shoulder.

Ramirez's grey eyes shifted from Rose's limp body to Phantom's fidgety form.

With a click of the door and a whisper he said, "Is your temper still present?"

Phantom gazed up at the old man. Ramirez was the only one to refer to Phantom's monster as his temper. He knew it to be something stronger, something deeper, something more physical than temper, but some part of Phantom always wondered if he was more correct than anyone.

"It is," Phantom breathed, half scared Rose was awake and listening, but she didn't stir in the slightest. He knew she didn't listen because her heartbeat was slow and steady. Too slow for someone feigning sleep. It was the same reason he knew the monster was still present.

"Yet you sit peacefully." Not a question either. It was wonder in his tone.

Phantom examined him. The man could read Phantom on a bad day and he didn't have many of those. He might have answered or ordered Ramirez away to take his opinions elsewhere, but he was too tired. He felt sleep heavy on his lashes, but for so many reasons, he could not close them.

The old man seemed to sense as much.

"You're needed on deck before we leave." His voice wasn't commanding. He wasn't telling Phantom anything he didn't know, but if he had to return to the deck, he'd have to leave her on the bed. Vulnerable. He went rigid at the thought.

Ramirez noticed. "Perhaps," he started. "I can watch over our guest."

Phantom lifted his head to refuse, but the man's eyes had melted. He imagined Ramirez to be what it was like to have a father, in some small way.

His Captain's lack of answer had Ramirez shifting to take up a position on the sitting chair beside the bed.

Phantom blinked at him, but still said nothing. Finally, he managed to peel himself away. The only allowance he could manage was telling the old man he would return as soon as the ship was at sea.

Nearly to the door, he turned to glance at her once more. The soft pump of her heartbeat was a comfort he'd grown used to. Her hand rested near her head, falling among her splay of blonde hair. He couldn't stop seeing blue. Blue everywhere, but especially in her eyes.

He shoved the image away before blinking at the sunlight pouring over the ship planks. Closing the door behind him, he took in the sounds and scents of a ship preparing to leave port.

With his beast still present, everything was too loud, too strong, too much. The scent of salty air and fishy aroma swelled. All at once the scents of each of the devils slammed into him. Jon's scent was sand, sun, and musky sweat. Hyne's scent was lemon and green tea, followed by Tick's smooth fresh water stone scent. Black smelt of jasmine and leather.

All of it were scents he could smell, provided he was close enough to the devil, without his beast form present, but with the monster humming under his skin, the scents were strong and collided all at once.

The noise was worse. Barrels rolled. Men shouted. Ropes snagged on wood. Footsteps reverberated.

Phantom placed a hand to his head where a headache had formed. The tell tale sign of controlling the beast for too long, keeping it at bay. He breathed heavily. This was one of the reasons he had not wished to leave his quarters. To leave her.

"Captain." Jon spoke and it was too loud. Like Phantom

had woken from a drunken splendor and was paying the price. He glanced at the brute with a tense brow. Jon narrowed his eyes, no doubt seeing the still blackened eyes. "Earhart would like to see you."

In the midst of everything, Phantom nearly forgot about Earhart and the wife Rose nearly brought back from the dead. *Angelica*. What would Earhart had become if she had died?

"Is she well?" Phantom breathed, half believing the scene he witnessed to be a dream, even if he never slept.

Jon let a twitch of a smile hit the corner of his mouth. "She is more than that. She keeps saying she has more to do. That she needs to see to her children. Earhart has insisted she remain in bed for now."

Phantom let his own smile break. "Of course he has." Earhart likely had his own trouble believing in her recovery.

Jon whispered, "Some are asking how she recovered so quickly."

Phantom didn't have to look to know he was being watched. By other devils, by angels, by villagers saying their goodbyes on the docks. "She was not as badly injured as we first thought. That is all they need to know." With Jon's inscrutable gaze he added, "For now."

That seemed to satisfy Jon enough because he nodded. He held out his arm. Of course, the brute had every intention to follow his Captain to Earhart's hut. In a normal circumstance, he wouldn't need or allow the escort, but with the beast below his skin, he had no choice. He couldn't afford a beast incident to happen today.

When they reached the hut, Phantom knocked on the door. Earhart opened it with a rustle. The open door showed a glimpse of Angelica Earhart, standing in the kitchen, cooking breakfast. Apparently, she had made herself useful despite her husband's insistence. She stood in a new dress that wasn't stained with blood and with all the grace she normally held, as if nothing life threatening even happened to her.

Earhart closed the door and whispered, "Is she awake?" Phantom shook his head. "Give her my thanks then. Although—" he glanced at his wife, a crinkle appearing between his brows. "I don't think any thanks could ever be sufficient." Phantom nodded, understanding him deeply.

"You're not coming with us?" Phantom blurted. He knew. Of course, he knew Earhart would remain at his wife's side. Help the Kalonite slaves settle into the village. Be sure no Brettanian soldiers survived the attack, but Phantom had not come to terms that he would have to face Ashby without Earhart. It seemed incomplete to finalize their freedom without Earhart at his side.

Earhart turned his tired gaze to Jon. "Jon can secure my duties, Captain. I am needed here for now."

When freedom rang and the time came for each of the devils to choose how they would spend it, Phantom knew his first mate would end up here, with his family. Even if some selfish part of him wished for them to sail the seas forever.

Phantom lifted his brow. "Take care of her, Earhart."

Earhart lifted his own brow, imitating his Captain. "You take care of *her*, Captain."

Phantom froze. But it was not lost on the two devils before him. Phantom had no idea what to do with the kidnapped stowaway songbird that calmed his monster and healed the wounded. A woman who held his ticket to freedom. An infuriating woman who he dreaded parting from.

The Captain clapped a hand on his first mate's shoulder. "May you have smooth waters," he started, reciting a goodbye Phantom would never forget.

"And open seas for all days," Earhart replied, patting him on the back.

Jon and Phantom left their friend to his wife who strode back into the room— back to his *tresora*.

———

At the dock, Arita was saying goodbye to her brother. There was an air that passed between them as they spoke their native language. A prideful gleam appeared on Wilson's face. Arita would stay to protect the people of Kheli with the rest of the angels and Phantom never felt more confident in that decision.

The little boy, Karasu, had grown an entire inch since Phantom had seen the boy last. There was a gleam in Wilson's eyes whenever he looked at the boy and told him all about his adventures aboard *Nemain's Revenge* with the silver-tongued demon.

Russet boarded the ship, but his eyes trailed Arita, her eyes returning his gaze while Wilson's attentions were on the boy. The two had been circling each other for awhile.

Wilson grunted when he noted the exchange.

Phantom chuckled to himself as he passed them. He took two steps onto his ship before a blur of black hair and leather sauntered past him. Sophia Clare strode onto the ship deck as if she owned it. A pack strapped to her back along with her bow and full quiver. Gone was the barmaid dress. She was strapped in as much leather as she could manage with trousers and a puffy red undershirt. Her black hair was braided to one side and her features were as still as stone.

"What do you think you're doing?" Phantom said, forcing his tone to be calm.

"I'm coming along," she said with no room for argument.

Phantom narrowed his eyes, trying to piece together who she thought she was talking to. "You are not a sailor, Miss. And we are pira—"

"And you are down a man. It's an even exchange. An angel for a devil," she interrupted. Her features settling remarkably harder with determination.

"We don't need—"

"I'm better with a bow than anyone here and you know it."

Phantom let a whisper of a smile lick his lips. He did know it. He wanted to ask her to join the devils the moment she displayed her skill, but she wouldn't find a pirate's life easy.

"If you are coming, you have to understand the rules."

Her face softened a bit, but it was replaced with something just as determined. Perhaps the huntress still had something to prove.

"You do not interrupt your Captain. You follow orders. Mine and my first mate, which is now Jon." Her eyes shifted to the brute who curled a hand in a mock wave. "You do not hesitate. And you do not argue. Or you will be tossed onto the closest island until I have the patience to deal with you. Is that understood?"

"Yes, Captain," she replied, her tone dutiful.

"There's room on my bunk," Black hummed from the railing of the ship where he leaned.

She tensed at the sight of him, but if the barmaid couldn't handle Phantom's swordsman, she wouldn't have invited herself aboard *Nemain's Revenge*.

Phantom tossed his arms out. "Welcome aboard, Miss Clare."

CHAPTER 22
LIEUTENANT

S alty sea air mixed with a foggy breeze from the North as they sailed away from Kheli's shores. Seagulls cooed above the sails, flying with them, likely drawn by the fish breakfast Wilson distributed to the devils. They were wasting their time. He'd sooner shoot the birds than let them steal food from the ship.

Phantom stood on the quarterdeck looking over the crew busying themselves with duties or shoveling food into their mouths. It didn't matter if Wilson was in a sour mood, the food would always be good. It was a pride he carried with him. Some part of his village, his country he could keep alive.

Clare had settled in with the crew easily enough. Black had mercifully kept his distance. Phantom knew that wouldn't last long, not with the glances exchanged by either one of them like sharks, circling each other.

Jon spouted orders the moment he stepped a boot on *Nemain's Revenge* as its first mate. The other devils took no hesitation in obeying his orders. On a good day, Jon was a fearsome pirate to behold. No other man would be more well suited to the job.

Finally, they were out to sea, Kheli a speck behind them, and Phantom couldn't muster up the strength to reenter the cabin. Would she be awake? He had so many questions and he wasn't sure how to ask most of them. When he glanced at the blue sky above them all he could see was the blue that glowed in her eyes, on her throat, down her arms, on her fingertips. The light that wrapped itself in ribbons around her form as she sang. And her voice— he'd never forget it.

A throat cleared beside him and he snapped his attention to Jon. The man's dark brown hair hung to his shoulders, his barrel large arms exposed to the elements, and his knives strapped to leathers across his chest and sides.

"We're steady, Captain." Jon stated, but a coat of curiosity engulfed his tone.

"Good," was all Phantom could bring himself to say. His voice seemed to struggle with words the more he thought on blue light, on Kalonite slaves and Brettanian soldiers, and Rose Davenport.

"You've had a long night, Captain. Perhaps it's time you get some rest." Phantom laughed, a cool sound holding no joy. "You'll need to be alert to negotiate with the Minister."

He spread his arms, facing his new first mate. "It would be lovely to sleep, however, the act would be lost on me." Phantom could still smell scents everywhere. He knew Wilson was preparing fish before he ever emerged from the main cabin. Every heartbeat, every sound was deafening, overwhelming.

Phantom met Jon's eyes and the brute audibly sighed. Not only at the stare of struggle, but at the blackened eyes that were surely still there. They didn't risk sailing while

Phantom's beast was so close. With no where to go, the crew would not survive. Yet, here they were.

"Should you even be on the ship right now?"

He had considered it, staying on the island while Jon delivered Rose to her father. He'd likely manage the negotiations, but this newfound information about the Stone would likely serve its purpose best if Phantom was there to bargain with it.

"And where else would I go, Jon?" Phantom snapped, louder than he intended, but he didn't care. The leash on his monster was growing more and more taut. *The longer I'm away from Rose*, he thought with a shudder. "Should I banish myself to a longboat, float behind the ship?"

"You'd tear the longboat apart, Captain." Jon said with no emotion. It was a clear fact. Jon had witnessed the beast first hand, as did Earhart. If Phantom was left to his own devices, with no way to settle the beast, he'd tear the boat apart and have to swim back to the ship. If he didn't, he would risk tearing someone apart.

"I could do a lot worse, Jon." He caught the brute's gaze again. "Much worse."

Jon snagged his lip in his teeth. Phantom watched the struggle on his mate's face, odd for a man who was normally so stoic. Perhaps, after all this time, he read the man like a book. Not unlike how well he read Phantom.

"You should return to her."

Phantom's jaw nearly dropped. "I'm in a very dangerous state while she remains in a vulnerable one. How exactly do you see that ending for us?"

The brute crossed his arms. He made Phantom feel short and small, even if he wasn't. He'd felt the beast settle in her presence at the waterfall, but it was only one instance.

Would it happen again? Was it worth the risk? If she died—everything would be lost.

"I have a theory," he stated again, returning that stoic gaze.

"Does your theory involve how long we can run from the Navy before my ship is at the bottom of the ocean?" But it wasn't just the devils the Minister would come after. The entire village would be forfeit.

The thought made Phantom's head hurt, pounding on the exhaustion building ever more urgent. He rubbed his hands over his face, banishing the thoughts from the forefront of his mind.

"Go see her," Jon whispered. A glint in his eyes had Phantom releasing some tension from his shoulders. Jon was usually insufferably right. It was usually exhausting, but there was a part of Phantom that urged him back to the cabin— back to Rose.

With a heavy breath, Phantom peeled himself away from the attention of his first mate. His boots clamored across the floorboards before reaching the Captain's quarters. He contemplated knocking, but decided against it. He didn't have Ramirez's talent for soft knocking, especially with a beast pounding beneath his skin.

The scent of cooked fish hit first, then a signature smokey sweetness, along with Ramirez's citrus and woldenberry scent. An almost unbearable combination.

Through the door, Rose sat up in the bed, nibbling at the fish on her plate. She smiled, laughing softly at something Ramirez said to her. Her smile was potent, relaxing a great deal of pressure off his shoulders.

Her smile faded when she caught his gaze, but it didn't disappear completely. It only grew hesitant. He was not the only one concerned. She revealed a very large secret, risking herself in the process. Now, she would wait for whatever consequences her actions would bring.

"Captain," Ramirez prompted when Phantom said nothing. Perhaps he had already been speaking to his Captain.

Phantom coughed, clearing his throat. "My apologies, Ramirez. Can we have a moment?" It wasn't an order, because in this moment he felt very small. With all he owed to the woman laying in his bed, he should be accepting her orders. Without her, those slaves would have been sold to Brettania. Then again, Angelica would have perished without her. It felt wrong to spout orders before her.

"Of course, Captain," Ramirez mumbled, picking up their empty plates before exiting the room.

Rose let her gaze land on him, taking him in. He flexed and unfurled his hands beside him, feeling all too seen, but he didn't move from his spot near the door.

Not until she patted at the blankets beside her. "Come," she purred melodically like the sirens in those old sailor's tales. The way she drew him in, she could have put them to shame. "Sit." He obeyed, sitting upon the bed, leaning his weight on one arm. If he wasn't so hyper focused on her, he'd fear he'd fall asleep.

"How is Angelica?" A hint of concern etched the skin at her eyes. She didn't know if the Stone's magic had worked, or maybe she did know and that was the concern.

"She is fine. She was—" Phantom found it hard to speak. "She was cooking when I visited her. On her feet, as if nothing happened." His brow furrowed, still not understanding how. He was never one to just accept things on faith, but he didn't see himself ever understanding how a dying woman was on her feet only hours later.

"Good," was all the songbird said, as she averted her eyes to the floor.

Phantom let his eyes roam her skin, searching for a scratch on her light skin. Skin that held a touch of red from sun exposure, but nothing worse. All she accomplished and there wasn't a scratch on her.

"How?" Phantom found himself whispering before he could stop it.

The gold coin eyes caught his again and the image of blue faded. All that was left was her. "Surely, you understand, I cannot say." Her voice was soft, like a prayer, like a plea.

"I know now why the Stone is so valuable," he started. "I know you can control it." He sighed. He could use the Stone against her, but a day ago she was willing to risk losing it to keep her secret. He doubted the leverage would have any effect now. "Will you answer any of my questions?"

She blinked, not expecting the sincereness in his voice.

"I cannot answer any that have to do with what transpired last night," she said gently, but slightly more sure of herself. Sure that he wouldn't force answers from her, he realized. The idea of forcing her created pinpricks across his skin.

"Why do you not leave Samsara?" It was not one of his most pressing questions, but it swirled among the others. She blinked again, leaning back slightly. "When you ran into the solider's camp, you showed no fear, even though you understood the danger you put yourself in. Yet you speak of the sea— as I do." The words stopped short on his breath. "You speak as if you want to see every inch of the world, yet you haven't seen a neighboring island." It wasn't something he knew, but he guessed. The resignation on her face confirmed it.

Rose drew her hands to her lap and stared at her palms. "I can't leave," she whispered. The statement was both unfamiliar and familiar. Then he understood.

"There are people to protect on Samsara?" He guessed and she straightened. He was right again. It was the same look he had on his own face when he spoke of Kheli, of the people to protect there. People she felt responsible for too.

She nodded, but didn't add to the statement. Instead, she asked, "Who are you really, Captain Phantom?" Her eyes were sharp and narrow on him.

He smiled crookedly at her. "You wish to know the great secret carried by *Nemain's Revenge*?"

Softly, she said, "I heard Sebastian call you James."

The joy fell from his face, but he didn't relax. The memories splashed up to him like the rouge waves of high tide and he was the helpless rock, slowly eroded by his past.

"I haven't heard Sebastian's name next to my old one in quite some time." The reminiscent memories crashed over him again, children playing in the street, covered in mud. Him and Sebastian were not those children. They were the children who pickpocketed the parent's coin purses. It was never enough, but it got them and the other orphans by. "To answer you, no, James is not my name. James Hawkins was a useful name when I was a child and when I applied for the Navy. Nothing more."

Her eyes grew wide. It turned his smile back up.

"You were in the Navy."

"Quite," he stated. More memories crashed, carving

away a bit of the wall he'd used to keep them out. A younger, skinnier version of himself, standing in white and blue with every other new recruit, right along Sebastian Ashby before he became the Commodore.

"How did you become—" She fell short, the words falling from her lips.

"A pirate?" Phantom offered.

She tightened her lips, nodding.

He let a breath fall. "I'm surprised you didn't hear at least a version of the truth." He rubbed his hands over his face before continuing. "Of the crew you've met, only Earhart was on the Naval force with me when we were ordered to the Scillian islands. A group of Kalonites, not much different from the ones you helped save, had taken refuge there." Something akin to guilt flashed over her face when he mentioned her part in saving them. "I don't know why they are valued so much, but the Prime Minister ordered their capture."

She froze. Her father ordered their capture. A man no different than those Brettanian soldiers. At the very least, the soldiers acted out of desperation.

"In the dead of night, Earhart and I, commandeered the ship you are currently sailing on. We packed up the Kalonites and sailed them home. We—" he paused, knowing he could not include Earhart in the blame. "I killed every solider still on the ship when we left."

He moved his head to Rose, dreading her reaction to the information. It was a moment he often regretted, yet he would never change. Her face showed no hint of disgust, but she offered no reassurance either. Not that he expected her to. He understood. He chose to be the villain because it was the only way. He couldn't bring himself to regret it, but he didn't expect people to understand.

Since she had no reply, he continued. "Tick and Ramirez were part of the group we saved. With the new information we learned today, I know they would have been killed by the Minister as soon as we docked in Samsara. So I could never regret my actions in the Scillian islands that night." He spoke with certainty, even if the faces of the naval soldiers he killed crashed into him. Men he once considered comrades, but he keep his face straight, determined.

"I give you a choice." His voice was low and unfamiliar. The monster was so close, he could taste the officer's blood on his tongue. He desperately clung to that control as he waited for their responses. "Live by my command or perish at my hand."

Not a single officer chose to follow Phantom that day, so they perished under the teeth of the monster. The very first legend born, since Phantom allowed the youngest to live. He was dropped at the nearest Samsaran village to make sure the Minister knew who he had to answer to if he tried to take slaves again.

"Tick?" She asked, snapping him from the memory of blood and screams. "Why doesn't he speak?"

Phantom came into that cabin expecting to ask her a thousand questions. Instead, here he was, answering hers and unearthing painful memories.

"In all the years I've known him, he's never spoken a word. He was a very scarred man, Rose. I believe he is old enough that he was a child when the war began."

Her eyes went wide again. There were very few children who survived those days.

"I drug Hyne's hungover ass out of a back alley in

Samsara not long after that. The two have been inseparable since." Phantom shrugged, but there was nothing casual about it. Tick was jumpy and shaky before Hyne came along. It was Hyne who taught him not to be scared anymore. Sometimes Phantom wondered if it was from watching Hyne's sheer stupidity or his unending bravery. Either way, Tick started to smile when Hyne arrived.

Rose glanced to her hands again.

"I have a question for you," he said. Her eyes slowly raised to meet his. "If you could go anywhere, no consequences, no limits, where would you go?"

A small, delicate smile crept up one side of her face. A sense of pride washed over him, like he leapt from a rocky cliff face into the waves and found them to be warm and sweet.

She looked out the tattered glass window, watching the horizon and all its secrets. "I want to see Kalon." She smiled again and it was larger. Beautiful. "My mother used to talk about how beautiful the ruins were there. She loved the Kalonite people."

"I'll take you," he blurted, but he would do anything, go anywhere if it meant that smile would not leave her face.

It didn't. "What?"

"I'll take you to Kalon. To Draiochet, where the ruins are even more magnificent. To Atlas. To the Wynnlow fields of Koi No Yokan. Anywhere you want." He should have stopped at Kalon before promising the world when he couldn't grant it to himself, but he couldn't stop. "We could sail so far off the edge of the map that we'll have no idea what we'll find." With every word, her gold coin eyes lit up a little brighter. "Anywhere you want to go."

Then her smile dropped and reality snapped back to

him too. He hadn't even realized he leaned closer to her or her to him until she straightened herself away from him.

"I'm still your prisoner."

The word bit like a bucket of ice cold sea water, even though she said them with no mirth. She understood his reasons now.

"You will still ransom me to my father." Her eyes fell to her hands in her lap again.

"You could leave," he whispered, as if he dared not let anyone hear. "Once Kheli is free, you could leave of your own accord. Go to Kalon on your own, but always know there will be a place for you on my ship."

Her smile did not return like he hoped it would and the hope that she would spend more time aboard *Nemain's Revenge* died with it. She would not leave on her own. He could see it in the way her eyes set strongly, but he meant the words, he'd make her a devil right there if he thought she would stay.

She lifted the blankets from her legs and jumped off on the opposite side of the bed from where he sat. She cast him a knowing look. "Rest, Captain Phantom," she said sweetly and it was the first time he'd ever heard her use his chosen name without a hint of mirth or malice. Without biting out the word *Captain*. Instead, there was respect in her tone and a hint of something else.

When he didn't move she added. "There are bags under your eyes. And I know you haven't slept all night. You'll want to be fully rested to face my father."

He nearly flinched at the thought of having to negotiate when he would do anything to keep both his freedom and hers. Although, he knew it would not truly be freedom if she didn't pay for it herself. Not for her.

Phantom cleared his throat, suddenly raspy. "As you wish, love." He attempted his old smirk, but when the charm fell short, she pinned him with a raise of one eyebrow. She swept past him, her scent wafting with her, but the smokiness of her scent was gone. Only the sweetness of flowers lingered on her.

She opened the door and he was no longer hit with a cacophony of scents and smells. Only a soft sea breeze and murmurs. The beast was gone. His monster had completely settled, awaiting to be summoned once again.

Wide eyed, he stared back at her as she glided into the light. Awestruck, he fell back onto the bed. Asleep in seconds.

CHAPTER 23
BASHTIR BONFIRE

T he island of Bashtir was in sight, as the sun was about to set. Another ship, smaller than *Nemain's Revenge* sat on the opposite side of the small sandbar of an island. Captain Phantom had kept his end of the bargain. Show up at Bashtir with one unharmed daughter of the Prime Minister. A task that proved more difficult than he could have imagined.

Phantom had slept most of the day, but by the time night settled on the shore, his nerves were shot. Even with the restful sleep that came with calming the monster, he dreaded the sunrise more than anything.

Samsara sat in a foggy shroud in the distance. The Minister's Keep was a force to be reckoned with. Its large grey stone walls were unbreakable. Even with every storm that came and every army that sought its protection. Its walls stretched to protect the entire city, shrouding the city in a sea of grey.

It reminded Phantom of a prison. He supposed to Rose, it was. Although he may not understand why she choose to stay there, he'd always see the fortress as a prison. After all, he was once locked away in it too.

Rose Davenport was currently in the middle of a Kazeboon match with Robin. The boy needed practice anyway. He wasn't a fantastic liar, but the boy's honesty was something Phantom admired, especially, with the cards Davina had dealt him. No one would blame the kid for lying, but he didn't. It wasn't in him to.

Phantom watched the boy's small nose wrinkle as he wracked his brain for the answer to the puzzle Rose had laid out for him. Phantom was too far away to see what tiles they played or what names they claimed, but Rose's smile was hard to look away from. She only spent three day aboard *Nemain's Revenge* and she fit like she was born to sail with pirates. Although, he couldn't picture the identity attaching to her. She was too graceful to be a pirate.

No, she's much more of a siren. A vision of blue ribbons of light flashed across his memory.

"Captain." Ramirez approached with a piece of parchment in hand. A white wax seal of a mermaid adorned the rolled parchment, how fitting. "It's from the Minister." A hawk flew by the ship, back to its master.

Phantom reached for the parchment, broke the seal, and unfurled the concise note.

COMMODORE ASHBY HAS ARRIVED IN MY STEAD UNTIL DAYBREAK.

AT DAWN, WE SHALL HAVE A CHAT.

PRIME MINISTER DAVENPORT

Phantom curled and crunched the parchment under his palm. Ramirez and Jon stiffened beside him.

"The Minister has chosen to delay his arrival to

daybreak," Phantom bit out. He knew the power games the Minister played. He knew Phantom would do nothing to harm his daughter. Not if he wished to survive this encounter with his life. Nor would he leave, because the Commodore would pursue.

The Commodore possessed a fancier ship than a few days ago. The hull was painted with a red wash, clearly Brettanian made, but the Brettanians built ships to last since they had many enemies and much distance to travel. The Samsaran Navy got a hold of one sooner than Phantom expected. They could not outrun a Brettanian ship.

The Prime Minister had outwitted Phantom with only a couple of minor maneuvers, yet he possessed the upper hand. He had the Minister's daughter, the Stone, and the secret they both possessed. At least enough about it to imply he knew more. It would be hard waters to maneuver nonetheless.

Even with the games beginning between him and the Minister, he couldn't help the relief that flooded over him. They'd have one more night with Rose Davenport, rather, he'd have one more night with Rose.

"What do we do until then?" Jon asked, since he'd soon have to prepare the men to drop anchor.

Serena trilled overhead, flying over the crew to reach the powder monkey, but the little beastie had little control over her landings. She barreled into Robin and Rose's game, ruining their piles. They rolled with laughter in response as the beastie complained.

It brought a smile to Phantom's face.

"We haven't a proper bonfire in ages, Jon." The idea bloomed into his mind. He knew how to play the Minister's games. At Jon and Ramirez's confused faces, Phantom turned to face the small island they approached. Not a single soul lived on Bashtir because it could easily plunge into the sea with a storm or a very high tide. It was the prefect location to showcase how little the Minister's power play worked.

"Get the men ready to weigh anchor. We're going ashore. We'll need rum and that red moonshine we stocked." Jon's face nearly went pale, which was impressive for his coloring. Red moonshine was a sure way to make any man howling drunk in no time.

"Aye, Captain," Jon chimed when Phantom's features showed no sign of jest. He stomped away to get started.

Phantom spotted a particular doctor. "Smith." The doctor immediately turned his attentions to his Captain. Phantom dipped his head toward the beastie. Smith understood immediately.

Serena was precious beyond measure, worth more than any treasure Phantom could possess. If the Minister discovered Serena's presence, the results would be catastrophic. Particularly, if the people of Samsara discovered she was imprinted to him. Although, he would pay good money to see the Priestess's face when she found out.

Dragons were creatures of Davina. An imprint was as good as naming someone a leader, but that was the last thing Phantom wanted. The Minister could keep his island, but he couldn't have Serena.

If only he could say the same about a certain songbird.

Smith whistled for Serena. Reluctantly, she pulled away from licking Robin's face to land on Smith's arm as he descended the main cabin steps.

Tonight, he would let his men have their fun. The

Commodore wouldn't attack, for several reasons, one being the implied *parley*. He always did follow the rules. Another being the Minister's disappointment at the missed opportunity to speak with Phantom himself, even if he did receive his daughter back.

The third and most important reason being that if he attacked he could very well harm the songbird in the process. Whether it be for the power she possessed or his fondness of her or sheer duty to his Minister, he would not allow that.

So, they dropped the anchor and rode the longboats to the nearest beach on Bashtir.

Phantom ordered that they make the bonfire larger, more extravagant. He had absolutely no problem with burning down what few trees were left on Bashtir's precarious shore, though that was not the purpose. The purpose rested in the Commodore being able to see exactly what they were up to. There was no doubt in his mind that Ashby would report it to the Minister.

Clare had taken a boar with her on the ship when she boarded. It rested over the bonfire, providing the perfect feast for the devils. Although drinks were plentiful, some chose to refrain due to constitution or nerves. Sophia Clare being one of them. The woman had not fully integrated with the devils. Though, he suspected she wouldn't remain aboard once they docked in Kheli again.

Ramirez and Smith refrained from drink as well. They remained on the ship, guarding it and the little beastie.

Jon put a bottle of rum in Robin's hands. Precariously, he gulped down a swig then promptly coughed. "Ah, why do you drink this?"

Jon and Hyne rolled with laughter. Hyne seized it from the boy. "More for us then, lad."

Jon clapped a hand on Robin's thin shoulder. "One day, boy, you'll drink like the rest of us."

Phantom hoped for Robin's sake that wasn't true. The Captain laid on the sand, propping himself up on his elbows while Jon sat crosslegged on the sand.

Much to Phantom's surprise and utter joy, Rose took little convincing. She plopped down in the sand next to Phantom and he got the feeling of a cat choosing his lap as its nesting perch. The feeling made him freeze, as if any shift would cause her to walk away.

"I do actually enjoy rum," she stated.

"Do you now?" Hyne said before Phantom could beat him to it. "I didn't know the Minister would allow such a thing."

She raised a finger to her lip with a soft *shhh*. "He doesn't. My lady's maid brings the drink to me every once in awhile."

Hyne feigned surprise. "Whatever do you threaten her with?"

The songbird narrowed her eyes at the devil, then to Phantom's complete delight, she leaned forward to shove him over. He willing accepted the shove and fell back into the soft beige sand. Jon chuckled softly beside him. Tick on the opposite side of Hyne, broke into a smile.

Rose tipped the bottle back to guzzle more of the spiced liquid. He knew it had to burn her throat, but she seemed to relish the sensation. She wiped a drizzle of the amber liquid from her chin once the bottle returned to her lap.

"Captain," Hyne called. Phantom tipped his head in attentiveness. "You need to make her a devil. She belongs with us." His tone held every note of sarcasm and jest, but Phantom wished severely that he could.

She made an adorable round shape with her mouth instead. "I would not—" her words slurring, "—not fit in with you filthy lot."

"Oh," all three men said at once.

"Yes," she insisted. "You are all the most filthy—" Her voice inched higher. "Foul-smelling, ill-mannered creatures I ever met." He might have believed her if she wasn't smiling. The sight bright and full, warming the air more than the bonfire could.

Hyne lifted his arm to smell himself and apparently coming to the conclusion that she was right.

Phantom curled his head back to look at Rose, placing an earnest palm to his chest. "You wound us, love."

"You—" She hiccuped. "Are quite possibly the worst of them all," she added before downing another swig of the bottle she commandeered.

"Am I?" He nearly burst with the excitement, leaning on one elbow to face her more fully. The gesture didn't seem to intimidate her in the slightest. "Tell me, love, what have I done to offend you?"

"You," she said, taking a breath to clear her head. She wasn't quite drunk enough yet, which was perfect. She was just intoxicated enough to be truthful. "You made me kidnap myself."

He nearly snorted with laughter. Jon and Hyne chuckling along with him.

"And," she continued, loudly. "You beat me at the game with the lying."

He laughed again. "Forgive me, love. I shall let you win next time."

"And," she said again, completely ignoring his promise. "You locked me away."

He narrowed his eyes for a moment. "I never did find out how you managed to get past my devils," Phantom said, shooting a glance at Robin then at Russet who rolled with laughter at the opposite end of the fire, talking to Black and Clare.

But Rose ignored him again. "But you don't smell horrible," she said softly.

Phantom perked up. "You hear that, devils? I do have *one* redeeming quality."

They snickered at the implication that they still smelled badly, until she spoke again. "You smell like salt and oranges." She said it so softly that it was nearly a whisper on the sea breeze, but Phantom heard it loud and clear.

He caught her gaze as it went wide. "Do I, love?" A wash of embarrassment reddened her cheeks or maybe it was the rum. She downed an even larger gulp of the liquid courage. Surely, she hoped it would erase this moment from her memory. He hoped it didn't. He wouldn't forget it anytime soon.

He nearly reached for her, to wrap his arm around her and seize the bottle.

To Rose's luck, Clare came stomping toward their sitting group, abandoning Black, Russet and Wilson. Her bow absent, but she still kept an arsenal of knives on her person. Her hands flexed and relaxed. Clearly, she itched to reach for them. He wouldn't blame her. After all, she was an angel surrounded by devils with the exception of a songbird.

Black chased after her.

"May I join you?" Clare asked flatly.

Phantom frowned before putting a welcoming hand to the empty space in their circle.

"Thank you," she said before plopping into the space.

"Clare, come on," Black called, but he wasn't saying it with humor as usual. There was hurt across his beardless face. "I—" he started. "I'm sorry. It won't happen again."

"Forget it," she snapped, but she made no move to stand. The other devils stirred, unsure whether to help their friend or help the lady. A quick condemning look from Clare to each of them had them planted where they sat, leaving no room for Black to join.

He uncurled his fists then defeatedly turned from the group.

When Black was out of earshot, Hyne spoke in a hushed tone. "What did he do?"

"Nothing," Clare snapped. Hyne seemed as though he wished to join Black.

Rose extended the bottle she had been coveting to Clare. She didn't speak to the angel, only raised her eye brows in offering. With the barest hesitation, Clare accepted the bottle and downed more gulps than he thought she could. Then he thought *he* could.

Phantom raised his own bottle to the air. "To freedom!" He shouted above them. "And to the seas we shall soon see much much more of."

"Aye," the men said in varying points of unison. They lifted their bottles with him and Clare shot the Captain a grateful tight lipped smile.

"To freedom!" Rose declared, seizing Phantom's bottle from him before raising to her wobbly feet. He'd pray to any Goddess that would listen that she got that wish.

When she nearly toppled over, Phantom sat up, putting

a hand out to steady her. "Careful love, that is red moonshine, much stronger than the rum you've taken a fancy to."

She waved a hand in his direction, dismissing his warning as she tipped the bottle to her throat. The crimson liquid only touched her lips before she spurted it out into the flames beside them. The bonfire reacted, building higher into the sky with the newfound fuel, the red licking crimson in spots as the moonshine burnt away.

The devils tossed their heads in roaring laughter. Some of them with a hand on their bellies, trying to ease the hurt of harsh laughter. Rose flushed completely, but again, it could have been the alcohol.

Phantom only chuckled since he was half worried that she was about to fall right over. He stood, seizing the bottle back from her hands. "It's best to leave the Goddess spirits to us, love." Her eyelids were heavy and her feet unsteady, so he passed the bottle off to Jon before putting his hands at her waist.

It was a relief that she had made it known to him that touching her was not off limits as he promised. If the promise held to his original intent, he might not have let her join them on the shore, but nothing replaced the trust she had given him in erasing that boundary line. In showing a piece of her to him the night she helped Angelica. It made him want to see what would happened if the rest of her walls came tumbling down.

The feel of her waist rested in his hands, then her arms came across his shoulders, steadying herself. He eased them to the sand again and she groaned with the movement. He felt for the canteen of water on his sword belt and extended it to her. "Drink this," he said, almost coming out as an order, but ending like a plea.

She made the most adorable scrunched nose face before accepting the canteen. He had to force himself to look away as she splashed the water down her throat.

Not far from them, Jon watched, contemplative. Almost sad.

Phantom raised his eyebrows at the man, but he turned away to resume his conversation with Hyne and Clare. Apparently, they had decided to ignore Phantom and the slumped Rose in his arms, making the moment more intimate than he first believed.

She handed the canteen back to him and he set it aside. The songbird still held to his arm, a hand curled around his bicep. The intoxication hindered her enough, because she squeezed it slightly. He suppressed the masculine urge to flex at her touch. They weren't exactly facing each other, but they were still on their knees.

Rose's gold eyes tipped up to him, widening a fraction. "I— um," she said, losing her thought as her eyes descended to his arm, where her hand gripped him. "I'm sorry." A bit of sober understanding glinting through the foggy drunken haze, but she did not release her hand.

"I'm not," he whispered, softly enough that the words were only hers. She glanced up again and he let a devilish smile split his lips. "When I mentioned my promise before, I had no intention of you returning the favor." She blinked for a moment, so he added, "You, love, may touch me however you wish."

She froze, unwilling to remove her hand, but also not willing to let it travel further. Even with present company, he would have let her touch wherever she wished. Not only would he have reveled in the touch, but he would have relished the curiosity on her face. He would have enjoyed watching it grow.

But he also saw her confliction, even inebriated, so he fell away, offering her space to choose.

Phantom curled back into the sand, landing on a sand drift a bit further away from the rest of the group. It propped his head and shoulders up enough to observe the rest of the crew. He spread one arm out in invitation. Then he waited.

She sat, still on her knees, studying him. Her eyes fixated on the space he left for her at his side. It wasn't permission that he asked for. It wasn't the consent to have a dalliance in his cabin before daybreak. In her current state, he wouldn't dream of it.

No, this was still about trust. All he offered her was rest and warmth. Tentatively, she crawled over and he swatted away the idea of her doing that in a much more private setting. She lowered herself into the crook of his arm and he held his breath.

One arm she tucked into herself, the other glided onto the black silk of his shirt. A single finger brushed the skin at the "v" of his open shirt. She was both fearless and careful. Then one leg— One soul-focusing leg came up his thigh and rested at his hip. He nearly grabbed the underside of her knee to pull her more flush to him, but decided against it. The moment seemed too new, too fresh to test limits such as that.

Instead, he folded in the arm she laid upon, curling it into her body. It circled around her back, landing on her waist, his fingers barely brushing her hip.

"Is this too much?" He asked, suddenly unsure of himself.

"Don't you dare move." It was enough to make him freeze and relax all at once. She wanted and welcomed his touch, she didn't flinch at it. It was enough where he wondered if she knew touch at all. Was she deprived of intimacy? Was she abused by it?

Then absolutely nothing was there. There were no pirates laughing and whispering nearby. There was no ending to the night. No daybreak that would end the moment. It was him and it was her. Her gold eyes sparkled in the firelight.

A soft flute hummed from the devils at the fire. It was Tick's instrument of choice, since he could not join with his voice. The notes floated over the smoke of the fire with ease. Jon banged on soft drums with him as Clare carried the song.

WHEN THE LIGHT HAS DIED AND THE EVENING
GROWS
SHALL WE RAISE A GLASS TO FRIENDS AND FOES

The angel sang with ethereal grace. A light airy voice that held stark contrast against the men's rough, low notes. The song carried on like a funeral march, but with a lighter air. As if it represented peace and mutual understanding.

FOR THE FATHER LAID HIS PENNIES BARE
THE MOTHER SINGS SOFT THROUGH AIR
ON THE SHORES OF GREEN AND GOLD

The song continued on, but Phantom no longer paid attention because the song lulled the heavy lidded songbird at his chest. Rose attempted to keep herself awake, but with the rum softening her insides, the song coaxing her to sleep, and Phantom's warmth pressing into her, she didn't stand a chance.

He watched her eyes grow heavy enough to flutter shut. He felt her body go limp and heavy, signaling the final piece of her guard melting away.

It was the most devastatingly beautiful thing he'd ever seen, because come daybreak, she would be gone.

You foolish bastard. What have you done?

ON THE SHORES OF GREEN AND GOLD

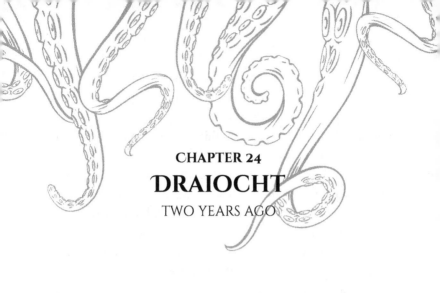

CHAPTER 24

DRAIOCHT

TWO YEARS AGO

P hantom rushed onto the camel Earhart held the
reins to, his breath coming out harshly after
running for miles. Draiocht guards had the stamina
of horses.

"What the hell?" Earhart tossed the reins to Phantom
before they sped off, kicking the flanks of the camels,
regretting not getting horses to mount, but his pursuers only
had their feet, for now. "I leave you alone for a couple of
hours—"

He paused at the look on Phantom's face, clear even
with the bobbing of his body against the gait of the beast
below him. Earhart tossed an exasperated look behind him,
watching the determined run of the palace guards. The
kind that protected Draiochet's most important officials.
"What did you do?"

"The usual. Drink. Princess. Brawl. Jail. Escape. Now,
guards."

Earhart's mouth dropped open and Phantom let out a
bellowing laugh.

Sand curled in the air around them. The deserts here were long and unforgiving. The sun was high in the sky, beating down relentlessly. Phantom's signature black was too unsuited for weather such as this, so he donned the classic white robes most natives wore.

The beating hooves against sand and sandstone rippled his body causing him to jolt forwards and backwards. The dirty, stinky beasts were a stubborn breed, but they provided an ample escape plan in the desert. Excitement laced Phantom's body, filling him with the thrill of adventure that only came when he broke the law. Or, when he sailed the seas during a storm.

This far south, the storms were more abundant, but they'd need to return soon. They'd been away from Kheli for a month now. The longest ever, but a particular storm had blown them off course and damaged the ship. They had to get repairs in Draiochet before making the journey back. A process that was nearly complete.

But it would have to do, if the guards planned to chase them all the way back to the docks.

"We have to lose them." Earhart used a small whip to urge his camel faster. "Hut hut!"A glance back told Phantom that one of the guards had gone to retrieve horses and caught up. Three horses were mounted by guards followed by commands and kicks.

Fear and excitement spiked Phantom's blood again. He couldn't get caught… again.

They approached a smaller village that served as a pit stop on the way to the docks. There were small huts made of sandstone and dried reeds lining the streets, people scattering along the sand roads.

"Left," Phantom shouted, directing his camel to turn the

corner. It groaned at the change in momentum, but took the turn, hardly slowing. These creatures weren't exactly meant to go fast, but their soft hooves took the sand more effectively than the hard hooves of horses. The guard's mounts slipped in the sand to make the turn, slowing them significantly, but they quickly gained momentum back.

Earhart cursed as the guards gained distance. Ahead, the villagers gathered in what looked like a market, selling and trading goods in bright colors.

"Move!" The first mate shouted. Neither of them had been there long enough to pick up on the native language. Brettania's influence was too far away for the locals to understand, but with the way Earhart was flailing his arms, they took the hint, moving to the sides.

They barreled through, running into tapestries and banners placed above and knocking over carts and stands. The village people cried out in protest. They weren't exactly making friends.

Phantom swiped a tapestry, laced with brilliant golds and whites, as they raced by. He turned in his saddle, facing the incoming guards before hanging the tapestry on a nearby banner. The first horse spooked at the hanging obstruction causing the second to slam into it. Both horses and their riders collided and fell through the tapestry, landing in a heap on the ground.

Phantom threw back his head, laughing at the sight, but the third horse jumped all four of them. He frowned as he realized the third rider was different. He was the one who brought the other two horses along for the guards, but he didn't wear a guard uniform. The rider was dressed completely in slate grey robes and a mask shielding his face from sight. Even through the clothes, Phantom could tell the man was large, very large. He made the war horse beneath him look like a donkey, making the Captain wonder if tales of giants in the South had any merit to them.

"Hurry up," Phantom urged, turning in his saddle to face forward.

"You're the one who insisted on the bloody cows!" The camel Earhart rode bleated its protest.

They rode on, toppling more carts and piles of goods before they cleared the market. A final mound of baskets sat at the end of the alley. Phantom drew his pistol, aiming for the landing. The shot popped into the air, eliciting screams from the natives, but the towering baskets fell to the sand in a glorious thud, just shy of their camels.

Phantom whooped at the sight as baskets spilled their grains, colored rices, and other goods into the ground, creating a barricade. But his excitement lasted for all of a second when the giant of a man and his horse jumped over the wall of baskets.

"Please tell me you have a better plan than that." Earhart shouted, irritation growing steadily stronger as he kicked at the groaning camel. The creature might buck him off soon.

Phantom stared ahead, an idea forming and a smile growing. "I have a better plan than that." Earhart glared at him with enough doubt to drown in, but Phantom only smiled at his friend. "Such little faith, mate."

There wasn't enough time to tease his first mate. He balanced precariously as he climbed to his feet on the saddle. "Grab that clothes line ahead, we'll swing to the roof."

Earhart's eyes widened in alarm as he spotted the line in

question. It dangled high enough that they only could reach it when standing on their mounts. "Are you crazy?"

"Quite possibly."

Earhart swore, cursing the Goddess of Fate for giving him such a reckless Captain, but Phantom was too focused on the task at hand. The saddle jostled below him, so he held the camel's hump firmly until they were close enough. The camel groaned at the increase of pressure.

"Sorry old girl," Phantom whispered before jumping off her back entirely. Earhart followed in time with Phantom's jump, grabbing at the rope above them. The camels ran off and the line sagged. The click of hooves told Phantom that the grey guard was behind them and the line didn't break as he planned.

"Now what?" Earhart asked with more agitation than curiosity.

Before he could answer, Phantom drew the dragger he kept in his boot and slashed the line. Earhart yelped at the sudden movement. They flew into the building's window, tumbling onto the rug of someone's home. The woman of the house screamed at the intrusion, yelling something in the native tongue.

"A little warning next time," Earhart grumbled, clamoring to his feet.

Phantom glanced out the window to see the guard dismounting his horse and marching into the house. His first mate attempted to calm the panicked woman who grew steadily angrier.

Phantom seized his barrel arm and pulled him to where he assumed the door would be, nodding apologetically to the woman. She screamed something that sounded like insults and curses as they ran into the building's hallway. Two glances and Phantom spotted stairs leading up.

Perfect.

"Come on." He tugged the first mate along, leading them up the stairs.

"I've never following you on a mission again."

Phantom laughed because he knew his first mate was full of horseshit.

They reached the roof, a sand covered flat surface with a couple of chairs and tables scattered about. All the buildings in Draiochet were boxy, making their roofs ideal landing platforms.

Phantom took a short scan of the building and its surroundings. No buildings were close enough to jump to and the height was too tall to land safely with a jump. They'd likely survive, but broken legs would make the chase abrupt and useless.

Earhart panted next to him. "Great, now we're trapped here." There was a sense of acceptance to his voice. "Angelica will kill me if I die here."

Phantom planted a hand on his panicking mate's shoulder. "Nemain cannot save you, my friend. I'm afraid you'll have to face your wife's wrath."

Earhart let out a huff, deciding if dying here was the better option. He raised an accusatory finger. "She'll kill you either way."

A loud crack and the door to the stairs flung open. The grey guard stepped through, a slight jingle to his step that only accompanied someone who was heavily armed.

Earhart raised his hands. "What do we do?" He whisper shouted.

But Phantom was distracted by the man himself who

pulled off his hood and mask to reveal darkened skin and even darker eyes. His brows were thick and furrowed as if angry was a state of being. From this close, his size was even more intimidating. His arms and shoulders were wide and thick, but his height was easily near seven feet. His hair was half tied back at his nape and there was a gleaming steel knife in his hand.

A feeling spread from Phantom's core to his throat like being chilled and warmed all at once. He knew what it meant.

"Captain," Earhart whispered with more urgency as the man stalked closer. A short glance at Phantom's awed grin had Earhart's jaw dropping. "No." He shook his head. "Him?"

Phantom stared back at the mountain of a man. "Him." He inched forward, shooting his hands into the air. "You caught us." The color drained from Earhart's face, so Phantom whispered back, "Trust me."

Earhart swallowed, clearly understanding he had no better option.

Phantom turned to the grey guard extending his arms to be bound. "We surrender." The man stared into his eyes, clearly seeing something in them too, but he blinked it away, grabbing Phantom by the wrists and turning him to bind them behind his back.

"You go," the man said in sloppy Brettanian, referring to Earhart. "I need only of Maahes." Phantom's brows clashed. The people of Draiocht weren't supposed to know Brettanian. This was no guard.

"Right," Earhart breathed, drawing his blade. "I'm not going to allow that."

A shot rang before Earhart could swing the sword, a

259

pistol in the man's hand. He shot the hilt of the sword, forcing it from the first mate's hand, but not killing him. "This, *I* cannot allow."

"Go," Phantom urged. "It's okay. Smooth sailing my friend." But that was far from a proper goodbye and Earhart knew it. Phantom winked to solidify the message.

He'd be back and with any luck, the brute would be with him.

CHAPTER 25
NIGHTMARES IN BLUE

When the night was old and the firelight had been doused by tired devils, Phantom scooped up a limp Rose in his arms. He held onto her the entire longboat ride, but had to wake her once they reached the ship. With heavy lids doused in sleep, she barely made it up the ladder to the ship's deck.

With a hand on her waist, he guided her to the Captain's quarters. The other devils only glanced briefly at her intimate touch on his arm before resuming their pursuit of a cabin bed.

"Lean on me, love," he offered. Rose leaned on him heavily as they reached the quarters.

Once inside, he let her fall onto the bed. He pulled the leather boots from her feet and gently took his longcoat from her back. She really was so beautiful. Her hair was plaited behind her in a golden tail. The gentle skin of her face shadowed in the dim light of the moons.

He leaned down to trace the curve of her cheek with his

knuckle, pulling away once he realized what he was doing. He had to let her go. Tomorrow he would be free and she would be back with her father. They may never see each other again. He would never know what this flicker of warmth, this swell of want and the unfamiliar sensation of need would grow into.

Some part of him hoped she would find her own freedom and come looking for him, but he knew better than to hope for the impossible. So he dropped his hand.

Warm, light fingers stole his, stopping his pivot in its tracks. Her eyes were open, glittering in the lilac notes of Macha's moon.

"Stay," she whispered.

He let out a breath. One simple word and it was his complete undoing, reversing all the walls he had built. He felt them tumble as he saw the sincerity in her eyes.

"Always," he breathed and it was a promise he would not let her break.

Not a single hint of a smile appeared on his face as he slipped his own boots free, shrugging off his coat. Normally, he hung it neatly, but with her gold coin eyes pinning him, he dared not move more than necessary.

Phantom climbed onto the bed that had gone from his to theirs in a matter of days. She shifted away from him to make room. As gentle as he could manage, he resumed the position they grew accustomed to on the beach, reaching out an arm for her to curl into. She did so without hesitation, curling into his warmth.

With a couple breaths, she was asleep.

He watched her for a moment, the slow even pace of her breaths that signaled unconsciousness, the glow of her skin under the silver and lilac moonlight streaming through the windows and he had to wonder— what on earth possessed this perfect creature to trust him?

Phantom could think of no legitimate reason for her to be so comfortable with him. To sleep peacefully in his arms. Perhaps it was the rum, but he knew from experience that it would take more than rum. For a moment, he thought he imagined it, but he didn't have nearly enough imagination to create the *feel* of her next to him.

Every soft curve of her molded to every hard part of him. His mind fixated on where her thigh, which was deliciously thick, weighed on his own. Where her hand draped over his chest and the cotton of his shirt. And finally — where her head was nestled into his shoulder and neck like it belonged no where else.

Bloody Hell.

He couldn't think like that. By the time morning crested the horizon, he'd have to let her go. It wasn't nearly enough time, but it was all he had. He rested his head against the headboard and let his eyes drift closed.

Thrashing and whimpers woke him from sleep. The hazy cast of drowsiness clearing to take in the blonde beauty at his side. She twitched and whined with her eyes closed as if enduring immense pain or reliving it.

Phantom placed a solid arm on her shoulder, hoping to ground her, but she thrashed further, jerking against him. Her brow was beaded with sweat and her face twisted in a wince.

"No," she whined in her fitful sleep. Her hands balled into fists, grabbing ahold of covers as if they would protect her.

Phantom seized her shoulder harder, shaking her. "Rose," he said, his own voice shaken. "Rose, I need you to wake up. It's only a nightmare." The words seemed to bounce right off her. Her thrashing and whines grew louder, more urgent, as if the villain of her dreams was drawing close.

Anger coiled hot in his core. He'd be the villain to whatever monster sought to torment her.

"Rose," he pleaded. "Please, Rose. Wake up." He put a hand to her cheek. "Wake up," he yelled.

She exploded. Blue light ribboned out of her to swirl around the room. She hummed in her fitfulness making the ribbons distorted and unclear. As if she wasn't singing quite right to harness them. For a moment, he thought those streams of blue light would reach for him, push him away on their own accord.

Instead, they curled around him, his arms, his torso, dusting his cheek, like a house cat showing affection.

The door to his room burst open, Jon entered, knives out. "Captain. What's—"

Jon's arms lowered and his mouth dropped.

Phantom put a hand out to reassure his first mate. "It's alright." The low humming still came from Rose as blue light curled around the room. He'd bet that if her eyes were open, they would be fully glowing blue. He checked his pockets, but the Stone was tucked away in his coat on the floor. No part of it touched her skin.

Her power was hers, not the Stone's. Unless it took her

awhile to shake the effects of it like it took him time to calm the monster.

Still, she hummed and mumbled as if there were words attached to the song, but the song became smoother, even as she thrashed, causing the ribbons of light to smooth.

Jon's near black eyes widened as he took a yielding step.

The ribbons widened and faded to transparency, filling the room like a blue colored wind. Some parts were more thick and brightly blue and others were a dark navy, like the shadowing in a painting. The different shades fashioned an image in a monotone of blues, but it moved.

They were in the middle of a forest, one that Phantom had never seen before. Beautiful tall pines and abundant foliage surrounded them, but among the trees, figures shuffled and stumbled. They bore no weapons, possessed no armor or formation. They didn't even appear to care that they had been spotted.

The figures didn't move correctly. They weren't human. Their clothes were dirtied and torn, their skin bruised and scratched, but no blood flowed from their gaping wounds. The creatures appeared to not care at all.

He knew what they were. Necromites.

They filled the mainland outside of Atlas and had slowly been taking over every other country. The very reason those Brettanian soldiers could never return home.

The necromites grew closer, increasing their pace once they spotted their prey.

Rose screamed and the image snapped away as if a large wind had come to blow the blue tendrils away, but that was what she saw in her nightmare. Even though her singing ceased, she was still trapped there. Trapped with those creatures after her.

Phantom rushed to her side again, attempting to shake her awake.

Jon stepped to help, but Phantom raised a hand that halted him. "No, fetch some water." When Jon hesitated, Phantom put urgency into his voice. "Now."

Jon stepped out from the room.

Phantom turned his attention to Rose again, grasping her hand in his, surprised to find it ice cold. He knelt there at her side with her knuckles pressed to his lips. "Rose, please," he mumbled against her skin. "Wake up." She thrashed again, and his heart dropped. Had the necromites reached her? Were they tearing her apart?

He held her hand to his chest, right where his heart threatened to rip right out of his chest. His breath was heavy and it felt as though the entire world shook, but then her body stopped.

The thrashing and whimpers ceased and her breathing slowed. The sight alone let him release a breath, but his heart still beat wildly. He held her wrist flush against him. If this was the action that grounded her, she could keep her hand there as long as she needed.

Her eyes snapped open. No blue covered those gold eyes. He released another breath. A longer one that finally let his heartbeat settle. Until her eyes locked on her cold hand. A hand that was being thawed by his abundance of heat. A hand that felt the pulse and blood of his flesh coursing through his veins. She froze, hesitant to remove her hand.

"What—" She started, but her voice was shaken, so she cleared her throat. "What happened?"

"You were having a bad dream, love." For a moment, he was about to tell her about the blue light and the moving painting it made. "That is all," he added. She hadn't offered him the information yet. He wanted her to give it to him willingly. Perhaps that was a selfish reason for keeping the information from her.

"Oh," was all she said. He let his hand drop from her wrist, no longer needing to keep her hand in place, but she didn't move it. It was half across his cotton shirt and half across the hairy skin of his chest. He was surprised to find she didn't lower it. Surprised and delighted.

His earlier panic melted into something lighter, more tangible. "If you wanted to touch me, all you needed to do was ask," he purred. Partly, for his own amusement. Partly, to distract her from the recent horror she endured.

It was that moment that Jon barged in, pail of water in hand. "Here you are, Captain."

Rose snapped her hand away, but Phantom was unsure if it was due to the interruption or the words he spoke. It didn't matter, because he missed the feel of her hand so much he nearly whimpered.

"Place it on the table, Jon." Phantom attempted to keep the mirth from his voice, but Jon understood the dismissal well enough. Seeing that Rose was awake and seemingly fine, he exited through the door again. His eyes wide.

Phantom glanced to the window. It was still incredibly dark, but the barest hints of dawn coveted the sky. He turned back to the songbird, who sat up against the headboard.

"Drink some water, love." This could be their last moment together. No, he wouldn't allow it. "I must prepare to meet with you father." He shifted to stand and something shifted in her face. Disappointment perhaps. "You'll be home soon." The words came out flat as if that night had meant nothing to him. He nearly winced.

Maybe be expected her to ask for him to stay again, but she only nodded. With a heavy heart, he stepped back into his boots and swung his coat onto his back.

With one more look, he left the cabin.

CHAPTER 26

A NEW DEVIL

TWO YEARS AGO

A brown sack that once held potatoes was firmly situated on Phantom's head to prevent him from knowing where they went. Not that it was much use, they never mounted a chariot or a steed so Phantom doubted they went beyond the outskirts of the village.

He was shoved onto a chair and tied to it, weapons released from his person before the man decided to lift the bag.

Phantom blinked at the sunlight streaming into the room. "Interesting choice of rendezvous." His eyes trailed the plain sandstone walls. They were near completely bare, but this was impromptu. A guard would have drug him back to the city by now or killed him on sight. "I, myself, would have chosen a destination a bit more romantic in nature." Phantom grinned at his joke, as if they were secret lovers looking for a quiet place. The grey guard's face was impassive, clearly unbothered by his attempt. Phantom turned his head.

I do love a good challenge.

"Your mouth will get you killed." The brute's accent was deep and heavy, but he knew how to enunciate to make Brettanians understand him.

"Come now." Phantom spread his arms as best he could in the restraints. "We're really past strangers at this point." He glanced down at the ropes pinning him to the chair, pitching his voice deeper. "Although, I usually prefer the roles reversed." He let his eyes draw up, catching the brute's understanding of the double meaning in the scrunch of his nose. "Now, why don't you tell me how you know Brettanian so well?"

He didn't answer. Instead, he breathed deeply and crossed his arms, somehow seeming impossibly larger.

"Not one for conversation? It's alright, I like the shy ones." There, the man's jaw tensed. Phantom reveled in getting a rise out of him. "Was that question too personal? Let me try another." He cleared his throat dramatically and the man glanced at the ceiling as if asking his gods for strength. "I know you're not a palace guard." The man showed no reaction. "So what are you and what business do you have with me?" His tone snapped, letting the man see that he did possess an iota of seriousness.

"I am *cerbalus*." Phantom blinked at the unfamiliar word. "In your language, how do you say— bounty hunter." The man snapped his fingers at the realization of the right word.

"Ah, how much am I worth to you, *cerbalus*?" Phantom lifted his brows at the prospect. He respected a man's pursuit of riches. Bounty hunters weren't much different than pirates.

The man stepped down, bending at the waist to be eye level with Phantom.

"Freedom."

His respect for the man went so astronomically high that Ramirez would have to include it in his chart of the stars. Freedom and bounty. The two things that motivated himself.

Phantom smiled broadly. "We're much alike."

The man huffed, turning from Phantom to place his head in his hands. There was more though. What purpose did he have in bringing Phantom to this abandoned corner of a small village? If he sought freedom and bounty, he'd have Phantom on a horse ready to ride for the city.

"We are not alike, Maahes."

Phantom smiled again, if not a bit grimly. "Perhaps, you caught the wrong prize. That name holds no meaning to me."

The man snapped, coming closer to Phantom than he had dared before. "Lion of the sea. A demon created by Nephthys herself. The trickster. A phantom and a pirate."

Phantom blinked, unsure how to process the words. He wasn't sure his legend had reached this far South, but apparently it had. Or the *cerbalus* heard of him the same way he knew Brettanian. Still, the pieces didn't fit together.

He laughed, the sound hollow. "It's really unfair that you should know so much about me and I haven't the faintest idea about you." The brute grunted, irritation prickling. Phantom mulled around the information he did have. "Why does a *cerbalus* require freedom?"

His eyes grew dark. "I killed wrong man. Your capture makes my sin clean."

"Naturally," Phantom murmured, turning his head. "Then why am I not on a horse right now? Or on one of those delightful spitting creatures?" The man actually bared his teeth, as if he was a wild animal. Phantom would know what that was like. "I think, you don't want to go back. I think you want out of wherever they imprisoned you, but you aren't exactly eager to return to your captors."

"Your mouth will get you killed, Maahes." He repeated, face still impassive, but Phantom could sense the doubt in the man.

"No, no I don't think so. You see, you know I have a ship and no matter who you believe I am, you know I will go very far away from this Davina-forsaken sand rock."

The man's lips tightened and Phantom knew he had him.

He leaned in as far as the rope would allow. "I have one condition." The man's eyes narrowed. "You become a member of my crew. Become a devil that discovers the world under red sails." The man scoffed, clearly needing more convincing, but Phantom wasn't done. "You travel yourself, don't you? That's why you learned the most prominent trade language in the world? But travel is expensive, *cerbalus*. If you board *Nemain's Revenge* as a devil, you can go anywhere you want, be anyone you want."

"And become a pirate?" The man snapped with distain.

"Is it that much different than being a *cerbalus*?" A pregnant pause filled the dry air. "The world is at war with the dead and consequently, each other. With us you will be joining a family and you will have freedom. Devils can leave anytime they want. All I'm asking is a couple of months to prove to you that you do in fact belong with us." He let the offer settle. "Freedom is worth its weight in gold, mate."

With a brutish grunt, he came around Phantom to release the bonds, but they were already loosened. Phantom slipped free with the ease of an alley cat. The man raised a brow at him.

"Come now, did you really think you had me? I had you." Phantom extended his hand. "And you are?"

"Jon," the man stated, accepting Phantom's outstretched hand. "You call me Jon."

CHAPTER 27
NEGOTIATIONS

A nother ship joined the Commodore's. It was encased in painted gold trimmings and shimmering sails, but smaller and, from the rounder shape of it, slower. A ship not intended to pursue, only to lounge.

The Prime Minister had finally arrived and not a moment too soon. The Eastern sun breached the horizon on the starboard side. Phantom knew not to bring too many men with him, so he brought Jon and Black in the longboat. There weren't many others he could trust to keep their mouths shut when needed. Tick being the exception. But as they loaded the boat, Clare appeared with a bow and quiver strapped to her back.

"Absolutely not," Phantom ordered, losing the one angel who volunteered to board *Nemain's Revenge* would be a tragedy Kheli may not recover from. Especially, *this* angel.

"This—" She put her hand out to the sand bar island before her. "This is all for the people of Kheli. One of them should be present if you wish to negotiate."

Phantom let his voice drop. "If you die—"

"I won't," she interrupted and Black tensed beside her. "This is why I wanted to come in the first place." Briefly, her gaze flicked to Black, but refocused so fast, he nearly missed it. "Those are my people and when you leave to gallivant the seas, it will be *me* in charge of protecting them."

Phantom smiled. It was exactly what he wanted to hear. It's why he would never offer her the chance of becoming a devil. He needed her to be an angel. Kheli needed her to be an angel.

Phantom gestured to the longboat. "Our carriage awaits." She jumped into the longboat without hesitation, her head held high.

Black opened his mouth, but shut it with a silencing look from his Captain, but then decided against it. "You've been planning this."

"Of course, Mr. Black." He moved a hand to the devil's back, leaning in to whisper. "From the very moment she shoved you away before shooting. I very well might end up calling them 'Sophia Clare and the Eleven Angels'." He shoved the man with his shoulder in a playful manner.

A singular glare from Black had Phantom lifting his arm away. Black may not like it, but Clare and her crew were now responsible for Kheli.

A couple steps on the sandy shores of Bashtir and Phantom could see the Prime Minister of Samsara. He was perched on a lavish chair before a large elaborate table. Everything was white, gold, and blue, as if the colors of Samsara didn't make him sick every time he saw them, he straightened his back and sauntered through the sand.

On the table was an array of food and drinks, goblets of wine, mounds of cheese and bread, bowls of fruits from Kheli. Fruits that could not be found on Samsara. A roasted boar sat at the very middle of the table, nearly blocking the Minister from view, but the boar had no hope of blocking a man such as the Minister.

He was the epitome of gluttony. The excess dripped from his person in spills of jewels and fine fabrics. A line of women stood behind him. All of them dressed, but barely so. Gauzy gold and white hung loosely around their curves and their eyes were downcast. They each varied in size and skin tone. The Prime Minister might have been a man of prestige, but he never denied something to himself that was beautiful.

Behind the girls was a line of Samsaran naval soldiers, Commodore Ashby among them. They wore the naval colors of blue with white and trimmed in gold. The Commodore had replaced his coat with a higher quality one. One that contained pins and medals of honor. Phantom even knew what a few were earned for.

The entire display was intentional. The Prime Minister never did anything that was not on purpose. The food was temptation. An invitation into his own lavish lifestyle. A promise of wealth that would be promptly seized with the first oath that left a solider's lips. Or a fifteen year old orphaned boy.

"Minister," Phantom addressed with his hands firmly planted before himself. The Minister enjoyed his power games, but they weren't for show. This was about more than returning his daughter. He knew that the moment the

Minister had delayed his presence. Phantom evaluated the scene again, trying to understand exactly why he chose to tempt them. Or was there another purpose?

"Lieutenant Hawkins. It's been far too long." The Minister stated with a mouthful of boar. His voice muffled by the interruption in his mouth.

"I prefer Captain now, Minister." Phantom forced his hands to remain steady. It was instinctive to shove his hands to his side. The same way the line of naval officers stood behind the Minister.

He didn't even bother to raise his head. "Captain Hawkins doesn't have the same ring to it."

"Captain Phantom," Black interrupted. A bit out of turn, but his correction was a show of loyalty, so Phantom allowed it.

The Minister paused briefly before lifting a goblet of wine to his clean shaven face. His silver hair and eyes were an epic contrast to his daughter's lustrous gold hair and eyes. He blinked away thoughts of Rose.

"Yes," the Minister mused, finally setting his cup down and examining his opponent. It was the way one would evaluate a liar in a game of Kazeboon. Whatever he saw in Phantom or his companions lacked because the man frowned. "I heard you were going by that name now. *Captain Phantom*." He raised his hands in mockery of the name Phantom had chosen for himself. The Minister's mouth curved in an amused smile. "The infamous pirate who stalks the waters of Samsara." His voice held a note of jovial humiliation that made Phantom's skin prickle. "Who preys on the people. Renowned for unspeakable acts. Who shows no mercy to those he meets?"

Phantom only held the man's gaze. He'd let the Minister

believe every word produced by rumor. Let him think that the devils would pillage to their heart's content. That their lust for gold and blood was unmatched. Phantom waited for the fear to descend on the man's face. He wanted it to darken the man's features, but it did not.

Instead, the Minister looked bored.

"Where is my daughter?" He asked while shoving a shiny red grape into his mouth.

Phantom let a smile tug at his lips. "I believe I may have caught a bigger prize than I first intended." The Minister froze. *This.* This is why he didn't want Rose present for the negotiations. Phantom crept closer to the table, his devils followed and the officers tensed. Phantom held up a hand to stop them and they halted. The display showed exactly what he wanted, power and control. Their loyalty was strong enough to give him that.

Phantom inched his way to the Minister until he leaned forward against a chair, only a table's length from the Minister himself. The Commodore was there instantly, his sword half drawn.

But in mimic of the power Phantom displayed, the Minister held a hand up to halt his Commodore, narrowing his eyes. It was another look Phantom was familiar with in Kazeboon.

"Your daughter," Phantom whispered, soft enough for only the Minister and the Commodore to hear. "Has the most beautiful singing voice." The Minister's breathing seemed to halt altogether. "Wouldn't you agree?"

A muscle flickered in the Commodore's jaw. Unlike the Minister, Ashby was all too easy to read. His thoughts and feelings were always written all over his face. That's why the poor man was never able to beat Phantom. Not when it came to a liar's game.

The Minister set his fork down gently, seemingly contemplative as if reevaluating a player. A player that was dealt a better deck than he had expected, but then he exhaled loudly and it melted into a laugh. Not a loud or obvious laugh, but a breathy, joyless, demeaning laugh.

"Do you really think you can blackmail me, Lieutenant?" His eyebrows raised. "Do you really believe that you have any information you could hold over me?" The man called his bluff, but he wasn't bluffing. Perhaps, the Minister was unaware of his daughter's power, or he called Phantom's bluff to challenge him. "Bring me my daughter." It was said with the tone of an order, which sparked every instinct in Phantom to disobey. To reject the order completely, but the negotiation could go no further if Rose Davenport was not present. The Minister had to see that his daughter was unharmed.

With a glance back and a flick of his head, Black moved, hesitating as he glanced at Clare, who stared bullets across the table. At the Minister, at Ashby, at the officers, even the girls serving the Minister. Her arms were tense, ready to snap to her bow and knock an arrow in the blink of an eye. Phantom knew, all he had to do was say the word, and there would be an arrow in the Minister's chest, but sadly, they would not make it off the island.

He resisted the urge to tell her just that as Black trotted back to the longboat to retrieve Rose.

Phantom turned back to the Minister. "These are my terms," Phantom said and the Minister's brow rose so far it wrinkled the lines of his forehead extravagantly. "I want Kheli's independence from Samsara." He took a breath to continue, but the Minister's eruption of laughter halted him. The sound contained no warmth, but it was abundant, lavish, and full like the items spread across the white tablecloth. It jolted Phantom upright.

"Oh," the Minister said, taking a breath between his laughs. The Commodore was unamused at his side. "Oh, you're serious." The Minister attempted to school his features, but failed and rolled into laughter once more.

Phantom tossed an egregious look back to Jon and Clare, their features surprised but firm. Phantom's light sting of humiliation melted into true anger.

"You come here with a Draiocht brute and a girl with a few sticks and you think you can force my hand?" The laughter faded out and Phantom felt his own temper bubbling. "No." The Minister slammed his hand on the table, his fork and crumblings jumping to the sand.

"You do not wish to receive your daughter back?" Phantom bit out. A spark of selfish hope filled him at the possibility of keeping the songbird. A hope he discarded immediately.

The Minister's thin mouth scrunched. "What will you do Lieutenant?" His brows rose again. "Will you kill her?"

Phantom steeled his features, even if the very thought of spilling Rose Davenport's blood made him want to rip out his own heart. "I don't have to," he risked. Showing unwillingness to carry out a threat could damn them all. "I could take her back to the ship. Give you more time to think. A week? Perhaps a month? It could be very difficult for her on a ship with all that time."

He'd make certain it was the best damn month of her life.

The Minister chuckled. "Difficult for you and your crew

perhaps." Phantom blinked. This man was not fond of his daughter at all. In fact, he seemed to loathe her presence. "But you will still return her. To this very beach and we will once again have the same conversation. So I ask again," the Minister said, his voice firming and hardening. "Will you kill her?"

Phantom prayed to Nemain for the strength. He steeled his features further, until they were as hard as stone. "Yes," his voice came out low, deadly.

The Minister studied him for a moment, then began to smile. "You know you have a tell Lieutenant?" Phantom resisted the urge to blink. "It is precisely what you are trying to avoid. Whenever you are trying to sell a lie, you harden your features so thoroughly that most would not be able to tell. But I can. Because you come up with some tick you don't possess when you tell the truth, or use some small lie to throw off your opponent." Phantom ceased breathing. "You see, but when you lie, you void yourself off all tells. And *that* is precisely your tell."

The unspoken air between them told the Minister what he needed to know. The exact thing that Phantom couldn't admit to. It didn't matter if the Minister believed he had affections for his daughter or simply was not as ruthless as the rumors claimed. Both were enough to gain the Minister the upper hand. His eyes shifted to the space behind Phantom. "Ah, Rose."

A glance behind him told Phantom that Rose strode right beside Black. She was adorned in full pirate garb. There really was no repairing her dress.

The Commodore rounded the table to retrieve Rose. A flick of Phantom's hand and Clare's bow was aimed at his head. He froze.

"Nothing personal, brother," Phantom mused. "But I'm not willing to part with her quite yet."

Phantom resisted the urge to turn back to see if Rose attempted to walk to the Commodore. To run to him. If Black or Jon had to hold her back from doing just that. His more cunning voice told him that's what he wanted. That a Rose desperate to be reunited with her life would serve his purposes. But another voice betrayed him.

"Haven't you heard?" The Minister cooed. Phantom's clear ignorance amusing to him. "Tell him, Commodore."

"She is to be my betrothed," the Commodore stated officially as if the words held no meaning, no depth, no damnation. No more than a business contract would.

"Soon, I will make the Commodore my successor and he will be the new Prime Minister. "

Phantom tilted his head at the man. "That's not how a Prime Minister is chosen." It was known that a Prime Minister had to be elected to rule, not named as a successor. That's what Kings do.

"It is if I say so," the Minister bit out, but he spent no time explaining himself to the pirate before him. His face grew disinterested. "Rose, darling," he started, looking past the pirate Captain. "Why do you insist on trying my patience?" His eyes burned with disappointment and something else more lethal. A look that had the beast inside him waking.

A look over his shoulder and he saw Rose breathing rapidly, her cheeks flushed, her gold eyes blazing. As if her father was the very thing that had attacked her in that blue nightmare.

The tang of fear hit his nostrils. *No. Not now.*

The monster thrummed in his head, demanding release.

It wanted to be present. It wanted to be out, ripping apart the Minister and his officers. Especially, when the source of that tangy scent came only from Rose Davenport and it was most certainly caused by the gluttonous man sitting at that table.

The Minister flicked his hand above his head. The movement effortless.

Officers pulled a gagged flailing body from behind him, Phantom's vision went entirely red. It was all he could do to keep the monster under his skin. One inch of the monster's leash and the Minister would be dead, but so would he, and so would his powder monkey.

The Commodore stepped up to the line of officers, seizing the boy by his arm and dragging him to the Minister's side. Phantom heard his devils flinch behind him, stepping in the sand, ready to launch themselves at the Commodore, but he had a knife to Robin's throat before any of them could take a second step.

"Unlike you, Lieutenant," the Minister mused, seemingly disinterested. "I am willing to carry out my threat. So is the Commodore." Robin sniffled and whimpered under the Commodore's blade. Phantom knew the boy reminded him of a young version of his old friend, but seeing them together, he couldn't have been more wrong. Robin's young freckled face was stricken with fear, that tangy scent swelling in the air around him. The Commodore's face was stoic, no different than what it was while he watched his Minister eat. Even with a knife to the boy's throat, Ashby had not a hint of hesitation. It was the same look he had when the Minister ordered for the Kalonite's capture all those years ago. By some small mercy,

Phantom thanked Nemain that it was not Tick under the Commodore's knife.

"Let my daughter come to me, and I'll let the boy live." No mercy. No other option. No turning back.

Phantom glanced back to his devils. Clare stood with her bow knocked, ready to strike the Commodore in the head. She would hit true, but it would only risk another solider ending Robin's life instead. He was too far away to make a decent escape. Clare must have realized this, but she held the bow taut and Phantom knew, she would release the arrow with no hesitation if he ordered it.

Jon's muscles were tense and rippling, even through his shirt and his eyes promised death. If Robin died on this sand, Jon would perish with him. No matter if Phantom attempted to stop him. If it were anyone else below Ashby's knife, he would follow Phantom's order, but for Robin, he'd risk anything.

Black kept his face stoic with one arm on Rose's forearm. Not that it made a difference. She made no effort to return to her father. To her betrothed. Her face was dumbfounded and perhaps a little disgusted. She should be. He wanted to scream at her. *Look what your father is capable of. Look what your betrothed is willing to do for him.*

The Minister clicked his teeth. "Tiktok, Lieutenant," he mocked. "You try my patience."

Rose blinked. Once. Slowly. Then, she strode away from Black who made no effort to seize her arm again, not with the commanding look Phantom cast him. She walked in the sand as if it were a death march.

"Rose," Phantom whispered when she was close.

"Don't," she said so softly it nearly died on the wind, but

he saw the tears trickling down her face even as she let her hair drop to cover them.

The sight nearly making him feral.

She marched on, rounding the table to stand at the Minister's side. The grin on his face was near blinding. He got exactly what he wanted and he paid for it with nothing.

Phantom's voice was a low growl in his throat when he said, "Let the boy go."

"I seem to recall that I said the boy would live," the Minister mused, laying a hand on his daughter's back. She tensed at the touch. "I did not say I would let him go."

The red in his vision grew spotty. It was near impossible to focus on anything. Anything but Robin's frantic breathing and the bead of blood dripping down his neck.

"What," Phantom bit out, "do you want?"

"Like you don't know." The Minister shoved bread down his throat. A hand pressed between Rose's shoulder blades. He nearly missed her flinch. "The Stone." The Minister pointed to a spot on the table. "Leave it there and I will let the boy go."

Phantom pressed his lips together. Even with his vision red, he knew any other choice would result in Robin's death. He stepped up to the table. The line of officers moved, drawing their pistols in a standby attack position. If Phantom even moved too quickly his and Robin's life would be forfeit.

Slowly, he released the Stone from his coat pocket, his hand closing around the black velvet pouch it resided in. He began to set it down when the Minister demanded, "Open it."

Phantom froze.

"I know your tricks, show us it's the Stone."

He coaxed it from its cocoon, glittering light swirling around his hand. The brilliant lilacs and silver shining true. There was no mistaking the Stone. No way to duplicate its life like patterns.

The Minister's eyes still did not stare in wonder. Only disinterest and something else Phantom couldn't quite place. He set the Stone on the table. When he leaned down, his eyes locked to Rose's, but she broke the contact, turning her gaze to the sand.

Phantom shifted his stare to the Minister, who grinned wildly. His teeth had spots of food where he hadn't quite finished chewing.

The Commodore released his grip, slashing Robin's bindings instead. The boy nearly toppled to the sand in an attempt to rid himself of the officer. He ran back to Jon as fast as his feet could carry him, but Phantom's eyes were locked on the Minister.

Finally, he broke the eye contact. He had nothing left to bargain with. Nothing that the Minister wanted. So much so that he began to wonder why they stood in the sand without being pelted with bullets.

Phantom turned, walking back to his devils. Each one of them harbored a solemn face.

"Oh, Lieutenant," the Minister cooed. A swift metal *click* and Phantom knew that everyone of those guards held their guns up. Only a finger twitch away from ending their lives.

But the red was too vibrant. The monster was too close. "It's Captain now," Phantom snapped, pivoting to see the Minister standing before the table. His wild grin still present.

"No, Lieutenant, it never was." The Minister nearly choked on laughter at the sight of Phantom's confusion.

"Did you really think you would get away with this for so long without consequences? The escapades. The pillaging of my great city. Sailing my ship like she's yours." He muffled a laugh. "No, you have been doing exactly what I wanted you to do."

That tangy scent filled the air around him, but it was not his men, or the angel with the taut bow beside him. No, the fear radiated through him, dulling the red around his vision.

The Minster pointed to Clare and she tensed. "Those people you steal for. I can wipe them out in a day and have twice as many Samsarans ready to work the land instead. I do not need the villagers of Kheli." Clare went absolutely still. Or maybe it was Phantom's own body.

"What I do need is something for the Samsaran people to fear. I need them to fear the infamous Captain Phantom and his Eleven Devils. So they will believe in me. In my Navy."

Phantom spat out a laugh. "You've truly gone insane if you believe I will help you trick your people into respecting you," he growled. The monster barely leashed.

The Minister pointed a finger to the Brettanian ship behind him. "That ship will leave now if I give the order and slaughter the entire residence of Kheli. Another ship will leave tomorrow with willing participants." Clare's bow shook, near ready to snap under the pressure she applied. "Of course, this would be after your entire crew is hung publicly. The witches burned," he said, waving a hand to Clare and to Black, who tensed so harshly he shook. "You, Captain," he said in a tone of pure mockery, "would watch it all."

His vision turned wholly red. The monster was ready to lash out and drag every last officer into the depths of the ocean. He'd throw them onto Nemain's carriage himself if he had to.

After a beat of deafening silence, the Minister sat down again, clearly reveling in the win. "Come to the fortress alone tomorrow at dawn, Lieutenant. Or I shall find out exactly which Kheli savage is your favorite."

The silence fell over him again. He had nothing to say. Nothing he could say. His body ached and begged for action. A knife to be thrown into the Minister's throat. A sword in his belly. A bullet through his head. He'd tear out the man's throat with his bare hands. With his teeth.

"Captain," Robin said, near frantic. "We need to get to the ship." One look down at the powder monkey and his vision cleared a bit.

Wordlessly, Phantom turned to walk back to the ship, his devils and angel following suit. Clare managed to loosen her bow without shooting an arrow for the same reason Phantom retreated. They had no other choice. There was never freedom here. Not in Samsara. Certainly not in Kheli. Not even aboard *Nemain's Revenge*. The name seemed to be a mockery of the ship's current purpose. It would be used to trap, not only himself, but the people of Kheli and Samsara as if they were game pieces on the Prime Minister's chessboard.

Phantom turned to look back in time to see the Minister's hand land on Rose's bare arm. He lifted the skin there and she flinched. Not a reaction of new unfamiliar pain, but pain nonetheless. He pinched her. The Minister pinched his own daughter and she seemed to be used to it.

Do you have a death wish?

Phantom did not think. He reacted, lunging for Rose. For the Minister. He would rip the man's throat out. Damn the consequences. Jon's firm, strong arm branded Phantom's shoulder before he could take another step, gripping his shirt. Black came up beside him to seize the other shoulder.

"Live," Jon bit out, his voice low, deadly. "Live to fight another day."

Then the Commodore's hand was on Rose's back, leading her to the ship that awaited them.

CHAPTER 28
A BEAST OF BURDEN

E verything was red, the longboat they boarded, the morning sky which clouded over with fog. Red had completely overtaken Phantom's vision. It took every ounce of his mental strength to keep the monster at bay. To not think about the trickle of blood down Robin's neck. Or the despair on Clare's usually stoic face. They only reminded him of the pounding in his head.

I failed.

Davina must hate him. Not that he would blame the Goddess. He belonged to Nemain anyway, but now he'd drag his devils down to the depths with him.

He lost. He lost everything. He never had anything. The ship. The devils. All he had won for himself and anything he was ever proud of was never his. Every coin, cloth, or food they stole furthered the Minister's purposes. He spent the last three years working for the very man he thought he escaped.

The thoughts coaxed his monster into action, but it was manageable. Enough to get him on the longboat. Enough to remove his pistol, knife, and cutlass, passing them to Black. Enough to not rip the floorboards from the bottom of the longboat or tear out Jon's throat for looking pitiful. No, that was the tangy scent of fear.

Jon was afraid. He should be. But there was a sense of power that fueled the monster with the idea of the great *cerbalus* quaking in his boots.

Once reaching the ship, Phantom precariously climbed to the deck and Jon's knives were out before his boots scraped the dewy deck floor. Black had a sword drawn in the next instant, handing Phantom's removed weapons to Ramirez. It was Ramirez who took one look at Phantom and all the color drained from his face.

Phantom knew his posture was menacing; the hunched back, the lethal stillness of a predator, and the tension racking his body. But he knew, it was his eyes that gave him away.

"I take it things didn't go well," Ramirez chimed, a hint of hope in his tone and a citrus scent curling around him mixed with the cigar smoke the devil was so fond of.

Jon didn't move an inch. His weapons were firm and steady in his hands. Even as the stench of fear ripped off him in waves. It was pungent enough to make Phantom's nose itchy. "Worse than we could have imagined."

A small, sturdy voice said, "But you are all alive—" It was Smith's voice. Footsteps clomped against the deck and Phantom's head whirled on the doctor, but Black's blade was there to block him. The doctor flinched, near mortified by the haunting image Phantom presented. He didn't know, but by the blood draining from the man's face and the fear soaking his scent, he must have felt the incoming death.

The doctor had stopped before Robin, seeing to his neck.

"Everyone," Jon shouted, commanding. "Clear the deck. Do not come out of the cabin until I or Black say so."

Every eye turned to Phantom. It appeared as a mutiny, even if it was far from it. If they wanted to rid themselves of a captain, they would have left him on Bashtir to rot. They probably should have.

A low, unnatural, rumbling laughter rolled from Phantom like a sneaking wave. There to rip the living from shore and swallow them whole. "They don't answer to you, mate," the words came out all bite. Each word sharp, growling, and so very low. Phantom turned to Jon, a sliver of that humanity still in him. "Let them see what I become."

A keen sense of awareness led Phantom's gaze to the man with a stick. Wilson was leaning against the ship railing, observing closely.

"They will not abandon you so easily, Captain," Black announced. Of course, Black knew what Phantom wanted. After everything, knowing his devils were caught in this snare same as him would drive him to madness. This was his mess and his consequences would see all of his devils to Hell with him. He couldn't allow that. With the monster, he could scare them away. "The devils do not scare."

But he could bloody well try.

A menacing grin filled one corner of Phantom's mouth. By the scent of fear in the air, scared was exactly what the devils were. Since Black was still so close, Phantom whispered, "Are you willing to bet your life on that?" His eyes shifted to Clare. "Are you willing to bet her life on it?"

Sophia Clare froze where she stood. She smelled of the

woods and fresh rain, but nothing tangy. Not yet. It would come. It would come with the coppery scent of blood.

"Captain," Jon spat, his bulky arms tense as Phantom's head snapped to him. "You are not gone yet." His voice evened out as if calming a mad bull. Such a waste. "Imagine the lake on Kheli. The waterfall and the moons. Whatever calms you."

For a moment, he stared at his first mate. He was too far gone, the monster was too close to stop. The small amount of holding back he managed was only delaying the inevitable. He knew it the moment he saw the color drain from Ramirez's face. There was only one time the old man held so much fear.

Phantom's eyes must have glowed red.

It was the reason he knew he belonged to Nemain, because everything was red like the light of the crimson moon. The moon of death and the color of blood. The floorboards of the deck were red. The devils surrounding him were coated in red. Even the glint off Jon's blades cast a bloody glow. This is what it looked like when Nemain's moon was full in the sky, but it was only him who cold see it now.

"Have you told them?" His voice changed, echoing in his own throat. Jon somehow managed to grow tenser. "Did you tell them how you came to be a devil?" He didn't look to see, but he felt the attention of his devils, on himself, and on his new first mate. When Jon didn't answer, Phantom continued. "Did you tell them that you were sent to kill me?" His voice lifted in a "hmm?" sound, but it came out closer to a growl. "That you were paid to bring my head," Phantom snapped, his head tilting to the side.

Fog rippled through the ship, lowering visibility, and making the morning sky dark.

Jon still didn't answer. He didn't even dare to look at his fellow devils to watch the shock on their faces.

Phantom moved. A few long strides and he stood before his first mate shouting with many voices. "Do you wish you would have killed us now?"

The final sliver of humanity dropped away like the drop of an anvil. And we were free.

Jon's blades weren't quick enough. He'd never be quick enough. With inhuman speed, both knives clattered to the floor and our hand was around Jon's throat, closing in on the delicate skin there. We'd never thought of Jon as delicate before, but here he was, fragile as a flower. A little more pressure and he'd wilt.

We had him pressed to the rail of the ship. His burly, hairy hands clamped around our arm. An arm that was both ours and not ours. It was veiny, and flexed so tightly, every muscle was tensed from the power of the beast inside us.

We licked over our top row of teeth which told us that our canines had elongated. They came to deadly points. Blades meant to slash open flesh and rip it to the bone. We scanned over our victim and were deciding which part of him to sink those fangs into first.

A quick jab at our back told us that Black had not forgotten his place. Jon went limp in our hand so we released him, letting his body drop to the deck. Black had a spot of blood at the end of his sword. A faint prickle of pain came from our back.

Black lunged to slash open our naval, but we caught the blade in our hand. He shoved down his tangy panic and pulled back on the blade, slicing our hand open. More red filled our vision. We snapped forward, seizing the blade again and ripping it from his hand. More blood spilled from the wound on our hand, until it stopped and closed up.

We watched the despair settle on Black's face as we bent the sword, folding it in half. The metal groaned with the unfamiliar pressure, until it snapped apart completely. The color drained from Black's face. He'd never faced the monster before, only directed us somewhere to be subdued. There was no where to go now.

Not for us. And not for him.

As fast as lightening, we swiped at Black, digging a palm into his throat, but something sharp drilled through the flesh of our wrist, prying a roar from the back of our throat. We snapped our hand back to release the arrow from its perch.

A sharp snap of our neck and our eyes were pinned to the angel. Her bow was knocked, aimed at our head. Finally, she too smelt foul. She smelt of fear, horridly mixing with her pine and rain scent.

"Sophia, don't!" Black shouted, putting a hand up to halt the angel's next attack, but it was too late. Our eyes locked on the angel, sizing up exactly how fast she could release that arrow. We'd dodge it easily enough. She wouldn't get the chance to surprise us again.

Before we made another step, something knocked into our head. We whirled, facing a stone faced, clear scented man. A staff primed in his hand. The stale scent of steam and dumplings coated his clothing, but at his core there was no discernible scent. Nothing about him gave away his fear.

"*Enu hyeo tashin*," Wilson spat. *Silver-tongued demon.*

We smiled, letting him get a good look at the points exposed from our mouth. At how right he was. We are the demon. And of course, Wilson knew that. That was why he did not show surprise. Why we could not scent the fear on him. There were evil things in his religion after all. *Us.*

On the deck of *Nemain's Revenge*, Wilson kept his staff up as he circled his new opponent. One quick movement and we could snap the staff in half. We could have him flat on his back with our fangs buried in his neck before he could know what happened.

"*Jigoku kata.*" *Fire stance.*

The man spun his staff in the air then landed it before him, slamming it to the deck. Then he let out a roar and pounded the staff to the deck again.

We moved, but Wilson was quicker, knocking our hand away. Then with equal swiftness, knocking the other end of the staff into our back, shoving us away. It was enough force to knock us off balance, but not to the deck.

Wilson straightened with his staff poised in his right hand and arched into his back. The other hand was out, as if feeling the air, but it was for balance, giving Wilson the swiftness of a feline. The man was harnessing air stance too, combining speed with strength.

We moved again, coming to separate Wilson's hand from his arm, but the staff came down again. It snapped into our neck, forcing us back, then it swept across our legs, knocking us to the deck. His staff was aimed for our throat to keep us down, but we knew not of threats. The only way to beat the beast was to knock us out or kill us.

We grabbed hold of the staff, forcing him to yield a couple steps, but he slipped it free of our grasp before we could shove it into his neck. Or snap it across our leg.

He straightened again, gaining balance and footing, that somehow earned him an advantage. His movements flowed

297

as he rolled out a full kata, starting with the staff along his body, then beside him, then before him, then finally slamming into the deck.

Water. Air. Earth. Fire.

But we knew the movements well. He taught us.

This time, we strode for him unevenly to throw him off, snapping at the last possible moment. His staff was too quick, then it was too slow and he too ended up with a palm around his throat.

We leaned into his quickening pulse, surprised to still find his scent clear. The tips of our fangs only just brushed the sensitive skin of his neck when a sharp pain exploded at the back of our head. It was followed by shattering glass.

We released the neck of the man and whirled to find Hyne with a broken bottleneck and wide eyes. Apparently, he thought that would work. Our lips peeled back in a snarl, changing our target to the trembling man. Fear wafted easily from his skin like the stench of sweat as his eyes widened in surprise.

Pain exploded again as another glass shattered.

Then everything that was red went black.

CHAPTER 29
WHAT'S A MONSTER

An exploding headache was the first familiar thing to greet Phantom upon waking. The next was the cool bite of shackles clamped around his wrists and ankles. The chains rattled as he tugged at them. For a moment, he didn't understand why he sat shackled on the floor of his ship's brig with a splitting headache.

But the memories flooded back to him. How he wanted to sink his teeth into a devil. He took a cursory glance around the brig. It was barely used for prisoners. It was kept as a storage room more than anything. Piles of old clothing and barrels of rum littered the floor around his feet. A moldy stench berated his nose.

It was a miracle the monster was settled because the shackles and the metal bars would have been no obstacle. Earhart would have known that. His old first mate would have dropped him on Bashtir and let him settle on the island. Even if it meant risking his Captain to the waves.

"Awake, I see," Jon said, rounding from the corner. Phantom didn't know he stood there, which was good. It meant the beast was not close enough to scent the man. Phantom blinked at him. The light from his lantern was too bright, too much. If being in full beast form was akin to being drunk, this was the hangover. Except much worse.

"You survived I see," Phantom choked out as Jon leaned his forearms on the bars of the brig cell.

"Narrowly," he stated. No bitterness, but no forgiveness in his tone either. Phantom noted the bruise darkening Jon's neck.

Phantom moved his finger to his brow, pressing hard on the pressure building at the center of it. "My apologies, Jon," Phantom said cooly. "If I had known our negotiations would have gone so poorly, I would have made a plan to handle it." Handle the monster. Settle the beast. Perhaps, killing himself would have been the only option. The notion didn't sound terrible. Not as the gravity of those "negotiations" came crashing down around him. How he managed to fail so spectacularly.

He managed another breath. "How many left?" It would be the final straw, knowing that he had lost everyone. Every devil he'd ever acquired, saved, or freed over the last three years. It would convince him to end his own life. If not for his own safety, but the safety of those around him.

Phantom expected his first mate to say he was the last one, that everyone else jumped into the longboat and rowed to Samsara. Instead he said, "All of them." It was worse. So much worse. "Every single man or woman who boarded this ship on Kheli is accounted for." All except Rose, he wanted to say, but kept his mouth shut. "I asked each one, none plan to leave."

Phantom shook his head before the words had completely left the devil's mouth. "No," he breathed.

"They are loyal, Captain. We all may follow you for different reasons, but we follow you. If anything, seeing your power and strength made them more eager to follow you."

"No," he said again. Images flashed in his head. Some were nightmares, some... memories. His hand wrapped around Jon's thick neck, stifling him, forcing him to hold his breath. Blood spilling and flesh tearing. An arrow pointed at his head. She should have shot him. She should have let her arrow fly. "No."

The shackles rattled with him as he shook his head. "No, they deserve better than this."

Jon stepped back as if Phantom had physically hit him.

Phantom let gravel coat his words. "They deserve better than a captain who would kill them on a whim."

"That was not a whim."

"They deserve better than to watch their backs for an enemy onboard. Jon, with the Minister's new agreement, the risk of my *temper* taking over is higher. You know it," he bit out.

He wished they had left. Every single one of them. He had hoped he'd wake up to an empty ship. He'd waste away while they found their lives somewhere else.

"We did not stay solely for you, Captain," Jon bit back. The last piece of the puzzle snapped into place. Kheli. Many of them had grown attached to the island people. The cost of their own safety or their own lives would be the lives of every villager on Kheli, including Earhart and his family.

"Is the beast settled?"

"Yes," Phantom said and no sooner did Jon unlock the brig cell. He went to work on the shackles containing his limbs next.

"Then there is something else you should know."

Phantom tensed, preparing himself for the blow. What could possibly be worse?

Jon swallowed once before speaking. "Serena is gone."

Phantom blinked. The little beastie couldn't be gone. She had imprinted on him, even the monster wasn't enough to scare her away.

"Robin said the Commodore stole her when they took him. The poor lad blames himself."

He itched with the thought of what they had to do to keep the beastie quiet enough to smuggle off the ship. His eye's reached Jon's, full of his own rage. A rage that had nothing to do with the color red.

"I will get her back."

———

All the devils waited above deck. Each one stood and straightened when they spotted Phantom climb the steps of the main cabin, his breathing labored. The splitting headache was still intent on torturing him, but luckily night had fallen. Only the light of two moons shone over the eerie deck and illuminated the crew.

Phantom swallowed. He didn't realize he was searching for Rose until he couldn't find her, but she was long gone. It was truly a miracle that she did not witness what he became when the monster took over. They might have stayed, but she wouldn't have. All she needed was a reason to believe the worst of him. Not that it mattered.

Hyne tensed not far from where Phantom stood. "At ease, devil. The monster has passed." They seemed to relax, but only slightly.

"What happened?" Clare chimed, before Phantom could muster the courage to explain. Her voice was stern, angry.

Phantom raised a hand to calm her, a sign of peace. "I know you're all scared and angry." He turned to the rest of his devils. "I should have told you all about this so long ago, but truthfully, I don't understand it myself."

"Try," Black spat. Black knew the monster existed, but he never knew why. He never knew how bad it could get. Only Earhart and Ramirez had seen it before, but Jon knew it could happen.

Phantom licked his lips. "When I was a boy, I was an orphan. I never knew my parents and I spent most of my childhood on the streets, picking pockets and begging for scraps. No different than many of you standing before me today." There were so very many devils with bad childhoods standing before him. He wasn't looking for pity. "One day, I picked the wrong pocket and ended up in an ally, beaten and bloody. When the men came at me again I knew they wouldn't stop until I was just another small body found in an alleyway in Samsara. I could see their intent to kill when they approached and I knew Nemain was close."

He took another breath as the wind silenced. "Then there were these voices screaming at me." He raised a hand to his head. "In here. I knew one of them had taken control when the men started talking about red eyes." He swallowed again. "That was the first night the monster had appeared. It ripped those men apart as if they were made of nothing more than pillows."

Everyone had stopped breathing. The only sound audible was the creak of the mast and the sway of the sails. Even the birds had ceased their gawking.

"The monster is not the only voice that haunts me, but it is the only one that had this affinity for killing." He was sure every man or woman there remembered exactly what that looked like. The elongated canines, the speed, the strength, every bit of it solely belonged to the beast.

A soft, small voice said, "What did you mean when you said Jon was paid to kill you?" Robin's eyes were still wide, as if Phantom would snap his neck right there, yet he refused to run.

Phantom let a smile tug at his lips. "I believe the best person to answer that question is the first mate himself." He took a couple steps to the side until he could lean against the railing of the stairs, allowing Jon the unwanted spotlight.

Every eye turned to Jon, leaning against the ship's railing with his arms crossed before himself. Those knives were firmly placed back into every sheath. His long hair hung loosely at the sides of his face, making him appear both strong and undone.

"In Draiocht, we have a legend. It tells of a lion that was cursed to be reborn. Unable to move on. Unable to reclaim his kingdom in the underworld. He'd only die again and again. Then live again until the Gods were finished with him." Jon's words were slow, but even. "My people believed that it was this lion that plunged the world into darkness. Or what you know to be the War. They locked up Phantom for brawling in the city when he visited. Then the people started calling him Maahes because his eyes glowed red."

Phantom cringed with the memory. "It really was not my best night."

Jon ignored him. "I was a fellow prisoner in their stinking cells. I was a bounty hunter and had just killed one of their priests. Phantom had escaped before the next morning hit."

Only a smug grin decorated the Captain's face.

"The city buzzed with the tales of Maahes, the cursed lion god. He was too much of a liability to the people to allow escape. So the priests bartered with me, offering freedom if I brought him back, dead or alive." The devils were silent again. "They needed a body to show the people that he was not a god and could not hurt them."

Robin's curious gaze landed on Phantom again. "Then how are you alive?"

Phantom nearly laughed. The notion mockable. "He wouldn't have stood a chance."

Jon ignored him again. "I had every intention of bringing him in cold, but rather than pleading for his life, he offered me a position on his ship. He told me freedom was worth its weight in gold." His dark eyes found Phantom's. "And I've never looked back."

There was no response Phantom could make that would quite encompass what that meant to him. So he only nodded. It was curt, but Jon nodded back all the same.

"That doesn't explain what that thing was," Clare spat. A fear response no doubt. He could see it in her eyes even if he couldn't scent it on her.

"That thing was me," Phantom breathed, regretting the truth as it spilled from him, but it was the truth nonetheless. If these people were truly to follow him, they had to understand. "It was just as much me as the version standing before you now."

Clare's lips were a solid line. She was good at hiding that fear of hers, but it was there. Present in the tension of her body. Black appeared at her side, putting a subtle touch at her side, reminding her that she was not alone.

Phantom raised his brows. "And it does explain it."

Robin was a shadow beside Phantom, looking up at him. "You are Maahes."

Phantom let a near sinister smile break his lips as his crew held their breath again. "It's one of my many names, yes." He pushed off the stair rails with his fingers up. "Although, the Draiocht people do not get it all right, my curse had grown popular enough to earn names in many religions."

"*Enu hyeo tashin*," Wilson spat. *Silver-tongued demon.* The sentiment made Phantom believe that maybe Wilson knew what he was all along.

Phantom's smile faded as he stared at the man with the staff. "Yes, Wilson. The title of demon also belongs to me, but I think you already knew that." He narrowed his eyes at the man, but Wilson said nothing as he let his stare communicate.

"Then what are you?" Smith chimed in. His long white hair neatly tucked behind his hat, but his eyes were blazed, unbelieving. "God or demon?"

Phantom let out a sigh. "Neither," he said, even as he questioned the truth. Eyes around him squinted or narrowed. Confusion and doubt. "At least, not to my knowledge." The air around them turned tense. "I have the memories from some of my past lives, but I cannot recall my original self. Or the curse of rebirth being thrust upon me. All I know is that I live a human life, I die, and I live again. With the one exception," Phantom paused. "The earliest memories I have belong to the beast you witnessed. During his life we—" He paused on the word *we*. It was such a simple word that referred to himself as both whole and broken. One person, but part of many. "I— was a creature driven by instinct alone. An instinct that seemed to center around death and bloodshed. I let the beast come out during battle." He blinked long. "He's the reason we never lose."

The tension on the deck snapped like a fallen branch. Every eye was on him, but they didn't look. They didn't see him. They looked inside themselves, remembering the battles they had fought together. To the close calls and the victories. They never did lose. At least— until yesterday.

Robin's voice rang again. "Now what?"

"I assume Jon and Black recounted the failure of the negotiations with the Prime Minister?" Phantom said with his head down. He considered hanging this event up as one of his greatest failures. Over many life times.

"They did," Clare bit out, her tone rough. Her entire village's survival depended on a band of pirates. It was bad enough dependency already, but if they failed to deliver what the Minister wanted, it would be Kheli to pay the price.

He looked to each devil and angel individually. "Now, we do exactly as we did before. Protect and supply Kheli. Pillage Samsara. We'll scare the Minister's people as much as we want and I'll visit the Minister in the morning to see what else he wants." There was a beat of silence. They expected more. A plan to get them out of this. A way to buy back their freedom. He had to come up with something. Eventually, they'd run dry of their usefulness.

"I'll think of something," was all he said as he watched the disappointment flood their faces.

The night was still young as Phantom stumbled into the Captain's quarters. He dreaded it, wondering if the bed still smelled of her. If smokey sweetness was embedded into the sheets. He also couldn't decide if that was a good thing or not.

Would he be disappointed or relieved?

He'd refused other devil's questions. Not because he didn't welcome openness. It was because he didn't know. *Why do you reincarnate? How do you remember past lives? Was that creature once a living being?*

The very same questions he'd been asking his whole life. Still, the openness was strange. Earhart was the first person he had ever shared knowledge of the beast with. Jon had put the dots together.

Thoughts of Rose kept pelting him. The way she moved on his ship, like she was born to ride the seas. The beauty in her angelic voice, even when she wasn't singing. Her generosity to risk herself for people she just met. Then, to risk exposing her most guarded secret for a friend she barely knew. How she let loose around that bonfire and every other moment that happened that night.

Then, the Minister's fingers pinching her pale, reddened skin. How she winced at the pain. A pain inflicted to control her. The memory of it made his skin crawl violently. He'd storm the Fortress for that image alone.

Jon leaned against Phantom's desk as he entered. Ramirez stood beside him with his arms tucked in front of himself. Their faces were stern, but concerned.

Phantom narrowed his eyes at them. "Whatever it is you have to say, I am very tired and need my beauty rest for the

Minister." It wasn't untrue. Even though he missed most of the day, he spent a lot of energy holding back the monster that morning.

When their expressions didn't change, he added, "If you're going to tell me not to go—"

"It's her," Jon stated, plain as day, his face hardening further.

"No," Phantom breathed. His eyes slid to Ramirez. To the one man who could tell him it wasn't true. To the one man in the world who could deny it.

"He speaks the truth," Ramirez spoke like it both enchanted and haunted him.

Phantom froze, letting the words crash into him. The bite of it as cool as ice water.

"It can't be," he gritted out.

Ramirez took a step toward him, lowering his arms and painting a sympathetic look on his face. "I saw it in her. The spirit of Isabeya. She even told me how familiar I am to her, but she couldn't quite remember."

"The nightmare confirmed it," Jon stated. Phantom's breathing halted altogether. "The land was clearly Eveleigh, but it wasn't what we know as the mainland. Those trees were from Kalon, skitter trees, they disappeared soon after the War began, but Isabeya would have been alive to see them. As your counterpart was."

As Rourke was. The voice that lived in his chest and every beat of his heart. The voice he'd taken to calling his conscience, telling him what he should do. The life that lived when the skitter trees still existed. The warrior who witnessed the War between the living and the dead first break out. The man who loved Isabeya.

"No," Phantom repeated, seeing her gold coin eyes

when he blinked, but they faded to deep brown. He rapidly opened his eyes, banishing the vision, but it lived with him.

"Why do you deny this?" Ramirez asked with a line wrinkling between his brows.

"Because," he bit out, "I let her go."

Thank you for taking a journey with Phantom and the Eleven Devils. If you'd like to find out what happens next, here's a sneak peak of Chapter One of THE SIREN OF SAMSARA.

OLD HABITS
BONUS CHAPTER

I t might have been the longest longboat ride of Phantom's piracy career. The Fortress stood high above him on the cliff top. Part of the cliff *was* the Fortress, fog circling the stones in a lazy haze.

It reminded Phantom of when he was first brought here. The memories crashed into him. He was a boy, no older than ten when he was dragged from the streets of Samsara and into the Fortress's thrown room. Every forgotten boy of Samsara kneeled before the Prime Minister that day. There was no shortage of orphaned children in Samsara. The War made sure of that.

The Minister liked to groom young boys to become officers one day. Boys who had nothing and no one were given a place and purpose. It made them strikingly loyal. Especially since they had no families to return to. Those boys were tested in every manner of the word. Mentally. Physically. Politically.

Phantom was called James Hawkins at the time and James Hawkins was a favorite of the Minister's. During the years of grooming, James had come out better, stronger, faster, smarter and the Minster had noticed. He gave James all kinds of rewards for doing well. Often times, James wouldn't even try. Many of the tests came naturally.

Until one day, a Mokshan boy was brought in. His brown skin was dirtied and his eyes were dark and scared. A look he would see on Tick one day. Even for an orphaned boy of Samsara, the Mokshan boy wore rags. The Minister stood before James, handing him a leather whip.

It was another test. A test much graver than any that came before it.

It was a test of obedience.

"This boy," the Minister had spat, his wrinkles much less pronounced and his eyes brighter. "Is guilty of trespassing on Samsara. Whip him until I tell you to stop." With the dark look in the man's eyes, James knew that he would only stop when the boy was dead.

James refused, tossing the whip to the ground. He could nearly taste the disappointment rippling off the Minister that day. "Are you sure you want to be doing that, Hawkins?"

James narrowed his eyes at the Minister. A man he had felt indebted to. Who brought him food and sweets and told him he'd be great one day.

The Minister's eyes shifted from the Mokshan boy to him. "He will be whipped whether you do it or not. Your choice is if you will join him."

When James had said nothing, a frown appeared on the Minister's face. He bent down to retrieve the whip and tossed it to his current Commodore. A tall war weathered man with grey hair and a permanent frown.

James stepped in front of him, not letting the

Commodore gain one inch over the boy. This Commodore did not care who stood in the way of his whip.

Phantom could still recall the first stinging bite of the whip, the crushing defeat it inflicted on its victims.

Scars he'd never be rid of decorated his chest and back, but the Mokshan boy still lost his life that day. The Prime Minister carried on with the needless tests, but he removed his favor and instead placed it upon James's best friend, Bash.

Sebastian Ashby was only known by the boys on the streets of Samsara as Bash. A fleeting word. A passing glance. Nothing noble or worthy of note. Not until the day the Minister drug in another boy, this one was from Draiocht. His skin darker than James had yet seen. His eyes like pools of ink. And scared. So very scared.

Once again the Minister shoved the whip into the hands of a boy, but it was Bash who was given the decision. James had searched for his eyes, begging his friend to look at him, to choose something else. But he also knew, the Minister would not allow a defiant officer in training to be pardoned for disobedience again.

Bash wouldn't make it out of there alive if he choose to stand up for the Draiocht boy, but James fumed from the balcony they trapped him on, far enough away that he could not intervene. He would find a way to save Bash. To save both of them. He'd risk everything just for the chance. He'd let the beast out and they could—

But Bash didn't allow him the chance.

With every ounce of strength he could find in his teenage arms, Bash whipped the boy bloody. The sound of the whip hitting flesh had remained in James's mind much more putridly than the sound against his own flesh.

It was that day that changed both their lives. Bash stepped onto the road that would lead him to become Commodore Sebastian Ashby.

And James would become Captain Phantom of the Eleven Devils.

Mortal enemies.

The large stone doors to the Minister's sea prison of a fortress opened and it was as if he were ten all over again, but there wasn't a cavalry of orphaned boys behind him. He entered not as a boy, searching for a place in life, but as Phantom, a pirate clad in black. Silver buckles lined his sword belt and leather coat. Silver and black rings decorated his dirtied fingers. There was so much evidence of what he had become, what he had fought for, and what he had earned. Especially, the tattoos circling his flesh. He had so much more than the boy who first entered those doors.

But that boy had Bash.

Now, Commodore Ashby stood decorated as well, but in the uniform of a naval officer. His coat was white with embellishments of blue and gold. The blue to symbolize that he belonged to the Prime Minister's Navy, but the gold warned passerby's that he earned a good position. That his stoicism and strength were not only earned, but used often. He was the Minister's personal killing machine.

Ashby only nodded at his old friend upon entering, but through his mask of obedience he huffed. The only indication that he didn't agree with the Minister. He likely wanted to see the pirate captain hang, easing the people's mind from pillagers. Instead, he became part of orchestrating their fear.

Ashby put a hand out to stop his old friend. Phantom was giddy with the attention. With a sideways glance, he let a smirk paint his face— right before it shifted into fake innocence.

"What seems to be the problem, Commodore?" He purred, letting the title leave his lips like an insult, not a hint of respect showing. Any admiration he might have held for his old friend faded the moment he let Robin bleed under his knife. It was the moment he knew Bash no longer existed. He was only sorry it took so long.

Ashby tossed his head to the nearby table.

"Disarm," he commanded, letting his gaze fall on Phantom's sword belt and pistol.

Phantom let a single eyebrow raise. "Make me."

Ashby's eyes narrowed. Clearly, he was tempted by the notion.

"Play nice, boys," a sensual, irritating voice slammed into Phantom. The voice made every muscle in his body go rigid. A voice that belonged to the Priestess Ravana. Better known as Samsara's Mistress.

Phantom struggled to keep his easy demeanor as she approached. She dripped in jewels that dazzled in the new morning light. Her silver simmering dress hugged her generous curves as she walked. And she always walked with a prowess. There were only three colors she could wear. Silver. Lilac. Crimson. The color choice would occasionally relate to phases of the moons, or what the Goddesses supposedly told her. But mostly, they reflected her mood. Silver told Phantom that she felt powerful, untouchable, and controlling.

Her vibrant red hair was a silken sheet that fell down her back. For a woman, she was tall, making Phantom feel short in her presence, but that wasn't the reason he disliked her. The woman had a liking for the orphaned boys the

Minister brought to the castle. He was not the only one to groom the boys.

"Yes, Mistress," Ashby cooed out of habit. When Phantom was still living at the Fortress, Ravana had taken to Bash. No doubt she instilled more than respect into him.

Phantom met her with a straight face. The beast nearly huffed at the sight of her.

She kissed her teeth at him. "Always were the defiant one, James," she purred.

He stiffened further as she encroached into his space, circling him with a hand on his shoulder. She let her hand drag with her around his shoulder, across his back, then to the other shoulder. No doubt, she was mentally undressing him. If it was any other woman, we would have flirted back, he would have teased her. But it was *her*. He'd rather shove her off a cliff than give her one ounce of satisfaction.

She breathed out. "Oh I've missed you, James." The words sent a shiver along his spine. She let a hand squeeze on his bicep. "My my, you've grown into a man." She finally rounded, facing him again. If it weren't for the Commodore's presence, he'd gut her right there. Her breath was too close as she leaned in. "I will enjoy reacquainting myself with your"—she trailed off— "talents."

Finally, Phantom let a smile break his stoic stare, but it held no warmth. It was only a mockery of a smile. "You're fooling yourself Ravana, if you think I'd ever invite you into my bed."

The Priestess's eyes did not fade with disappointment, instead her eyebrows rose in challenge. "We shall see, Captain," she hissed, but she somehow managed to make it sound sensual and bitter all at once. Her hands were on his sword belt, unbuckling it. She took her time, letting the leather slither from his pants, brushing a finger along the edge. Bile rose from his throat.

Her eyes snapped to his as she handed the entire sword belt to Ashby. He would rather the Commodore rip it from him than this.

Her hand curled around the pistol at his side. The beast growled in his core and he let a bit of it come out his throat. Her answering smile was sickening. Once handing the pistol to Ashby, she took a step back, examining Phantom with a hand on her hip.

As quick as a minx she swiped the small blade from inside his boot and grinned devilishly. "You may look different, James, but you're still up to the same tricks." With the dagger's hilt between her pointer finger and thumb, she delicately handed that to Ashby too.

"Anything else, pet?" She purred.

Phantom sliced her a look, wishing he could unleash the beast on her. He'd enjoy the second it would take to rip her throat out.

"No?" She turned to the Commodore. "Sebastian," she said his name slowly, like it was a poem. "I'll let you take it from here." She turned, walking away with a swish of her hips. He thanked Nemain that she had not sported crimson that day. It was a disgrace to the Goddess of Death when she did, because it meant she was in the mood for chaos.

ACKNOWLEDGMENTS

If you've made it this far, I want to thank you for taking a chance on a debut novel. The dreams and passion I have for this project wouldn't be possible without people like you reading these first books. I hope you stay with me, because I have A LOT more story to tell.

Thank you to my beautiful and wonderful editor, Rachel Ohm, not only for polishing my work until it sparkled, but also for your reactions to my story. For all the times you love it and for all the times you hate it. Without your hard work and encouragement, I would not be here publishing my first book. You truly have been my first mate when it comes to steering this ship.

Thank you to the authors who shaped me. Bryan Davis. Sara J Maas. Jennifer L Armentrout. Brandon Sanderson. Raven Kennedy. C.S. Lewis. Caroline Peckham and Susanne Valenti. Jenna Moreci. Abbie Emmons. H. D. Carlton. My dreams began because of you.

Thank you to my beta readers from TikTok.

@alexoverbooked & @bri.and.her.books

And finally, to Brenton, for being my everything. You are my support, my soundboard, my beta reader, my cheerleader, my fight scene expert, and the one who believes in me more than anyone.

ABOUT THE AUTHOR

McKenzie A Hatton's ideal night is a glass of wine and a good book. She grew up in the rolling hills of Oregon, spending time with family at the beach, and petting every animal who would let her.

McKenzie is a world traveler with a town in Ireland, Killarney, being her favorite. She is lucky to have the chance to travel and to write, the two things that make up her passions.

For book updates visit her website and sign up for the newsletter.

www.mckenzieahatton.com

CPSIA information can be obtained
at www.ICGtesting.com
Printed in the USA
LVHW020138051022
729964LV00014B/605

9 798986 449609